Praise for

# Sheila Kay Adams

"Her stories may be localized or carry you back to the thirteenth century, but their lessons, poignancy, and humor have no boundary, real or artificial." —*The Washington Post*

"Sheila Kay Adams is the real article. . . . Her traditional ballads go hand in hand with her songs and stories of her own life, like they're of the same cloth. They are. When Sheila does her work, I imagine the mountains breathe a little easier, knowing there's someone out there, speaking for them."

—BILL HARLEY, author of *Mistakes Were Made*

"Adams can make you laugh. And she can make you clear your throat and wipe at the corners of your eyes from emotion. This is no small thing. She has the gift." —*Chattanooga Times Free Press*

"Pure mountain magic." —*Life*

"We're all lucky that Sheila is willing to share her heritage with us, in song and story." —LEE SMITH

"*My Old True Love* sings and lives and breathes with joy and sadness and every emotion in between. Something ancient and wonderful resides in Sheila Kay Adams's heart, and we are lucky indeed that she has chosen to share this knowledge with us through the words of this fine, beautifully wrought novel."

—SILAS HOUSE, author of *Clay's Quilt* and *The Coal Tattoo*

*My Old True Love*

# My Old True Love

 A NOVEL BY

## Sheila Kay Adams

BALLANTINE BOOKS

NEW YORK

2005 Ballantine Books Trade Paperback Edition

Copyright © 2004 by Sheila Kay Adams
Reading group guide copyright © 2005 by Random House, Inc.

Published in the United States by Ballantine Books, an imprint of The Random House Publishing Group, a division of Random House, Inc., New York. Originally published in hardcover in the United States by Algonquin Books of Chapel Hill, a division of Workman Publishing, New York, in 2004.

Library of Congress Cataloging-in-Publication Data
Adams, Sheila Kay.
My old true love : a novel / by Sheila Kay Adams.
    p. cm.
ISBN 0-345-47695-6
    1. North Carolina—History—Civil War, 1861–1865—Fiction.
2. Triangles (Interpersonal relations)—Fiction.    3. Appalachian
Region, Southern—Fiction.    4. Ballads—Fiction.    5. Cousins—
Fiction.    6. Singers—Fiction.    I. Title.
PS3551.D395315M9 2004
813'.54—dc22                                        2003070809

Printed in the United States of America

www.thereaderscircle.com

2   4   6   8   9   7   5   3

Text design by Anne Winslow

This book is in loving memory of my parents Ervin
and Neple Norton Adams, who kept the family stories
and memories in their hearts and passed them on to me.
And it is lovingly dedicated to June Anders
and James C. Taylor—there could be no better in-laws.

Come in, come in, my old true love,
And spend this night with me.
For I have a bed, it's a very fine bed,
And I'll give it up for thee, thee.
I'll give it up for thee.

"Young Hunting," traditional ballad

My Old True Love

## 1

SOME PEOPLE IS BORN at the start of a long hard row to hoe. Well, I am older than God's dog and been in this world a long time and it seems to me that right from the git-go, Larkin Stanton had the longest and hardest row I've ever seen.

Granny had an old cow that was skittish back then that would kick anybody but her, so I knowed things was bad when she said to me, "Arty, go do the milking."

My heart laid in my chest as heavy as the milk bucket on my way back. See, my aunt Polly had been trying to have a baby for days and had screamed till her voice had plumb give out. I heard Mommie crying when I started up on the porch and just as I reached for the latch, the door opened and the granny-woman Hattie come out. She had a bright red stain on her forehead and try as I might I couldn't get my eyes to look nowheres else but at that red swipe mark. She never even had to say it. I knowed Aunt Polly was dead. Hattie's eyes was soft as a doe's as she took the bucket of milk and handed me the one she'd carried out of the house and told me to empty it at the far edge of the cornfield. Oh, Lord, I did not want to see what was in that bucket, but just like that red stain, I couldn't look nowheres else, and I gagged the whole time I was burying the afterbirth.

Even though they was a candle burning on the rough-planked table inside the cabin, it seemed dark to me. But there was that bucket of milk, and since they was all talking, I figured it fell to me to strain it. I kept looking at the bed where Aunt Polly was covered up by one of Granny's best quilts. It seemed like the gay colors caught what little light there was and I got sick to my stomach thinking about what lay beneath them. Mommie and Granny stood next to the bed and Mommie was still crying. Crazy-like, the words to an old love song run through my head.

> The doctor he come, to her bed he drew nigh
> Her chambers all parted and moved to the side.

And quick as lightning, another line from another song.

> No doctor's hand, just God's own hand.

Granny's face was so full of sorrow and hurt that I could barely stand to look at her, and I busied my hands to straining the milk. But that didn't stop my ears from hearing every word. In the softest voice ever was, Granny allowed as how Aunt Polly had plumb give up after Luke was killed. Mommie was holding Emily who had cried so long she had the snubs. Hackley had his fists twisted up in her skirt and when she started to say over and over, "My baby sister, my baby sister," he pushed his little face deeper in the folds. Right about then the baby started to cry, and everybody turned back to the bed. I took Emily from Mommie. It was when I set her on my hip that it come to me that I didn't even know what the baby was. But Emily was crying and fussing and Hattie was out the door and gone before I had a chance to ask.

Then Mommie said, "I'll take him," and Granny said, "No you will not." They quarrelled back and forth for a minute, then Granny said, "Thirty-five ain't young, honey. Ye've got eight young'uns and, God willing, soon to be nine. Ye have to think of your own." And what she said next caused a chill down the whole length of my back. "I'll keep him." And then her voice got real soft. "Till he dies, anyway."

Mommie's voice come out in a wail. "We can't let him die. He's all that's left in this world of Polly and Luke."

Granny held up her hands and said, "All right, all right." Then she said one of us needed to go to the spring and bring back water to wash Aunt Polly with before she stiffened, and my eyes flew back to the bed. I felt all done in and Emily was still making this tired little hiccuping sound like she wished she could stop but kept on anyway.

Mommie folded back the quilt from Aunt Polly's face. She tucked a strand of hair still wet with Aunt Polly's living sweat behind one ear.

"She looks young as a girl," she whispered.

Oh, but I thought I would die when she said that.

Then the baby cried again and Mommie got the funniest look on her face. Her chin jutted out, her eyes went to little slits, and she looked mad as hell. "Come over here, Arty," she said to me in a rough voice. She jerked Hackley loose from her dress skirt and knelt by the bed.

"That there is your cousin," she said. "He's ours to raise. He ain't got nobody in this world but us." Hackley made a little sound in the back of his throat and Mommie looked right at him. "He'll need a good strong name, now. You come up with a stout one, all right?"

Hackley looked at Mommie, then back at the baby. He nodded solemnly.

That must've satisfied her because she stood up, got the water bucket, and said, "I'm going to the spring."

And as Granny followed her out on the porch she allowed as how Mommie ought to take the pitch torch, since dark had probably come on down at the spring.

THE BABY MADE ANOTHER little sound and of a sudden I wanted to see that baby more than anything in this world. The quilt they'd wrapped him in had halfway covered his face and I leaned over and flipped it back. His big pretty head was covered in hair as black as a crow's feather. A tiny hand with fingers all spread wide reached out to us. Hackley stared at the hand, then shot a glance at the open door where Mommie and Granny stood backlit by the yellow light of the torch. I could see what he aimed to do and any other time I'd have smacked his hand. But, I didn't do or say nothing. I only watched Hackley's little hand move toward the baby. Quick as a snake the baby's fingers gripped it hard.

"Well, howdy," Hackley whispered. And I swear, that baby turned its head toward him just like he was listening. Hackley smiled. "Howdy, little feller."

IT WAS A GOOD summer for growing in Sodom, just the right amount of sun and rain. We would have plenty for the coming winter. Granny still spent a lot of time up on the side of the mountain where the garden was. With a sheepish look on her face and never quite meeting my eyes, she'd announce before the fog had even burned off that she had to go pull the biggest cucumbers or old bean vines to feed the hogs. She'd say this even though I knew for a fact she would never go in that garden with the dew still on. She'd stay gone until noontime and come in just long enough to fix us something to eat. She'd fuss the whole while about how everything in the garden was going to come in at the same time, which I had to laugh at because that's the way it *always* was. Then she'd head back out up the mountain, climbing hard to where the first row of corn started. She'd always stop there to bring her apron up to wipe the sweat that run off her face like little freshets, look back toward the house, then disappear in between the rows. But I could always tell where she was by the moving of the corn. And I could tell just as well when she'd leave the patch for the cool of the woods beyond, too. We'd had no fresh corn in many months, and my mouth watered at the thought of it and when she come in with the first little ears covered with watery blisters, we fell on them as though starving.

It was toward the end of August before I realized what Granny was doing. It was way up in the day and she was just heading back toward the house. She'd caught up the hem of her apron and had loaded it with potatoes. I had beat out a path on the porch walking the baby. He'd cried so much that day that even when he weren't crying, my ears rung with the sound of it. Granny was beelining it for the steps when he started to cry again. Her head come up and she made a sudden jag toward the springhouse.

She didn't want to sit here in the house and listen to him cry. It was then I knew it was going to be pretty much me for it. From the day he was born, my arms had carried him, but that very day was when my heart claimed him for my own.

In October, Mommie birthed a baby girl. We all crowded into the cabin to celebrate and to hang her with a name. Mommie said she'd be known as Martha Elizabeth, after Granny's mother and the queen of England.

We all shouted out, "Welcome to you, Martha Elizabeth Norton!"

Then Granny stood up and took the floor.

"When Polly's baby was born, Nancy told Hackley he could pick out a name for it. And now the little feller's three months old. It's time to hang him with a name, too. Hackley's been wanting to do this for a spell, but we weren't about to waste a perfectly good name on a young'un that might wind up carrying it to the grave, so we waited till we were certain he'd pull through."

I stood up next to her holding the baby. The room was quiet as could be and everybody was looking at us.

Granny went and put her hand on Hackley's shoulder. "All right, Hack. You hang a name on him, son. The time has come."

Hackley come right across that room and stood in front of me. He looked solemnly at the baby.

"I name you . . ." He looked around at everyone in the room, then back at the baby. "I name you Larkin!" he shouted.

The room rang with the shouts: "Welcome to ye, Larkin Stanton!"

OH, BUT THERE ARE no words to tell how Larkin grabbed hold of my heart forever when he was five months old. They was a big snow on the ground and Granny had just come in from milking the goat she'd got from Jim Leake. Me and Larkin was laying on a quilt in front of the fire and his little face was a constant wreath of the sweetest smiles and he was cooing at me for all the world like a little dove. And then he looked up at me with them big round black eyes and said plain as could be, "Amma." Tears come so quick to my eyes I was blinded. Though it pleased me beyond all knowing I tried to tell him, "No, no."

But Granny stopped me.

"Let him call you Amma, child." Granny's eyes were soft. "He's chose you to love best of all, and with good reason. You been all the mama he knows."

LARKIN TOOK HIS FIRST steps, just shy of nine months old, into Hackley's arms. From then on he was never still. He was slow to smile, but when he did his whole face beamed, and you felt blessed just to be in its light. He was quick to learn and I could make him mind with not much more than a smacked hand.

One summer evening me and Granny was on the porch where we'd be more apt to catch a bit of a breeze should one decide to come up the cove. I'd been trying to learn this really hard love song called "The Silk Merchant's Daughter," and Granny had already sung it through a half-dozen times. Larkin was in my lap, and halfway through her singing it yet one more time he started to rock back and forth in perfect rhythm. A low hum began in his throat.

"Granny!"

Granny never liked being interrupted mid-song like that so she was ill when she opened her eyes.

"What?"

"Watch Larkin," I said.

Granny began to sing again and the low humming started up again. She stopped and his humming stopped. Larkin's eyes were fastened on her mouth. She sang and the humming started again.

"Well, I'll be damned! He's trying his best to sing, ain't he?"

"He *is* singing, Granny. Sure as I'm setting here holding him. That's what he's doing." I turned his body until his face was close to mine, but he wanted none of that. He squirmed away back to Granny, humming impatiently in her direction.

Granny laughed with delight. "Looks like we got us another singer, Arty."

> He called for a knife his business to do.
> "Hold on," said the young maid, "for a moment or two
> It's a silk merchant's daughter from London I be
> Pray see what I've come to from the loving of thee."

Larkin's humming got all mixed in with our singing and it all eased its way into the dark there on the porch.

BY THE TIME LARKIN was five he had already learned every song I knew. Granny had to start reaching far back in her memory for them love songs that were so old she swore they'd come straight from the old country. I had to agree with her since they talked an awful lot about Scotland and England. It made me feel funny to think of singing songs that had been tucked away in people's hearts that had come all the way across the ocean.

But Larkin was too little to think about all that. He never cared where they come from. He was just always begging for one more.

"Lordy, honey." Granny said. "You have to give me time to study about it. You know who you ought to git to sing for ye is Hackley. He's learned from that bunch of singing Nortons, too. He's about the only one I can think of right off that can sing all day and not sing the same one twice't."

And so Granny pieced another square in the quilt that would bind them two boys together.

These were the days that I would look back on once I'd married with such a longing in my heart. Them were times that seemed almost magic—you know how it is when you remember your childhood. The sun is always shining or there's a big pretty snow on the ground, and you're young and never sick or tired, and everybody you ever loved is still living and your whole life is a big wide road stretched out in front of you just waiting for you to take that first step toward the living of it.

It was in the fall of my fourteenth year, just as the leaves had started changing on the highest peaks, when I really noticed Zeke Wallin for the first time. I'd knowed him all my life but this day at church I really *saw* him. Me and Granny were making our way through a knot of people that were still milling about in the church-yard after preaching and Larkin had darted away from us with the final *amen*. I watched his dark head move through the crowd until I saw him catch up with Hackley. Then I saw a flash of teeth from beneath one of the old oaks at the edge of the churchyard.

Zeke Wallin had the same spare build, fine bones, and square jaw-line of his older brothers. Never in his life would he tame his curly black hair, and on this day a glossy lock had sneaked out from under his hat. Oh, but his brows set off his best feature: widely spaced eyes of such dark blue they often looked purple, which they did now as he was looking at me. In that minute he was the prettiest man I'd ever seen in my whole life. He told me later my feelings was all over my face, and I blush even now at what he must've seen there.

His smile got even bigger as he swept off his hat and give me a little bow. A rush of heat started in my stomach and streaked out-ward. A line from a love song raced through my head, the words changing and reshaping themselves into the version I would sing the rest of my life.

Black is the color of my true love's hair. His face is like some rosy
fair
With the prettiest face and the neatest hands. I love the ground
whereon he stands.

It felt like my skin had caught fire and it was all I could do to keep
my eyes on the back of Granny's dress as I went stumbling through
the crowd. But as Granny stopped to speak to the preacher, there I
was face-to-face with Zeke.

"Howdy," he said.

"Howdy." All that fire felt like it had settled in my face and I knew
it were beet red.

"I wanted to speak to you before you took off. Tried to last Sunday, but you got gone."

"Last Sunday?"

He flashed me another smile, then his face went all serious. "See,
I wanted to ask if I could walk you home. Same applies to today. If
you'll let me."

He took a sharp breath. "It ought to be against the law of the land
to have eyes that color, Arty Norton."

It was all I could do to keep my eyes level on his, but after he'd said
that I weren't about to look away.

"So can I walk with you?"

I realized that I'd not be the same again, ever. Already I felt as
though my skin laid over my frame differently. I looked up at the tow-
ering peak of Lonesome Mountain, imagining the child I'd been a moment ago standing just yonder.

"I reckon you can if you want to."

ON THE COLD NIGHT before I was to marry Zeke, exactly three months from that warm fall day, I laid in bed listening to the sounds that were as familiar to me as the sound of my own heartbeat. I heard the soft snore from Granny's side of the room. The wood from the banked fire hissed. The wind moaned its way around the cabin. Out on the porch, Belle, the redbone pup Hackley had given Larkin, gave a few sharp barks, then was quiet. Larkin, caught in a dream, muttered something I couldn't make out and flung a hand in my direction.

I reached out and touched his shoulder. He rolled against me, and was still. Suddenly, scalding tears come pouring out of my eyes. I put my chin on top of his head.

"I won't never love nobody the way I love you, Larkin."

Outside, the wind stilled as though listening, then rushed up the mountainside. On its breath was the smell of snow.

## 2

THE ONLY MAN I'D felt love for was Daddy, and that don't really count. But the thought never crossed my mind that I'd *ever* love a man the way I loved Zeke. I am a hardheaded woman and speak my mind whenever I take a notion, and when we first married, I had the notion often. He was so good and tender and loving. I was bad to fuss and quarrel, not at him but just to be quarreling. At first he'd try to offer advice or try to help me somehow. But he soon figured out that the best thing to do was just let me blow and then I'd be fine. Then I fussed because he never listened to nothing I said.

But Lord, how I loved him.

There were times when we'd be setting at the table eating and I'd just have to reach out and lay my hand on him. Many a dinner went cold because of that. And I know he felt the same for me. We was lucky people. I've knowed some that's passion for each other turned to hate after they'd been married awhile or, worse yet, they growed indifferent to one another. I would've gladly took the hate if I'd had to choose. But they was never nothing between me and Zeke but love. Now that ain't to say we never fussed nor quarreled. I was more than a little jealous though he tried so hard to never give me real cause. It was just that I was not blind. I saw the way women's eyes follered him, but if I mentioned it he would sigh great big and say, "You are seeing what ain't there, honey," or even better, "If they are looking why would I look back when I've got the prettiest gal in this part of the world?"

Zeke knew how to handle me all right.

ANOTHER REASON I LOVED him so was that it was fine with him that I brought Larkin with me. He were five year old and I couldn't stand the thoughts of leaving him. He stayed with us for almost two years then he wanted to go back to Granny's. It used to make me mad as the devil when somebody would say, "You'll feel different about your own." I could not imagine loving my own any more than Larkin. And it weren't so much that I did. It's just that Abigail was born before we'd been married not quite a year and within four months I was breeding again with John Wesley. Too many babies for Larkin. He even said he wanted to go stay with Granny where it was quiet. And, truth be known, Granny was not young anymore and needed the help. I missed him and cried when he left but I was so busy. And I did get caught up in the loving of my own, but I still say I loved him just as good.

THAT SPRING AND SUMMER after he went to Granny's, Larkin and Hackley got to be as close as two beans in a hull. Granny said she would find them sitting facing one another, Hackley patiently singing verse after verse, Larkin with eyes shut, his face still as a looking glass, soaking up every word. They roamed the mountains in search of ginseng, singing the old songs. Hackley's voice was clear and strong. But it was Larkin's voice, high and pure, that seemed to have wings.

Several man-shaped roots of ginseng decorated the fireboard of Granny's cabin. During the long nights of that winter, the boys would often give the roots the names of people that lived only in the old songs. Lord Thomas "dressed himself in scarlet red and wore a vest of green," and all the other roots "took him to be some king." Little Margaret sat in her high hall and sadly watched her sweetheart, William, and his new bride come riding up the the road.

They was in and out of my house all the time and I wish you could've seen the two of them—Hackley fair and hair so blond it looked white, with short, stout arms and legs; Larkin so dark, long, and lanky.

A HEAVY FROST BLANKETED Sodom in late May of 1853 during a cold snap we called blackberry winter. The white blooms of the thorny canes covered the ground looking for all the world like snow, out of place against the backdrop of the greening-up hillsides. Granny said we'd have us a fine blackberry harvest since only the hardiest berries would survive. And by July she knew right where to find them.

Larkin ran ahead of us as we paused to rest. The hill was steep, and this was the second time we'd stopped. He reached the top and turned, black eyes sparkling. His short hair, so black it gave his scalp a bluish tint, was damp with sweat.

"I done beat you to the top!"

"Your legs turned eight year old as of today, son!" Granny called out. "Lot younger than ours, for a fact."

"Not much younger than Amma's," he hollered.

"But mine's got a lot more miles on them and I'm hauling two," I hollered back. I was just four months gone but already showing.

Granny reached into the pocket of her apron and took out a plug of tobacco, bit off a chew, then put the plug back in her pocket. She chewed vigorously for a few seconds, spat, and tongued the moist chew firmly between gum and cheek.

"Larkin?" she called, gazing at the mountains in the distance.

His head popped up from the grass at the top of the ridge.

I laughed. "Your head looks like a guinea fowl sticking up that-a-way!"

He jumped up and come careening down the hill.

Granny waited until he stood next to her, then pointed off into the distance.

"You know what that mountain is a-way off yonder?"

Larkin shaded his eyes and stared. "Ain't that Little Bald?"

"It is. And hit's all the way in Tennessee, honey."

We stood there for a long time without talking as the summer breeze come flowing up the side of the mountain and, finding us in its path, teased and petted us before rushing on.

"Well, now," Granny said. "Them berries ain't gonna jump off the vine and into our bucket by theirselves."

"And we need to make haste, Larkin," I said. "Mommie is probably right now making you a stack cake for your birthday."

"Love Aunt Nancy's stack cake, yes I do!" Larkin sang.

The blackberry thicket had been there for as long as even Granny could remember. Some of the canes were thick as Larkin's arm. The berries were big and sweet and it weren't long before our hands and Larkin's mouth were stained purple.

Granny smiled. "Believe you put as many in your belly as in your bucket, honey."

"Reckon he just might have." I patted Larkin's stomach. "See how big it is?"

She reached and thumped his belly. "Lordy! Tight as a tick! They might not be no room left for no stack cake."

He pulled up his shirt and examined his stomach with a worried look. Then his face relaxed.

"Aw, Granny. You're just deviling me. Anyways, Hackley says I can eat more'n anybody he's ever seen."

"Ah! That Hackley is a trick, ain't he? He's sharp enough to stick in the ground and green enough to sprout," she said. "Don't believe they's a serious bone in his body."

"I don't know, Granny," I said. "He's serious about singing them love songs."

"Honey, let me tell you something. You three young'uns are some of the best singers of them old love songs I've heard since my Pappy passed. Now, he was a fine singer, Pappy was. Mommie would try to make him quit singing love songs. Said it was a sin! Pappy was plumb insulted, I can testify to that. Told Mommie she might want to reference the Good Book. Quoted scripture to her right then and there. 'Make a joyful noise . . . come before his presence with singing,' he said. 'And now these three remain: faith, hope, and love. But the greatest of these is love.' Said if the greatest was love and for us to come before his presence with singing, what better way than by singing a love song! Said if God hadn't meant for us to sing them old love songs, why he wouldn't have give us sense enough to learn the words to them. Weren't much Mommie could say about that. Pappy knew the Bible like the back of his hand, better than anybody in this part of the country." She sighed. "He was a fine fiddler, too. When Pappy took to fiddling, why, I couldn't of kept my feet still if my life depended on it. And sing while he played. Now, that's harder'n hell to do. Yessir. Could sing and play the fiddle at the same time."

"Hackley can, too, Granny. Aunt Nancy said she'd never heard of nobody that could play like him when they's only a young'un."

"Pappy could play the fiddle when he weren't no more than a young'un, too. Must be something in the blood."

"What's that mean, Granny?"

"What, honey?"

"That it must be something in the blood?"

Granny looked at Larkin. "Why, it means it must run in the family."

"Oh." Larkin was quiet for a minute. Then, "Granny, have I got something in my blood? Other than the singing thing? Wish't I could learn how to play like Hack. He's trying to learn me but, for some reason, it just don't make no sense to me."

I knew just how he felt. Hackley had picked up the fiddle when he was five and had flew right into playing. He could pick the banjo, too. But, before I could say a word, Granny answered him.

"Why, I never could play nothing neither, son. Pappy tried to learn me too. Made no sense whatsoever. Pappy said my fiddle playing put him in the mind of two cats fighting." She chuckled, then reached out and give his ear a tug. "Why honey, don't fret, you got plenty of good stuff in your blood." She rubbed her hand over his hair. "You got your daddy's features. He was a dark-eyed, dark-haired, handsome man. You know his mama was a Indian. He was a big, stout man— and you're a big, stout boy. And you got your mommie's cleverness. You got a head full a sense, son. So I'd say you got plenty of good stuff, Larkin Stanton. Follow me around the side of the hill. I want to show you something."

I grinned because I knew right off what she meant to show him. It was one of my favorite places in the whole world.

Granny went striding off toward a big chestnut. Larkin bent to pick up his little bucket, and when he straightened up, Granny was nowhere to be seen.

"Go on, son. Go round the tree," I said.

As we rounded the big tree I heard him gasp. "A cave!"

"I used to play all over these mountains when I was a young'un," Granny said. "My own mommie showed me this here cave when I weren't much older than you." Her eyes got awfully bright. "Me and my brother Josie found all manner of stuff in here—little pieces of bowls, little purties. . . . Josie was closest to me. Lord, hit don't seem like he's been gone fer fifteen year."

We stood there quiet. We'd learned that sometimes many minutes would go by as Granny made her way back down the familiar path that was her long life.

She shook herself, sighed, and stepped away from the memory.

"Well, you know it's here now. You and Hackley can make it your own."

She walked back toward the chestnut tree, leaving me and Larkin at the mouth of the cave.

I looked down at him and couldn't help but smile at the shiny boy-wonder look on his face, but then again maybe it weren't so much a boy-wonder thing cause I'd seen the same look on Zeke's face and him a man grown. And then out of nowheres come this icy finger that laid itself cold right at the base of my spine. *Cat walked o'er my grave,* I thought and made the *X* sign over my heart against it. And in a voice sharper than it needed to be, I called out, "Come on, Larkin!" And then I wanted away from that place *bad*. I took hold of Larkin's hand tight and turned us both down the path toward home.

• • •

That afternoon me, Granny, Mommie, and Lucindy were sitting on the porch peeling apples. Lucindy had fetched them to Granny when she'd brought her young'uns to eat cake with the rest of us. The sun had been awful hot only an hour ago, but had now made its way behind the apple tree at the edge of the yard. A breeze picked up the fine gold hairs at the nape of Mommie's neck, and I just loved the way she brought her hands up all dainty-like to tuck them back into her bun. Mommie had the prettiest hands and when I noticed them I always thought of the line from "Pretty Saro," "My love she is handsome, all proper and neat." Her eyes were the same color as the little flower on blue-eyed grass just like Granny's. But they didn't have the big life in them that Granny's did. I'm sorry to say that but it's the truth. They didn't.

"I swan, that Larkin is growing like a garden weed," she said. "Why, if you didn't know it, you'd not believe for a minute that they was near four years' difference between him and Hack, would you?"

Lucindy looked up. "You surely can't tell my Mary is older — Larkin's bigger than her already. Hell, he's big as Jonah and him turned twelve. You remember the night Jonah was born?" she said to Mommie.

"Don't reckon I'd ever forget it. Wind howling like as to cut you in two! Papa swore the wind blowed a cow off the mountain above the house."

Granny laughed. "It was the truth. We heard a thump against the wall. Long as I live I'll never forget the look on David's face when he come back in. Never hurt the cow."

"Well, I was hurting!" Lucindy said. "By the time Nancy got there I was screaming bloody hell. If I could of got my hands around Andrew's scrawny neck I'd have choked the life out of him right there on the spot."

They all laughed. But I never. Even though I too remembered they was a brief time when I was laboring with Abby and John Wesley that I could've just squeezed Zeke to death. But somehow it weren't that funny sitting here with my lap budding another one.

"Speaking of birthings?" Lucindy asked me as she spit a brown stream off the porch.

"Due the end of November." Mommie didn't give me time to say. "Probably won't be a year between this one and John Wesley."

I shot a look at Mommie and felt myself draw up inside. She had that prim, hateful look to her, mouth all pursed up and her nose wrinkled like she was smelling something bad.

"Abby was a big baby and so was John Wesley. This one probably will be, too." Granny tossed a rotten apple to the big rooster prancing about in the front yard. "We always did have the biggest babies, 'cept for your Marthy, Nancy."

*Bless her for the saint she is,* I thought. Trying to get Mommie off the topic she so loves nowadays. That would be the "how-many-youngun's-Arty-has-had-in-as-many-years-talk." Which would be three if you're interested.

"Aunt Hattie said Larkin was the biggest one she'd ever caught." Lucindy examined an apple.

"Eight year ago today. Time goes by so fast."

Granny laughed. "That 'catching babies' reminded me of something my uncle Leland said. You probably don't remember him, but I know you remember Aunt Lily."

I remembered Aunt Lily. She called herself big and stout and she was both. She was a little over six feet tall and strong as a bear. Funny, that. Uncle Leland killed a sow bear and as he was skinning it out heard its cub crying off in the woods. He took it home to Aunt Lily and she raised it grown. She'd just had Little Jack and they said the two of them nursed right alongside each other. That bear follered her around just like a big dog.

Granny must've been thinking the same thing because she up and said, "Now, Little Jack, when he was a boy was a pure-D fool over honeycomb. Aunt Lily had to watch him like a hawk when they robbed a bee tree. He'd git in it and have it all over him. They's all gathered up at Pappy's and Little Jack got into Mommie's honey crock. Lordy at the mess he'd made. Uncle Leland never moved from his chair and Aunt Lily was just raising all manner of hell. Pappy was saying how Little Jack must be part bear, way he loved honey, and Uncle Leland rared back and said, 'Why, didn't you'uns know that's how we got Little Jack. Baited a bear-trap with honeycomb in the Pig-Pen Holler and caught him!'" Granny laughed. "Aunt Lily looked at him, popped them hands on her hips and said, 'Shut up, Leland, damned ole son of a bitch!'"

I got so tickled I couldn't stand it. I could just see all that in my mind. They said Uncle Leland was a fine fiddler and a real cut-up. He must've been awfully brave, too. Aunt Lily carried an awful scar above her right eye where an Indian hit her in the head with a rock. She killed the Indian with nothing but her bare hands.

Granny looked toward the barn where the young'uns were just going through the big double doors. "But Larkin is a big young'un. Like his daddy's people, I reckon. 'Course my Pappy was a tall man. Some of his bigness could have come through him. God knows it never come through your papa's side." She looked at Mommie and snorted. "They was everone little people, women, men, all of 'em." She grinned. "Little all over, too!"

Though I laughed with them, I was watching Hackley and Jonah heading for the lower stalls to hunt snakes while the rest of the young'uns went up the ladder into the hayloft. I knew what a fool Mary was over kittens and figured she was hunting for the newest litter. She told me what happened in the barn that day years later. Funny how I don't need these useless old eyes to see in my heart how it must've been.

The big boys wouldn't let Larkin go with them and I doubt that he cared much. Even then he was always hunting for a chance just to be able to look at Mary. She was such a pretty thing, redheaded and freckled like her mama but wispy, delicate, and small-boned. Of course Hackley claimed her for his own. That was no surprise.

But what happened in the barn that day *did* come as a surprise.

Mary said they found some kittens in the loft and she'd picked one up to pet. She said she happened to look at Larkin and he had such a look of longing on his face that she felt sorry for him. Oh, Lord, how that makes me feel even now. It makes my belly hurt to think of him longing for something, anything. And it makes me mad as hell to know she felt sorry for him. I don't know why, but it does.

She said she put the kitten down and eat some strawberries she'd put in her pocket. And then she offered to scratch his head. Oh, that burns me up. Like he was a dog or something. But that's not what she felt, I know that because she told me so. She said his hair felt coarse as a horse's tail and was black as a crow's wing. Larkin must've been purring loud as that kitten before him. He told her she smelled good. Bless his heart. I guess she did.

Larkin told me himself that he'd watched Hackley kiss her. Then Hackley had gone running after Jonah, laughing how he'd done it on a dare, leaving Mary standing there in the light-striped aisle. And then he'd asked if he could kiss her too, and she let him. Poor Larkin. Always second on the list.

He said I called for him right after and I remember it, plain as day. I remember seeing them big boys run out of the barn all red-faced and I hollered out, "Larkin." He come to me. He always did. He was such a good, decent, and loving boy. And I remember what he said to me his face all lit up and bright as a new penny.

"Mary smells like strawberries, Amma."

Fool that I was, I had no way of knowing that he was carrying with him her very breath.

## 3

Carolina was born on the first day of December that year and time for me after that melts and runs smearing all together. Having three under three is *not* the way I'd say to have them. Now, you talk about being tired, but I was slap wore out.

I wouldn't have thought I'd remember much about them times but it's always an amazement what I can reach back and drag up out of this tired old head. I can recall something that happened fifty, sixty years ago better than what happened just last week. Why, I remember words to love songs I learned when I was just four or five year old. Or stuff that ain't got to do with nothing, except maybe my heart, like how the sky colored up so pretty of a summer morning with that pale red and orange right before that big sun ball peeped its hot face up over the mountain. Or in the wintertime taking that first breath of air so cold that it caused my nose hair to brickle, and how the deep lavender light of dawn would be laying about in every crease and crevice there in the cove and the mountains off toward Tennessee would be wearing their misty shrouds. Or how I asked Granny one time if she thought green might be God's favorite color since he'd made so many different shades of it. I remember sweet things, too.

The way Zeke's eyes changed color with his moods, the wonderment on John Wesley's baby face when he found his hand, the sweet milk breath of all my children, the time little Ingabo pulled all the green 'maters and when I fussed at her she shrugged her shoulders and said, "I'll just have to take them and hang them back."

Maybe it has something to do with what's important to us, and what happens when you get old ain't too important. Granny said it was because them early memories was stored in the uncluttered mind of a child. I reckon that's one of the prettiest ways to explain it that I've ever heard.

CAROLINA WAS ALREADY A month old when the first deep snow of the season fell. It had stayed warm right up till then. Then it was as though winter had just been biding her time, saving it up. It snowed just about every day till way up in March. Most folks just hunkered down, waiting for it to be over. But weather never slowed Hackley and Larkin down even a little bit. They was always together and always out going and doing just like boys probably always have and always will. Some mornings just at daylight I'd look out and there they'd be heading down the main trace. I'd know they was heading for Big Laurel Creek. They had traps sunk in the deepest pools and went to check them at least every other day.

Oh, how I envied them two boys their carefree ways. It had only been four years since I'd gone traipsing along with them. It was *me* that learned them how to set their traps deep so only the biggest muskrats would go for the bait, *me* that Larkin come crying to wondering if the trap hurt when it closed on them, *me* that learned them to swim in the deep water of the Seward Hole, *me* that used to go with them to the creek in the still of a winter's snow. And it was *me* that was standing there with a great yearning in that cold little cabin my husband had built with loving hands, *me* that was now held back by the strong yet flimsy chain of flesh that was my own creation.

THEY WAS NO EASY way to get to the creek where it twisted and snaked its way around the foot of the mountain and was bordered on one side by a sheer rock cliff called Jumped-Up. It got named that 'cause it really did look like it had jumped up out of the water right on to the side of that mountain and it kept a stubborn grip for a hundred feet or more before it finally give way to the laurel hell that went the rest of the way to the top.

In the wintertime the clouds seemed living things that would lower their big faces right to the top of the mountain like they aimed to kiss it. As you went down the path to the only ford, they'd boil all about you, coiling around and sending out little ragged bits like arms and fingers, reaching and touching. Little towhees would come spiraling up off the limbs of the jack pines and dive right over what looked like the edge of the world. About halfway down you'd come out of a switchback and step right out of the clouds but they'd be right above your head, the bottom all bruised-looking with fat flakes of snow falling straight down. And as far as you could see, which was awfully far, was the world made soft by snow. "Granny's beat-up egg whites," Larkin would always say. God, I loved him and the things he'd say sometimes. And we'd all three just sing.

Hackley's voice was always certain, wrapping sure and confident around each note, moving along easy, up and down. Oh, but Larkin's was a wonderment, pure and clear, hitting them high notes and holding them, holding them.

Little Marg'ret a-setting in her high hall chair
Combing back her long yeller hair
Saw Sweet William and his new maid bride
Riding up the road so near.

She threw down her ivory comb,
Threw back her long yeller hair,
Said, "I'll go down and bid him farewell
And never more go there."

It was late in the night,
They were fast asleep.
Little Marg'ret appeared all dressed in white
Standing at their bed feet.

"How do ye like your snow-white pillow?
How do ye like your sheets?
How do ye like that pretty fair maid
That lays in your arms asleep?"

"Very well do I like my snow white pillow,
Well do I like my sheet,
Much better do I like that pretty fair maid
That stands at my bed feet."

He called his serving man to go
Saddle the dappled roan
And he went to her father's house that night
And knocked on the door alone.

"Is Little Marg'ret in her room?
Or is she in the hall?"

"Little Marg'ret's in her cold black coffin
With her face turned toward the wall."

"Unfold, unfold those snow-white robes,
Be they ever so fine,
For I want to kiss them cold, corpsey lips,
For I know they'll never kiss mine."

Three times he kissed her cold, cold chin,
Twice't he kissed her cheek.
Once't he kissed her cold, corpsey lips
And fell in her arms asleep.

Larkin never even strained on the high notes that had me screeching at the top of my lungs. It's a good thing he didn't have to study awfully much about the tune because he just lost himself in them stories. When he was little he'd put his own self *right there*, living it, breathing life into it. Listening to him sing never failed to jerk goosebumps up on my arms. Even Hackley, who went along not noticing much, would sometimes stare at him and say something like, "Damn boy."

But they was no beating Hackley when it come to a tune. He went whistling one all the time and once't he could whistle it good he could play it on the fiddle. Oh, how he could make them strings pull at your insides. "Your very guts," Granny said. When he took a hold of a bow, that fiddle might as well get ready because it was going to *weep*. Don't git me wrong, many was the time I watched all the girls go hungry-eyed when he'd commence to singing. But they went plumb foolish when he played. And Hackley loved the girls, any shape and any size. So he played a lot.

But even then, with Mary fixing to turn eleven and him just thirteen, Hackley told Larkin that day he wanted her for his own and aimed to marry her one day.

Larkin said they'd built a lean-to right next to the creek out of pine boughs and had a big fire going. Hackley was stretched out with his feet almost in the flames and Larkin was setting out in the weather.

"I can hear the snow falling all around me," he said. And Hackley had answered with the same thing I often said: "You say the damnedest things."

But if you think about it, you *can* hear snow falling all crackly-like.

They stayed around down there most of that day, playing in the snow, laying by the fire, eating what they'd brung with them. "I purely love this time of the year," Hackley said. And Larkin asked him, "Do you really aim to marry Mary?" Hard to think that even as boys she was always there between them, but oh, yes, she was. And when Larkin asked him if he'd thought whether Mary wanted to marry him, Hackley had shrugged and said, "Why, I reckon she does. I mean, I ain't thought about it much. Just figured when it come time, she would."

And Larkin said even then he wanted his mind off of that, so he'd asked Hackley to sing something he didn't know, and that was the day he learned "The Cruel Mother."

They was a lady who lived in York, all alone and lone-y,
She fell in love with her father's clerk, all down by the green
    wood-side-y.

They hadn't been courting but a year and a day, all alone and lone-y,
Until her heart he did betray, all down by the green wood-side-y.

As she was a walking across the bridge, all alone and lone-y,
She saw her belly were growing big, all down by the green
  wood-side-y.

She turned her back against the oak, all alone and lone-y,
First hit bent and then hit broke, all down by the green wood-side-y.

She leaned her back against the thorn, all alone and lone-y,
There's where her two purty babes were born, all down by the
  green wood-side-y.

She pulled out her snow-white breast, all alone and lone-y,
And bid them purty babes suck their best, all down by the green
  wood-side-y.

She took her hair so long and neat, all alone and lone-y,
To tie them with, both hands and feet, all down by the green
  wood-side-y.

She took a penknife keen and sharp, all alone and lone-y,
And pierced these two purty babes to the heart, all down by the
  green wood-side-y.

And with a napkin from her head, all alone and lone-y.
She wrapped them up when they were dead, all down by the green
  wood side-y.

She wiped her penknife on her shoe, all alone and lone-y,
But the more she wiped the redder hit grew, all down by the green
  wood-side-y.

She placed them under a marble stone, all alone and lone-y,
And prayed this murder would never be known, all down by the
  green wood-side-y.

I can just see Larkin, eyes shut tight, already making it his own, imagining that poor girl returning to her father's house pretending to be still a maid, thinking of the ghosts of the murdered children coming to call. Them children then telling their own mommie she was doomed for hell.

He'd be learning it to me in a week's time and asking, "Why do you reckon she let them suck if she just aimed to kill them?" I had no answer unless it was that she was a coldhearted and selfish bitch, which is just what I said to him. And he said he'd asked Hackley the same thing and I asked, "Well, what did he say?"

Hackley said just this: "Hell if I know. Just the way them old songs is, sometimes."

## 4

I HAD MY FOURTH child that we named Sylvaney the year Larkin turned thirteen, and that was also the year I was afraid he would never sing again.

Hugh Wallin's singing school met every summer where he taught the shape-note singing which went like this: a flag shape for fa, circle for sol, diamond for mi, and a square for la. When we all learned the music, we would sing the poetry. The church was always full to busting and we divided ourselves into the three parts, which was tenor, lead, and bass. The singing always started at 9:00 in the morning and more times than not we'd go straight through until suppertime with the number of folks singing ebbing and flowing as some would quit and eat and come back to sing again.

Every time Hackley got called on to lead a hymn the tenors, which was where all the young girls was setting, would go all a-twitter. He knew it, too; however much he acted like he didn't, he did. And this day was no different. He stood and literally flowed into the open center and even I could see what they did. He might have been little but he had that way of moving that women just loved. He held himself all loose and easy and his eyes looked lazy and quick at the same time. Even some of the older women set into fanning themselves. Maggie Hensley was like a worm in a hot skillet, and if I'd acted like that about another man Zeke Wallin would've slapped me blind. I would not have blamed him neither.

All but Mary Chandler. She set there with her hands folded on top of her book and never offered Hackley so much as a glance. And I believe that's why she was all he could see.

" 'Sacred Throne,' folks. Page thirty-five." He waited until pages had ceased rustling and all eyes were on him. Satisfied, he raised his right hand and began to beat out the time.

"Now sing your parts! Everbody sing!"

This was Hackley's favorite hymn and he had no use for the book in his hand. His eyes were never still as he began to sing the lead shapes. And each section in that little church began to sing in harmony so rich it caused my throat to swell up.

"Now sing the poetry!" He threw back his head, closed his eyes, and I forgot everything except the sound. There was a big silence when we finished. Hugh new what he was doing when he called on Larkin to lead the next. Not many people could follow Hackley.

Larkin stood and walked to the square.

"Let's sing 'Windham,' page two hundred and seven." All eyes gazed at him expectantly. "Let's pitch it." He closed his eyes and relaxed. His voice took the first note, then began the climb up the scale.

"Sol, fa, mi, la, sol."

On the high sol Larkin's voice sang out confident and full. Then it cracked. A little frown puckered his forehead and he cleared his throat and started again.

"Sol, fa, mi, la, sol."

Again he couldn't hold it. It was so quiet in there that I could hear folks laughing and talking out where they was eating.

"That's a good pitch, Larkin. Let's sing the shapes," Hugh said.

I could see his hand trembling as he started to beat out the time and sing the shapes to the hymn.

Finally he just quit singing but stayed on beating out the time for everybody else. I quit, too, and watched the sweat run down his face into his eyes. Then the song ended and he ought to have set down, but he didn't. Instead he brought up his book and stared at it dumb-looking as a cow, as though somewhere in there amongst the shapes he had memorized so easy when he was but a child lay the answer. He looked at me and I swear he looked like he was drowning.

Me and Granny both come to our feet but Hackley beat us to him.

"I'll lead the next one," Hack said, and though he laid a sympathetic hand on Larkin's arm, he couldn't quite hold back the grin that skittered across his mouth. And I thought, *Don't do this to him, Hackley, you little shit.* But he'd already done it.

Hackley give him a little shove. "It'll be all right," he said.

"Don't pay Hack no mind," I hollered right out. "Sing with the basses. Your voice won't break if you sing low."

It didn't. For Larkin did not sing another note the rest of that long day.

I DONE SOMETHING THAT day that I rarely did. I left Abby and Zeke to fix their own supper and mind the young'uns and I went over the hill to Granny's. I did take Sylvaney but would've left her too if I hadn't knowed my bosoms would give me a fit if she didn't nurse. And it were a good thing I did 'cause I was there a long time. Granny had her hands full of one awfully pitiful man-child.

He was setting on the porch, long legs drawed up, head resting on his knees, and he never even looked up when I howdied the house.

Me and Granny whispered around out back for a few minutes, then we both went out on him. Granny put her knobby old hand on his hair and her touch was so gentle it jerked tears to my eyes.

"Hit happens that-a-way, honey. Yer voice is changing into that of a man. You'll still be able to sing, just deeper and different. You'll see. Same thing happened to Hackley. 'Course hit went quick fer him. Didn't it, Arty?"

And I said, "Why, he squalled and screeched around at them singings for two, three months. Cut up and made such an ungodly racket just to draw attention to himself that Hugh had to make him hush up more than once't. Remember?"

His voice come out all muffled against his knees. "Didn't seem to bother Hack at all." He give a big heaving sigh and then said, "But what if I can't?"

Granny snorted, tugging at his hair a bit. "Can't sing, you mean? Raise your head and look at me," she said in her best no-foolishness voice.

Larkin looked up and my breath caught in my throat. He'd been crying and I thought, *Oh, honey, bless your heart.*

"Son, do you recall me ever lying to you?" Granny said in the softest voice I'd ever heard her use.

He shook his head.

"Then believe me when I tell you that this will pass. Time takes care of most things and hit'll take care of this."

She got down on her knees right in front of him and pulled him straight into her arms. She rocked him like a baby, singing to him the whole time. He let her do it too. And I stood there rocking Sylvaney and my milk let down and wet the front of my dress.

When she was done he pulled back and said, "What song was that, Granny?"

"Pappy called it 'The Blackest Crow.'" She smiled.

I said, "Aunt Vesty said it were 'My Dearest Dear.' Pretty, ain't it? You ought to sing it."

He said, "That's easy for you to say. But I can't." And he drawed his knees up and pushed his face back between them.

Now I'd had enough and I said so.

But Granny said, "You hush, Arty, and go set down over yonder and feed Sylvaney."

And I went because she told me to and felt foolish in the doing of it. Me a mommie four times and I turned right around like a slip of a young'un and set down.

"You will, Larkin. Don't quit trying. It'll come." When she went to get up her knees popped like a gunshot. "I promised you, didn't I?"

I reckon he needed something. So he held tight to her words as summer give way to fall.

EVERY OCTOBER ME AND Zeke had a frolic at our house. He was a fine banjo picker and loved to make music. We'd move all the furniture out into the yard so we could have lots of room for the dancing, which I loved to do. I will have to say that I was light on my feet and turned many a head when I hit the floor. I went by Granny's the night before to make sure they was coming. Truth be known, I wanted to eyeball Larkin. He hadn't come by the house in ages and my mind kept turning to him, worrying about him. And I do not worry well. I am as bad as a man to want to fix things.

When I went in the door Granny was mending a shirt by the light of the fire and Larkin was setting on the floor beside her. She lapped the shirt and leaned forward to spit in the fireplace. "Look what the cats drug in," she said, but I could tell she was glad to see me. Larkin never even looked up, just stared on like they was some big exciting thing other than the fire going on in the fireplace.

Me and Granny talked about this and that and when I just couldn't stand it no more, I asked both of them if they was coming to the frolic. But I was talking mostly to Larkin and he was the one that answered.

"No," he said.

I flew mad and opened my mouth to say something mean, but Granny stood of a sudden and set herself right down on the floor beside him. They was nothing then for me to do but set down on the other side. We set a while and the only sound was the hissing of the fire. Then Granny said in an easy, talky voice, and she did not even look at Larkin, "I was trying to remember the words to a love song yesterday," and then she stopped and never said nothing for a long time. I knowed she wanted Larkin to say the words but I can be right impatient at times and this was one of them. She give me a quick frown when I started talking but I was already in it now.

"Which song? I can't believe you've forgot words to a song."

She was still frowning at me when she started to hum the tune. I recognized it right off but knew better than to say anything else. I didn't even have Sylvaney to nurse this time and figured she'd just run me off.

"Yes, Arty," she said and her voice was not sweet when she spoke my name. "It is bad when ye get to where ye can't remember words you've knowed for seventy years." She began humming, stopped, shook her head.

"Real fine song, 'Pretty Peggy-o.' Recall the tune just fine, but the words don't come." She started up a low humming and started to sing. I was shocked at how phlegmy and coarse her voice was and tried to remember if it had sounded like this back in the summer and realized with a certain sadness that yes, it had been just this way.

Come a-trippin' down the stairs, Pretty Peggy-o
Come a-trippin' down the stairs, Pretty Peggy-o

She stopped. "That ain't right."

"That's the third verse," Larkin spoke like he just couldn't help himself. "First one starts out, 'As we marched down to Fennary-o.' "

I nodded. "That's right."

The fire gave a mighty crack, and a red chunk of wood shot out. Granny slapped it onto the hearthrock with her hand and at the same time give me such a look as would have shut the lying mouth of Satan himself.

"Saddens me to think I've forgot one of Pappy's favorites." She sucked in a big chest full of air and puffed out her cheeks when she breathed out, as she was wont to do. "Sing it for me."

Larkin's eyes went back to watching that miserable fire.

"You know I can't sing no more. Voice won't do a thing I want it to. Breaks and wobbles around. Sounds sometimes like a girl's."

Granny give a big snort. "My voice ain't likely to grace no stages neither, and I ain't gonna git mine back. This singing ain't about purty voices, nohow." She reached out and grabbed his chin, made him look at her. "It's the story what's important, Larkin, not how purty you sing it."

Something moved in his eyes. Whatever it was, it wrenched my heart and I would have said something but I did not and was later glad that I held my tongue, which, as you have probably figured by now, could be sometimes sharp.

"Sing it." She weren't ordering him to do it, she was pleading with him. "For me."

Finally he began to sing in a low, soft voice.

> As we marched down to Fennary-o
> As we marched down to Fennary-o
> Our captain fell in love with a lady like a dove
> And they called her name Pretty Peggy-o.

And though his voice was uncertain, cracked at times, bounced back and forth between that of man and child, we both could hear what it would become. Granny began to cry and it was this that was his undoing.

"Granny?" he said, coming up on his knees.

She laid the rock hard palm of her hand right on his cheek. "My Pappy has been gone from this world for nigh on sixty years now. I told ye a while ago that I can't remember much a'tall, and that was the truth. They's times when I'm hard pressed to recall Pappy's dear old face, try as I might. But just now, while you was singing, his face come to me so sharp and clear it near about took my breath away. It were your singing, child. You sounded just like him."

"I'm sorry, Granny."

Now Granny was staring at the fire, but she turned from it and looked him right in the face and her face just beamed. "Oh, Larkin, honey, it were a good thing. Just fer a minute I had my Pappy back. Ye give me something just now that I never thought I'd hear ever again." Her bright eyes moved around the cabin then came back to him. "When you're young it's hard to believe when somebody dies that they are gone forever, Larkin. You got nothing to lay forever out next to, nothing to measure it against." Granny hitched a bony shoulder. "You don't even know what you'll miss about them. Oh, you have some notion, I reckon. You figure you'll miss seeing them everyday, stuff like that. But, ye've no idea about them little things—Pappy was deaf in one ear and had a way of turning his good ear toward whoever was talking, sort of cocked his head to one side. He was a big man, and when he walked his feet would slap against the floor real heavy-like. Couldn't sneak up on nothing, that's why he had to be such a good shot with a gun. And, law how he'd laugh. Big booming sound. Why, he'd get so tickled sometimes that his eyes would just pour the water. And he was hot-natured and whenever he's out working he'd sweat enough fer two men. He'd cuss them gnats something fierce." And though her eyes were pouring water she laughed plumb out loud. "Called 'em dog-pecker gnats."

I couldn't help it. I laughed too, and so did Larkin.

Then she said, "I never knowed how quiet my world would be without him in it."

Larkin spread his fingers in a gesture of awkward compassion. "Granny, I—" he began.

"Shhh. I'm studying about things, Larkin. Leave it be."

I KNOW THIS MIGHT sound funny, but what I remember most about that winter was how quiet it was. Always before, and I really do mean most of the time—and especially in the cold weather when sound carried best—you could hear Hackley or Larkin, and usually both, singing all over the cove. But Hackley had set in to some serious sparking with Mary, and though I'd bet you a hundred dollars that if Larkin was trying to sing, he was not doing it where anybody could hear him. He drug around like a whupped dog as Christmas come and went and a new year started. Though I felt sorry for him, it got to where I could not hardly stand to be around him. Granny said it didn't seem to be hurting how much he could eat, which I witnessed firsthand when he come by the house to help Zeke slaughter a shoat that got its head hung between the bars of the hogpen and choked itself. He could flat put it away and was getting way tall and his shoulders was broadening up. He was going to be a pretty thing, but God, he was not pretty now. He slinked around looking like death warmed over, all hunched up and pulled in on himself, never looking nowhere but at the ground. I just wanted to wring a chunk out of him and say, *Larkin Stanton, you straighten up,* or something along them lines. But Zeke told me to let him be, that he'd come along, and I could only believe him since I had no experience at being a big boy. And it was not that I did not already have my hands full of young'uns and work, work, work. I was proud to see spring come on and then the summer, even though it brought biting flies, more fleas, and bloodsucking ticks. I could slap flies, pinch fleas, and pull ticks off. At least now I could work outside and get out of that cabin that got smaller and smaller every year.

ME AND GRANNY WAS hoeing corn up in the Jimmy Field one day that was hot as Satan's house cat. The air was so heavy I swear you could've wrung water from it like wringing out a dishrag. I had this banjo tune stuck in my head that Zeke had played the night before and that always drove me crazy. He said it was "George Booker" and I wished I could've gotten my hands on old George. I'd have killed him as dead as a hammer. Of a sudden Granny stopped hoeing and cocked her head. She was one row down from me and I had been having to really bust it to stay out in front of her so as not to backtrash her row. When she leaned on her hoe you can bet I leaned on mine, too. Granny could hoe most folks plumb out of the field, but not me, and it was with some pride that I'd taken the upper row. But I reckon pride does really goeth before a fall as I felt like I was going to fall up at any minute. "What's the matter?" I hollered and she waved a you-need-to-hush hand at me, which I did. I heard nothing but the very first of the frost bugs starting to sing out in the oaks and then it come to me, almost like a whisper. Larkin was singing. And though he was not singing big and loud, he would have had to be singing a little loud since we could hear him from where he was up in the Dave Newground. Well, I knowed then for sure that the high pure voice of the boy was gone. And then he really let loose and the flesh pebbled up on my arms.

My dearest dear, the time draws near when you and I must part.
And no one knows the inner grief of my poor aching heart,
Or what I've suffered for your sake, the one I love so dear.
I wish't that I could go with you, or you might tarry here.

I wish't your breast was made of glass, and in it I'd behold
My name in secret I would write, in letters of bright gold.
My name in secret I would write, believe me when I say
You are the one that I'll love best unto my dying day.

And when you're on some distant shore, think on your absent
   friend
And when the wind blows high and clear, a line to me pray send.
And when the wind blows high and clear, pray send it, love, to me
So I might know by your hand-write how times has gone with
   thee.

And I knew he was *in* that song. Who knows what had gone on in his head to put him in it, but he was there. I know what was in my head, though, standing there in that hot field with Granny grinning like a mule eating saw briers right below me and this black cloud of gnats dancing a jig right in front of my eyes. And I swear I felt like somebody had took their fist and hit me square in the belly and I almost doubled up. Of a sudden I was in that song too and really knew it for the first time. They was coming a time when all of us would live in a world that Granny did not and I could not help it. I started to cry and Granny must have thought I was doing that because he was singing again. And she said, "Lord, it is really just like hearing Pappy again." And I commenced to hoeing because I could not for the life of me say a word to her.

## 5

THEY WAS NEVER A time when something was not happening with them boys. And I will not call them men, even though Larkin was fifteen and Hackley was almost nineteen. They is some men that will always be boys, and Hackley was one of them. Some of that, bless his heart, was the way his history wrote itself, but my guess is he would have always been that way. Though Larkin was big as a skinned mule, he acted like nothing but the young bull that he was. I swear him and Hackley had two or three fistfights a week back then. Not with each other all the time, though they did have one or two when Larkin either beat hell out of Hackley or he would let Hackley whup him 'cause he felt sorry for him, because it *was not* in Hackley to quit. One time they got into it down at the store and Larkin hit Hackley so hard both his feet come off the ground and he went over the bank right into the branch. Then here he come back and Larkin knocked him over the bank again and again here he come back. He done that four times and every time Larkin would say, "Stay down, Hackley," but Hackley would not. Finally Clee Buckner took ahold of Hackley and held his feet off the ground till he calmed down enough to be set down. And as soon as he was turned loose, don't you know that he went right back at Larkin. I saw the look on Hackley's face then and knowed what had to be, so I hollered out, "You're going to have to put him down, Larkin." And that time when he hit Hackley he went down like you'd throwed a sack of flour on the floor. It is a good thing for them both that they did not get into it often.

They almost come to blows about Larkin's name of all things. I always wondered when that would break out, and it happened right here at the house, too. We was having a frolic and Hackley had put his fiddle down and was out with the men drinking. Now, do not get me wrong. I am not above having a drink myself now and again, but I am not for getting knee-walking drunk. I never did see no sense in that and still don't. But the men had ganged up and Sol Bullman's liquor was flowing like water that night. And Sol's liquor went down sweet and you didn't realize it had you till you was plumb cross-eyed and talking in tongues. As you probably know, they is happy drunks and mean drunks and crazy drunks. Hackley was a crazy drunk and wanted to go to fighting every time. So he'd had him a few drinks and, foolish like, Larkin set in about his name. Why Granny had mentioned it in the first place is beyond me, but she did. Larkin set right in wanting to know just how it was that Hackley had come up with his name. And Hackley said, "It just come to me." Larkin's eyes was black as the night and he said, "Is that right?" Hackley allowed that it was. They went back and forth for a bit and of a sudden they was both mad as hell and right in each other's face. I run in between them and said for them to both hush. Hackley barked out a laugh and said, "Well, I was just four year old, what did you expect?" And Larkin said, "Something better than being named after a coon dog." And me desperate to keep them from fighting, blared out, "Well, he was a damn good coon dog," which set everybody to laughing including

Hackley and Larkin. Later I told Larkin he ought to have been thankful 'cause Mommie had told me Aunt Polly aimed to name him after Grandpap Shelton. And he allowed as how that might have been better and I allowed back as how no, it would not have, since Grandpap's name was Redderdick.

But they stayed into it with them other boys around home. Zeke come in laughing one night telling me how a bunch of them had got to playing poker, which I do not believe in because it is spending money that none of us has. He said Hoy and Roy McIntosh was there and I knowed what he was going to say before he said it. I really think Hackley just did not like the way they looked or held their mouths or something just as foolish because they got into it every time they run up on each other. That was the first time that I heard how Hackley and Larkin had took to fighting back to back. When I thought of how deadly the two of them would be doing that I got the cold chills. Larkin that had them big fists and Hackley that would not quit.

WHEN DECORATION DAY COME it seemed like everybody in the world headed out to Sodom. It was always on the second weekend in August and folks started coming in on that Friday. Everybody was in a right festive mood and we'd all gang up and clean off every grave in every cemetery. It looked so pretty on that Sunday with all the graves mounded and raked smooth. I have thought about that a lot over the years and know now that they had to have been graves we didn't even know about. When I think of all the folks that has died, been buried, and forgot about, it makes me know that our lives are but a flash in the pan and we really are a short time here and a long time gone.

I have to tell you now that this year was different. I felt it right off as soon as we got to the church. I am not saying it looked any different. The little church was no big fancy thing, just a little box shape with a steeple on top in which, I'm proud to say, was a bell that we had bought from up north. On the inside we had benches that didn't have splinters on them, which is a good thing. I have set on ones that did and that was not good, because if you study about it they is no good way to dig a splinter out of that part. At the front we had a pulpit and Zeke's brother Hugh had rocked in a pretty fireplace. Two big old sugar maples stood guard on either side and they were a sight to see in the fall of the year. They give shade in the summer, and that was a good thing since it was hot as blazes this year. The men had knocked together a bunch of tables and they were already swagging with food by the time we got there to add our load. I'd cooked late into the night and got up before daylight to fry chicken and I know heaven could not smell no better than it did under them trees.

A clot of men had ganged up on the porch of Jim Leake's store. Others stood about in the yard. I could not believe how quiet they was, so I just had to wander over there to see what and all was going on. They weren't even milling about much, and I could still see where the dirt showed marks from Cassie's broom.

I went over to where Larkin was leaning against one of the posts and leaned against him. He was as still as that post listening to Wade Hensley reading the results of the election for governor from the *Asheville News*. Nobody spoke until he finished reading every thing they was to read.

"Damned if Marshall didn't go big for Ellis. Says here a hundred and fifty-six for him and eighty-two for Pool."

"What about that!" Ruben Gosnell was whittling away and the head and neck of a little bird that looked like a living thing was coming right up out of that stick. "What do you reckon they was thinking?"

"Not much, you want my opinion," Shadrack said. I did not care for Shadrack even if he was Zeke's brother. He put on airs and I told him that one time. I also told him that he put his britches on just like everybody else, so they was no love at all lost between us. "How anybody could vote for that lying suck-ass is beyond me. 'Specially after he shit us with all them promises to git that road in down through Paint Rock."

"Bet Shelton Laurel laid it to Ellis's hide, didn't they?" Hugh said. I did like Hugh, and especially his wife Rosa. Me and her had been friends for all our lives and I knowed how good he was to her and their boys. They is something to be said about a man that is good to his wife and does not use his fists on her like some others I know—which would include Shadrack, I just might tell you.

Daddy was setting next to Wade and he leaned over and squinted at the little print in the paper. *Poor old Daddy,* I thought, *His eyes are getting bad.* "Ellis didn't git a single vote in Shelton Laurel. Pool got fifty-one." He looked up. " 'Course, Ellis got four out of thirty votes in our district."

Andrew Chandler give a wave of his hand that said oh-forget-about-that. "Bet that was them Eckerds off on Spillcorn. They been fools since God's dog was a pup. Can't even hold it against them. They can't help it."

As Wade folded up the paper, Daddy said, "Well, every other district in the county except Little Pine went big for Ellis, as did Buncombe County. It'll be four more years of the same old shit."

"What hurt Pool was that business about putting a tax on everything," Zeke said. Me and him had talked a long time about that over the last month and I had told him that them folks down east ought not to have to pay for our roads and such up here but they ought not to make us pay taxes on stuff we had to have to barely survive, neither.

Andrew snorted. "How exactly you reckon they was going to figure out what we had that they could put a tax on? Ain't nobody coming into my house and nosing about, making lists."

"Felt the same way, Andrew." Daddy said. "But they was no way I was gonna vote for them yeller dogs that's in, either. We was between a rock and a hard place."

"Can't trust none of them politicians far as you can rare back and throw 'em out in the yard, anyways." Ervin Ramsey leaned forward and spit off the end of the porch. "Old Pearlie, God rest him, used to say the only folks fit to be in charge of things is them what don't want to be."

"I really miss old Pearlie," Andrew said. "He had a way of putting things that went right to the quick."

Wiley Franklin wiped his face. He was bad to sweat and his handkerchief was already sopping wet. "Well, now," he said, "Pool said something a week or so ago that was right on the money. He said they's a time coming and coming soon when we're going to wind up gitting into it with each other over this slave thing. Said them what owns niggers here in North Carolina can't raise twenty thousand men." He waved his arm at all of us standing there, "Be up to *us* to come up with the rest of 'em."

Greenberry Chandler said, "Far as I'm concerned, they ought to take all the niggers, load 'em on one of them big boats, take 'em about ten mile out into that big blue ocean and dump the lot of 'em."

"Eh law, Greenberry," Sol Bullman said. "That's the most words you strung together at one time since you married that big-mouthed sister of mine!" We all busted out laughing, for he was married to Hattie. She come from a long line of midwives and she had a way about her that said do not mess with me in any shape, form, or fashion. Most of us had been brought into this world by the rough, work-hard hands of her grandmother, mother, or in mine and Larkin's case, Hattie herself. It was a good thing Greenberry was a quiet man.

"But what about Tillman?" Andrew said.

I had not thought of Tillman Chandler in years. He used to claim me for his sweetheart but I did not claim him. He was tall and skinny, and if you was looking at Zeke you would know that I like men of a different sort. I did recall that Tillman had married a woman from Asheville whose daddy died not long after they'd set up housekeeping and that he had come into over two hundred acres and most of it good flat bottom land. It had never even flittered through my head that he would have to have slaves. But then why would it? They was no slaves in Sodom unless you counted the ones what was white and female.

"Damned if I know what to do about it," Ruben said to them. His eyes never moved from the graceful curve of that bird's wing. "But I do know it's a mess, a pure-D mess. Don't believe I understand all I know about this nigger thing anyhow." He raised the bird, give it a good long eyeball, blew on it, and went back to carving. "Never seen a man of color myself."

"Saw two of 'em last week when I was down in Warm Springs." Zeke said. "Black as the ace of spades."

"Well," Ruben said, "I can just about guarantee it'll come to war. They's too much fussing back and forth amongst 'em in Raleigh and up in Washington."

"Goodness, fellers, I reckon not." This was from old man Swan Ray. He started just about everything he said with *goodness* or *here there*. "Here there, it wouldn't be nothing to us one way or t'other. War amongst rich folks, ye ask me."

"Mayhap," Daddy said. "But somehow it always manages to work itself back around to being a poor man's fight."

"If you'uns could hear half of what I hear on my drumming route," Wade said, "you would know it will come to war. That's all I hear, 'specially down south of here."

Wade was from off down toward Hendersonville and had married Vergie Ray, who was Swan's daughter.

I was so caught up in what was being said that I jumped like somebody had poked me in the ribs when Big John Stanton's deep voice come rumbling out right there beside me. The *Big* part of his name was put there for a reason but I swear he could slip up on you and you would never know it till he wanted you to. We was not related to the Stantons but Larkin's daddy was one. Their grandma was full Cherokee and you could surely see it in both of them. She was never heard from again when they was all rounded up and took off.

Big John crossed arms big as fence posts over his chest and said, "Let it come, boys. I for one wouldn't mind a good fight."

"Maybe so, son." Wiley took his hat off and went to smearing that wet handkerchief around on his shiny bald head. "You're young and most of us ain't. But you'd still have to fight one side or the other."

"Hell, Wiley, I'm for joining the side that looked like it were going to win."

Lord have mercy, did that not set everybody to talking at once.

And would you not know that it was just then that Hackley come up to me and Larkin. He was wearing the white shirt Mommie had made him. Last week I'd gone to see if her beans had come in and they had and I was stringing and breaking them up while she sewed the buttons on it. My John Wesley loves green beans and Mommie's big greasys are the best. I must say Hackley looked like icing on a cake. Right then it come to me that my brother was one of the prettiest men I'd ever laid eyes on, even if he was grinning in a not so pretty way.

He said, "Lark, look out yonder and tell me what you see."

"Don't see much, Hack," Larkin said, though he did not do much more than let his eyes skim over the crowd. I could tell that he was way more interested in them men what was still arguing there in front of the store because of what he said next. "Have you heard any of this talk about a war?"

"War?" Hackley said, and I could have told Larkin that my brother had not lost a bit of sleep nor one waking minute with thoughts about no war. And then he said, "I want you to look at the damn prettiest girl in Madison County."

And I piped right in. "You better be thinking about something other than your jewel among women, Mary Chandler." I was trying to be funny, and Larkin picked right up on this, but it was all lost on Hackley because he got real serious. That in itself was a wondrous thing to behold, because there was not much in life that roused Hackley to seriousness.

"She is just that, sister." He had not called me sister in a long time. Then I did know that Hackley Norton was as serious as the night was long about Mary Chandler. And what he said to us next sealed the deal. The crowd sort of parted, and though I could not see from where I was, Hackley could.

"Why, that son of a bitch! Look-a there!"

Like a shot I was up on my tippy-toes trying to see. "What, what?" I said.

Larkin, being a full head and shoulders over me, said, "Willard's trying to talk to Mary."

And Hackley went rushing off, saying real loud-like, "I'll whup his ass!"

Then the crowd parted like Moses had raised his stick and I could see Willard Bullman leaning toward Mary. She had on a cream-colored dress and her waist looked slim as a boy's. I knowed for a fact that I would never see my own that slender again but I would not have traded places with her if it had meant I had to give up my young'uns and Zeke.

Hackley went out through there like a little banty rooster and when Willard saw him coming he looked around right wild. I knowed what he was looking for was standing right beside me. Everybody with any kind of sense knowed that if you messed with Hackley you had Larkin to fight and that was no fun. This is not to say my brother was not a handful all by hisself. He was. But I had my suspicions that it was Larkin they really dreaded and then I knew it for a fact, because when Willard looked and seen Lark standing there on the porch he sort of slouched off into the crowd without so much as a backward look at Mary.

But Larkin was looking at her, they was no doubt, and if you could have seen the look, it would have tipped his hand to you as it most certain did to me. It was such a look that I swear I had to look myself. And I will tell you what I saw. She was not short but not real tall, she was slender and not busty neither. Her dark red hair kept catching the light that was sifting down through the leaves. She had freckles, but they was not so many and she had that real white redhead skin. Her hands were as slender as Mommie's and I could not help it, I looked at mine. I would never have hands like them, as my fingers were too short, and I would never have the slender waist neither. But I would not complain, since Zeke seemed to like the way I was put together just fine. But Mary Chandler was as close to being beautiful as any girl I'd ever seen and I had not even noticed it until that very moment in time. I must have had my head under a bushel or maybe I'd just been raising young'uns and living my own life, thank you very much.

I could not stand to see Larkin all but slobbering on himself. "If you are going to stare so hard, you ought to at least shut your mouth," I said to him. And then I could have just bit my tongue right off at the look of longing and misery that moved through his eyes. Oh, how I wanted to take him in my arms and say, "Do not let this slip of a girl cause this thing," but felt that I ought not because I'd been so hateful and because I did not want to shame him any more than I already had. Red as a beet, he turned back to the men that was now a big crowd and loud to boot. I was never so glad to see anybody in my life as I was to see that Fee had come up and was standing on the other side of Larkin.

"Howdy, Fee," I said. His big round eyes settled on my face then moved on. Poor Fee. Talk about that hard row to hoe, well, he'd had one too. He had been named Pharaoh of Egypt Gosnell. Now why you would name a child that you loved that I do not know, and you cannot call somebody Pharaoh of Egypt anyhow, so we all called him Fee. Everybody thought he was simpleminded, but he were not and I know it. He did not think like the rest of us is all. And even though he was younger than me, Granny said he knew more about which plants could cure you and kill you than anybody in this part of the world. And, Lord, but he had a way with animals that I have never seen the likes of. The big white dog at his side was a testament to that. She were not a hound dog but looked for all the world like a wolf and might well have been just that, for all I know. But she were a pretty thing with eyes that looked smarter than some folks I know.

Larkin and Fee was in a big way of talking, which meant they were standing around shuffling their feet since neither of them was big on talking and I sneaked a look at Fee. He was not the prettiest thing in the world. When he was just little, he was skinny and his head had looked too big for his body. But when he got to be a big boy, it seemed like overnight he started sprouting coarse hair and his arms and legs literally growed ropey strings of muscle. Now as a man grown his body had surely caught up with his head, and I will have to say that standing next to Larkin Stanton did not help his looks none. Lord, but Larkin was a pretty thing. Fee's big lips skinned back over big wide-spaced teeth that was already stained from chewing 'baccer, and I allowed once more to myself that I would *never* dip snuff or chew until I no longer had teeth in my head. After that I don't reckon it would matter none.

They was talking about the dog and I looked down at her. She was looking up at Fee like he was the best thing in the world and I squatted down next to her. "Hey there, you, pretty girl," I said and she set them eyes on me and her ears stood straight up on her head. Her big red tongue come out quick as a snake and licked me right in the mouth. I couldn't do nothing but laugh and that got her even more excited but all it took was one word from Fee to put her right back to setting. "Down," he said. And I allowed that maybe he ought to come to my house and learn my young'uns how to behave as good and we all three laughed at that thought.

YOU KNOW HOW THEY is things in our life that we always remember right up to remembering right where we was, who was with us, how the sun laid on everything, what people said? Well, this proved one of them days. I'd seen Granny reach and take hold of her back down low and rub since I could remember. She was always lifting something too heavy and straining around. But it was the way she done it this day that I knew something was bad wrong. And I knew it with my very heart. When she'd come from the barn two year ago with a funny look on her face and told me she'd seen blood when she'd wiped herself I begged her to go see Hattie. Hattie told us that she had corruption, that it would get worse, but would take its own sweet time. And it had took so much time that I'd forget about it for days at a stretch. And then I'd get reminded like when we'd dug up some lilac bushes from next to her porch and planted them next to mine. "There," she had said to me, "now every time you get a whiff of them lilacs you will think of this day and us planting them together." And I said, "Lord God, Granny, don't talk like that." And she said, "Why, honey, look at how long I've had. Eighty year in case you can't count that high. I am older'n anybody I know, 'cepting for Lige Blackett and I reckon they'll have to knock Lige in the head with a frying pan on Judgment Day." When I laughed she did, too, but then she said, "Don't you tell I said that. Them Blacketts is mean as snakes and dumber than four buckets of hair." We both snickered about that because it was the truth, and then she reached out and pushed my hair back off my face like she used to do when I was a girl. "Just remember, Arty." And I said, "What?" And she got the funniest look on her face and said just this one word: "Everything."

• • •

NOW HERE WE ALL was, and I knew with every bone in me that this would be the last time we was all together. And with the knowing of that, it seemed like everywhere I looked I saw something to store up to take out and study later on.

That was the first time I noticed that Mary's little sister Julie kept sneaking looks at Larkin. She was a real sweet girl and awfully clever, but Julie did not look like Mary is the kindest way I can think to say it. I recall thinking, *You poor thing,* because Larkin did not look at her even once during that long preaching. His eyes went nowhere but to where Mary and Hackley set. So mine did too and I had to hide my smile behind my hand when Hackley tried to put his arm up around her waist and her back went straight as a poker and he finally took it away and his neck got all red. And I thought, *Good for you, Mary. You keep that up and you might get him yet.*

Mommie was bustling about, making sure all the young'uns had plates and spoons. She'd turned fifty a few months back and was more grayheaded now than blond. She was right in amongst my young'uns slinging food like a crazy woman. I had told her to wait till I finished nursing Zeke Jr. but she went right on with her rat killing like I had never said a word so I let her do it. I leaned back against the tree and looked at my brood. Abigail was like looking Mommie right in the face. John Wesley had my brown hair and green eyes and so did Sylvaney. Ingabo had curly red hair and Zeke Jr. was going to be redheaded too. I had got real tired of folks asking where these two got their red hair. Lige Blackett come right out and spoke what I knew everybody was thinking: "Are you sure these two are Zeke's?" And I fired right back at him, "Don't you think I won't smack you just because you are an old man." But they is no doubt about who daddied

Carolina. She looked like she was picked right out of Zeke's hind end, right down to her shiny black hair and purplish blue eyes. She was a Wallin to the bone.

About then Larkin come wandering up and of course Carolina set up a howling for him to pick her up. She was crazy about him and he petted her something awful.

Mommie shaded her eyes and watched as he settled Carolina on his shoulders. "You have plumb growed up," she said. Larkin blushed like a girl. I couldn't help deviling him a little.

"You better watch out, honey. Won't be long before some of these little gals set their eyes on you and go running for their mommies' brooms."

Carolina perked right up on that and hollered, "Larkin has already promised to marry me, Mama. Ain't you, Larkin?"

"That's right, missy. You need to hurry and get grown 'cause I need me a good cook. You can cook now, I know. And course you can keep house and all? Sweep and scrub the floors, milk the cows, wash my clothes, see to the garden, hoe while I'm plowing, all that stuff? You can manage that, can't you?"

I busted out laughing. I could tell by looking at Carolina's face that she had not thought of all that. Larkin had just lost himself a candidate for wife, and I told him so.

Mommie held out her arms. Larkin bent down and Carolina fairly scrambled off and hit the ground running. I do not think she wanted to hear no more about marrying. But Mommie would not let it go. "She is way too young to be thinking about that stuff. And her and Larkin is too close a kin to even let her think on it."

And I thought, *Oh, no. Here is the pursed mouth and wrinkled-up nose look.* But I had got over that bothering me and could not help ruffling her feathers a little.

"Why, in six years Carolina will be old as I was when I married her daddy. By Larkin's age I already had Abigail and we was working on John Wesley. Not even a full year between any of my first three. We was working mighty hard."

I knew I had got Mommie's goat by how red her neck got. I was sorry the minute it left my lips, but even though Larkin shot me a look, I could not wrap my tongue around the words to tell her I was sorry.

"Arty," she said, and I could tell she was mortified. "Set there and talk about getting babies. I swear sometimes . . . ."

She did not say what. But I knew already. She thought I was way too much like Granny and she looked down at the very things in me that she loved in her mama. Mommie was awful bad to preach religion this and religion that. She tried to make everything you did fit in a right place or a wrong place. But that is not the way of it all the time. They is a wide swath of life that is lived right down the middle. I wished you could have seen her face the time she asked me if I had found Jesus and I told her I did not know he had got lost. Oh, but you should *never* say something like that to them folks what have strong beliefs. I thought Mommie's eyes was going to pop right out on stems. I will never do that again.

About then I saw Granny take a drink from her crock and Mommie seed her too and I thought, *Oh, Lord,* and I was right, because Mommie set in on her right off.

"You ought not to drink spirits," she said.

And Granny said back, "The gripe in my belly's worse. Liquor with willer bark tea is about the only thing that helps it."

Mommie looked right shocked at that but fussed at her, "That liquor ain't good for your body or your soul. You ought to drink tea mixed with water. I don't see how you hold all that liquor anyways."

And Granny said the funniest thing I'd ever heard, but I know exactly what she meant now because I am the same way. She said, "Hell, Nancy, I can hold my liquor a lot better than I can hold my water nowdays."

I laughed so hard that I had to lay down. Zeke Jr. fell asleep. I must've dozed a little, too, since the next thing I recall is hearing Mommie and Granny talking real low as they put food away and gathered up the dishes.

"Why do you reckon Arty won't listen to a word I say? I swear sometimes she acts like I ain't got the sense God give a goose and she just baits me."

Of a sudden I was wide awake and listening to every word.

"Nancy, Nancy, Nancy." Granny give that sound that meant she'd puffed out her cheeks. "Arty's just who she is. And it ain't just how she acts toward you. You got your ways too."

That was surely the truth.

Mommie put on her best I-am-just-killed voice and said, "I have always wanted to be close to her. She is my oldest daughter."

And Granny actually laughed at her. "Ye take yourself way too serious, Nancy Ann. Always your way or no way. Well, in case you ain't noticed Arty is as tough as a pine knot and she has her own way."

Mommie sounded so pitiful then that even I felt sorry for her. "Well, I can done see that you're just going to take her side of it."

I was plumb surprised when Granny cut her off. "I have no time for this. You and Arty need to come of it because it ain't going to be no time till it's just you and her for it. And I don't know what in this world Larkin will do when I am gone."

Of a sudden I felt selfish. All I had thought of was me, me, me, and it were Larkin what stood to lose biggest of all and he probably did not even know. I set straight up then and looked around for him. It did not take me long to find him. He was right back over there at the store where them men was still talking, no doubt that war business. And as if they had read my very thoughts I heard somebody holler out the word *War.*

Granny shook her head and her next words come out on a long sigh that sounded like it had whistled right out of her soul. "All this talk about war. The men might fight it, but it is always the women that suffers it."

And Mommie said, "They'll be no war. But even if they is, it won't be nothing to us."

"They will be sides took, and that will mean a fight," Granny said, and right then it hit me and Mommie at the same time because neither one of us had a word to say back to her. Zeke Jr. slept on, but my mind was flying. How old did you have to be before you did not have to go off to fight? Or how young? Would Daddy have to go? Surely he would not, as he were an old man of fifty-one. If not him, then what of my brothers David and Willy? They was both married and had a dozen young'uns between and surely they would not have to go. But Robert and Hackley would. And I almost laughed at the thought of Hackley in a war, but I did not because I felt that yes, he would have to go too. Then I felt cold all over because I thought of Larkin and Zeke. But I am not one to worry with something that I cannot wrap my mind around. *They will not be a war* is all I could think as I picked Zeke Jr. up off that quilt and hauled myself to my feet. *They will not be a war because Arty will not allow it.*

But they was nobody there to sass me back and tell me that Arty might not be the one in charge on that day.

# 6

GRANNY WANTED THE DOOR open and the light of the hunter's moon had come dashing itself across the floor like bright-colored water and had crawled its way up in the bed with her. If you had told me that corruption would lay waste to a body the way it had Granny's in just three months, I would have called you a dirty liar. But it had, and laying there in that bed she looked as little as one of my least girls. Larkin was setting in the doorway with his feet on the outside step. He had his elbows propped on his knees and his hands was hanging down loose between them. I almost wished that he had gone on hunting with Hackley and them boys that had stopped by here before good and dark. He looked pitiful setting there. The moon's light laid flat on his face, and had it been a summer moon, it would have been pretty to see. But they is something about moonlight in the fall that I did not like then and do not like now. Granny had twisted and turned and fought the covers so that I was just wore out with trying to keep her covered up. From up on the ridge above the house, a panther squalled and a hen in the chicken coop answered it with a nervous chuckle. Granny opened her eyes and looked right at me.

"That would be the little hen Hattie give me two year ago. She's a good layer and right pert for a hen anyways," she said.

Larkin got up and drug him a chair to set next to me. The slats squeaked as he leaned forward to take her skinny little hand in his big one. He brought up the crock of white liquor we'd been keeping next to the bed. He took a sip and tilted it in her direction. "You ready for some more, Granny?"

"Pour me some and help me set up," her voice come all whispery.

I sloshed a fair amount into a tin cup and Larkin helped her up. He looked at me and I saw his hurt plain as day. How anybody could be as little as her and still live was beyond us both. She slurped noisily from the cup. "Lay me back down now, honey. Hit makes me dizzy to set up long."

I took the cup and looked down in it a minute, then I turned it up and drunk what was left. It burned like fire going down and I was thankful for it. My belly got all warm and I felt a little light-headed and was glad for that as well.

He eased her back onto the mattress and I pulled the quilts up and made a big do of tucking them under her chin. She'd stopped eating a week ago and I kept piling on the quilts because I couldn't stand the thoughts of her being cold.

"Mommie will come tomorrow," I said to Larkin.

"It'll be too late tomorry, honey," she whispered, staring out the door.

We never said nothing and in a little bit she said it again and her voice was a little stronger.

"I said it'll be too late tomorry. I don't aim to be here when the day breaks."

And I could tell by her tone that she meant just what she said.

She dozed off, but Larkin kept on holding her hand. Of a sudden she roused up and her eyes flew open.

"Josie? Oh, Josie, look. Them cats has found the nest of baby rabbits back an under the porch. Oh, no! They've hurt one of 'em bad. Try to catch it. We'll nurse it back. Damn cats!" Her hands sort of twisted around on the quilt and then were still.

Larkin leaned back hard in the chair, brought his hands up to his face, and fisted his eyes. I thought he was fixing to cry and I wanted to say to him, *This dying is hard business,* but I did not because his head nodded forward and his chin dipped toward his chest and I knowed he was asleep. I was tired myself but knew I could not sleep so I set there still as a rock and waited—for what, I did not know. A stretch of time went by and up on the mountain the big cat squalled again and I thought, *If any sound could wake the dead it would be that,* and then I felt all funny because I had even thought it. But it did wake Larkin up. We set a long while with neither of us saying a word. Then I was so glad he had not gone with them boys and left me there by myself. When Granny spoke I think it scared us both.

"Larkin, boy? Carry me out into the moonlight. I want to see it all one more time."

I would have hated to have been the one that tried to stop him from taking her out. It was not going to be me, even if I did think it was too cold. He took her up quilts and all, ducked through the door and they was gone out into the bright of that October moon.

If I close my eyes I can still see it and it was a sight to see. He stood in the middle of all that light and it changed them both into something other than what they had been inside the house. Though I had never seen no haints I allowed as how they must look just like them and though I knowed it was Granny and Larkin I could not help my-self making an X over my heart.

Granny sort of sighed and said, "Ain't many folks gits to leave this world by the light of a blue moon. Two full hunter's moons . . ." Her eyes glowed with the light. "Sing for me, Larkin."

"What do you want me to sing, Granny?"

"Why, my favorite," she said.

And though his voice was soft, it was the best I would ever hear him sing "Pretty Saro."

When I first come to this country, in 1749,
I saw many fair love'yers but I never saw mine.
I viewed all around me, saw I was quite alone
And me a poor stranger and a long ways from home.

Fare-thee-well to old mother, fare-thee-well to father, too,
I'm a-goin' for to ramble this wide world all through,
And when I get weary, I'll sit down and cry,
And think of my darlin Pretty Saro, my bride.

Well hit's not this long journey I'm a-dreading for to go.
Nor the country I'm a-leavin' nor the debts that I owe
There's only one thing that troubles my mind,
That's leavin' my darlin' Pretty Saro behind.

Well I wish't I was a poet, an' could write some fine hand.
I would write my love a letter that she might understand,
And I'd send hit by the waters where the islands overflow.
And I'll think of my darlin' wherever I go.

Well, I strove through the mountings, I strove through the main,
I strove to forget her but it was all in vain,

From the banks of old Cowhee to the mount of said brow,
Where I once't loved her dearly, and I don't hate her now.

Well, I wish't I was a turtle dove had wings and could fly.
Right now to my love'yer's lodgings tonight I'd draw nigh,
And there in her lily-white arms I would lay there all night.
And I'd watch them little windows fer the dawning of day.


"Sounded so much like my Pappy," Granny said, and I could not help it, I started to cry. "Hush up," she said, and her voice sounded light as the air. "You ain't never been one to cry and carry on any such a-way." I straightened right up at that. Then she said, "Drop the quilts, Larkin. I want to feel the wind on my arms and legs."

"Granny, it's cold out here. Keep the quilts on." I don't know why I was so worried about them quilts but it was all I could think about.

The quiet got awfully big in the long time it took her to gather up to answer. "Let them fall, Arty. Hit don't matter no more. I feel warm as I did when I was a girl."

And the quilts slid off and I pulled them away from his feet and stood there with them balled up in my arms. The wind come up then and lifted her hair, worried at the hem of her nightgown, and she smiled at us. "My mammy used to tell me that they was no such thing as dying. Said we really was just born twice't. Once to this place, then again into the t'other. Said we entered both like newborn babies. And she said just like we waited for a baby to be born in this world, they's folks waiting fer us to be born over yonder." And her breath kept coming out and coming out, but it was only when Larkin called her name that it rose back up and her eyes opened and she stared right at me.

"You see to everything, Arty," she said.

I had such a knot of tears in my throat that I could barely say to her, "Yes, I will."

"Ye'll be all right, son? Tell me."

"I'll be all right, Granny. I swear."

And I said in a strangled voice, "No, oh, no."

Her eyes moved from his face and got all dreamy as they found the moon. Suddenly her eyes got big and wide and she said, "Oh, they are all here now! Pappy!"

And with them words Sarah Elizabeth Gentry Shelton was born again.

IT WAS FULL DAYLIGHT when Mommie stepped up on the porch of the cabin and saw the open door. She come pounding across the porch, calling "Mama? Arty? Oh, God."

I got up from the fireplace where I was laying a fire. "She's gone. She went last night, or I reckon it was really this morning."

"Oh, Lord, have mercy on her soul," Mommie said, then she went to crying like her heart was broke. I let her cry. Sometimes that's the best we can do for somebody, to just let them cry.

I had already sent Larkin to Greenberry's to tell him and Sol to start charring out the coffin and on to tell Hattie to bring her corpse herbs. While we was waiting for him to get back, I told Mommie what had happened out there in the yard.

"She was looking up at the moon, but her eyes weren't seeing no moon. They was looking far off. And then I got the feeling that the yard was full of people. They was swirling all around us just for a thought, petting her and easing her somehow. And then they was just gone. Her too."

We just set there for a while drinking our coffee and then I said, "Well, I ain't sure what to do next, Mommie."

Mommie looked at me and her eyes was as dry as dust and blue as the sky and she said, "That's all right, honey. *I* know what to do. We'll get through it together."

And she sounded so much like Granny I could not help it then, I started to cry.

Granny had buried Pap on the high ridge that looked out on the whole valley of Sodom. Mommie had fussed that it was too hard a climb and Granny had said to her, "Why, Nancy, they'll carry me ever step of the way one of these days. I want to be planted where I can see the whole cove and be able to watch my people light the lamps in the morning and blow 'em out at night. And bury me with my shoes on 'cause if they's any way to come back, I'm coming. And if I can't, then what better place than up there? They ain't no prettier place in the world."

So we climbed. Up past the blackberry patch, dried up and withered from the early frost. Up past the big old chestnut trees with their limbs almost brushing the ground with nuts. On up past the cave and across the gully wash that held the tracks of a big panther. On up to the very spine of the ridge, where, for all of her talk about it being the prettiest place in the world, all I saw waiting for her was a lonesome hole in the ground. Everybody sung as they lowered her, but I could not. They was not a single word that found its way from my hurting heart.

We'll camp a little while in the wilderness, in the wilderness, in the wilderness.

We'll camp a little while in the wilderness, and then I'm a-goin' home.

And then I'm a-goin' home, and then I'm a-goin' home.

We're all a-makin ready, oh ready. And then I'm a-goin' home.

And then Hackley stepped right up to that dark hole that was now full of her and put his fiddle under his chin and played "Pretty Saro" and finally I felt the tears that had strangled me all morning start to let down. It was like that fiddle reached right in my throat and untangled the knot and I thought, *Bless you, Hackley.* I was not the only one. They was not a dry eye amongst us by the time he lowered the fiddle to his chest and, still playing, closed his eyes and sung it through.

Nobody said a word as the bow stroked that final note. Not a single word. Then the preacher just said, "Amen," and the crowd give a big sigh all together and everybody started to straggle off back down the mountain. But when Larkin made to leave I said to him, "No, me and you will stay. She would not have left either one of us." And we not only stayed, we helped Fee and them shovel in the dirt. I had kept her covered with them damn quilts and I felt it was my job to help cover her one last time.

I think the eating and mingling that goes on when somebody dies is to keep everybody from thinking about the thing their mind most wants to dwell on. That would be the person you had just put in the cold ground forever and ever because if we tried to think of all them empty days and nights to come, right then we would all go completely foolish. So we eat and talk and eat some more. Back at Granny's house that day it were no different. Except that this time she were not there to see to things and my eyes would not stay away from her chair by the fireplace or her digging stick hanging by the door or all the things that called out to me, *Here I am, but where is she?*

"SHE WANTED YOU TOOK care of, honey," Mommie said to Larkin as she put out food back at the cabin. "She wanted you to have the home place and that clinches it for all of us. It's yours."

He stood there with the blush of a boy still on him, trying to be a man, and, oh, how my heart just broke for him. "You do not have to stay here by yourself, honey," I said. "You come home with me."

What he said next cut me to the quick because it were the truth. "You don't have the room, Amma."

I wanted to argue with him and did, but he were set against it, and I finally had to turn from him and go to helping Mommie lay out the food that kept coming and coming. I thought to myself, for a bunch of people that has no money, it is a wonder we are not all big as fattening hogs for all that we are rich in food.

Hackley come up about that time and I could not help but hear what he was saying. I swear Hackley never said the right things. But you always knew what he was thinking since that was just what he said. He was gnawing on a piece of cornbread while he talked. "I know you hated to see Granny go. But at least you can go hunting with us and stuff now."

I felt the itch in my hand to jerk him up and just blister him like I used to do.

He went right on, though. "I guess that scared you and Arty when she up and died on you. I don't cotton to being around no dead people."

Before I could open my mouth Larkin put him in his place and did a much better, or at least quieter, job of it than I would have.

"It was not a scary thing, Hackley. I would not have missed being there for nothing in this world."

I was about to put in my two-cents worth but did not have to, because Mary come through the door right then and I become invisible to them both. She come across that floor a girl with a mission, and you would have had to drug me away by the hair of the head.

"I'm sorry about your Granny, Larkin." She sounded all out of breath and I peeped a look at her and thought, *Oh, my,* because there she stood looking up at Larkin with that red hair all tousled by the wind up on the mountain and her cheeks all pinked up from the climb and the sun.

Larkin thanked her and Hackley was squirming around her like a big puppy. I thought he was going to go to pissing on the floor at any minute. But for once her attention was not on my brother. It was leveled right at Larkin.

"Sary was a fine person" was all that young'un said as she put one of them slender hands like I would never have on his arm, and I saw heat red as a flame lick its way up the back of his neck. It was a good thing Hackley was blind to everything except what concerned him and only him, or there would have been a killing right then and there. But I don't know which one he would have killed. I looked her hard in the face and will have to say I saw no sign that she had knowledge of what she was doing to either one of them. If she had a notion she could have fooled the devil himself, for her face looked innocent as the day was long. I thought, *Arty, you must tell her,* but I did not do this until years down the road, and by then it would be too late. But we look back with vision that is crystal clear and we have no eyes whatsoever with which we can see the future.

Hackley done what he always did do, which was turn her where only he filled up her sight. He was jigging about that girl grinning like a fool. "What about me, darling Mary? She was my granny, too, you know." Then he leaned in and I swear he nipped at her neck with his teeth.

Nobody saw it but me and Larkin, but Mary knew that we had. I know you've seen how a cat will scrunch itself up, tuck its head down, and its face will look all insulted. Well, let me tell you that Mary literally hissed at Hackley. She *hissed* at him. "Don't you have no respect for me nor nobody else?" She went flouncing off, and there was that spine as stiff as a poker again.

And I have to say I had a world of admiration for that straight little narrow-shouldered back that was going out the door.

Larkin, however, was completely bewildered. "Ain't you going after her?" he said to Hackley.

"She'll get over it pretty quick. Then there's the making-up part." Hackley sort of groaned.

I told him he ought to go on after her since he appeared to be primed and ready if the front of his britches was any proof of the pudding. And he went on with his tongue dragging out on the floor. Granny always said that most men could make pure-D fools of themselves in way less time than you could bring buttermilk in a churn. I would never see nothing to prove her a liar.

THE MOON WAS ALREADY riding the ridgeline of The Pilot when Larkin come to stand next to me on the porch. Everybody else was gone and I was fixing to leave. I picked out the two pines that marked the spot where Granny was spending her first night in the long time gone. I put my arm around him and snuggled up close.

"Come home with me, Lark. Don't try to stay here by yourself. You'll just be lonesome."

"I got to stay sometime." He took a long breath in. "Can't get my mind to take in that she's really gone. I catch myself listening for her."

My mind went back to all her things that had called out to me a while ago. "Granny's been a constant for all of us. I always knowed she was right here where I could git to her if I needed her." I thought of all the times I had come up that path yonder with my ass dragging behind me, heavy-hearted with all the troubles of the world heaped on my shoulders and after being here with her for just a little bit I went back down that path with a lighter step.

Larkin must've been thinking my same thoughts for he said, "Granny had a way of helping you to cut through stuff."

And we both laughed and said at the same time "Bullshit," because that is just what she always said whenever we was taking ourselves way too serious.

Up on Graveyard Ridge, the pines went to moving in the wind.

"Bet that wind's cold up there, Amma."

"She is not up there to feel it, Larkin," I said. I had never seen a more empty corpse than hers in all my life.

We were both quiet for a long time and then he said, "Where do you reckon she's at?"

"Now, that I don't know." I give a wave toward that big old sky packed full of stars. "Out yonder somewheres, maybe." And then it come to me and I patted the front of his shirt. "In here for certain." Then I laid my hand against the side of his head. "Up here forever."

"What about heaven?"

"Mommie would be the one to ask about that business. That's where she would say Granny is. As for me, I don't know what I think when it comes down to it. But I will say if they is such a place, then Granny is there with her Mommie and Pappy and her brother Josie, her children, Uncle Pete, Roscoe, your mommie. And she's right now telling all of them about all of us. And they's probably a big frolic going on, music being played, and old love songs being sung, and she's right in the midst of it all."

Then in the most pitiful voice he said, "It feels like a hole has opened up in my life, Amma. Will it ever go away?"

And though I hated to say it, I surely had to, because again I could only tell him the truth. "It won't never go away, honey," I said. "You will just have to figure out how to live your life around it."

## 7

Winter come roaring in early that November and four inches of snow fell just a week after we'd buried Granny. Though I had begged and begged Larkin, he had stayed on at the house and had not spent a single night with us. He had come by and eat supper several times but that was all. It was during one of them times that I found out that Hackley was bringing his women to the house. Usually as soon as he finished eating Larkin would be for the door, but this one time he set at the table until even Carolina had finally give up and gone to bed. He did not want to tell me but I finally wrung it out of him and it was like twisting a groundhog out of its hole. He said that he didn't want to go home just yet because Hackley was over there with Maggie. My eyebrows must have looked like they had took flight right off my head. I knowed what and all folks said about her, that she was trashy and loose, but I did not think that way. Maggie had hoed on her own long row.

Maggie was the oldest of Wade and Vergie Hensley's nine children. Her daddy was a big, barrel-chested man what laughed a lot. He had this real easy way with people, which was a good thing since that is how he made his living. His old wagon loaded down with all sorts of things you could buy if you had the money went all over, down into South Carolina and even down into Georgia. He could tell some of the funniest tales you have ever heard in your life. I would reckon it was from him that Maggie learned that the only way to make it in this old world was to laugh about things. But now her mommie was a pure-D trick if there ever was one. And it was from her that Maggie got her cleverness, because Vergie Ray Hensley was one of the smartest people I have ever knowed in my life. I remember asking Granny one time if she was crazy and Granny laughed great big and long and then she said, "Crazy like a fox."

THEY WAS NOTHING MUCH remarkable about Vergie there at the start. She was smack in the middle with two older sisters and two younger brothers. They said all she done for the first few years was run after them two little hellions that was her brothers, neither one of which growed up to be worth killing, though that is just what happened to them both. Carl Robert was hung for stealing horses over in Tennessee and Jessie got shot in a card game down in Warm Springs. But then one night Vergie come down with a bad bellyache and by morning she was howling with pain and couldn't even keep down water she was throwing up so bad. Granny said her nor Hattie neither one thought she'd live after that second day and Vergie's mama, who was a big one for churchgoing, hit her knees and prayed all that next night and lo and behold, it seemed a miracle when the next morning Vergie set up and said she was hungry. They was all the big talk in church that Sunday and Vergie got attention from everybody. I mean it ain't every day that common folks gets to see a living, breathing miracle. Even at home she was treated like the queen of

Sheba with her sisters as step-and-fetch-its and them boys was plumb cowed by her. But the days went along, and it weren't long before things was back to normal. Vergie found out the same thing that I have—folks forget pretty quick. She was back to minding them boys in no time at all. But six weeks to the day of her first sick, she woke up with the bellyache. And this time it come with the worst headache in the world. Them sick headaches come like clockwork every six or eight weeks after that, and every time her family thought she would surely die.

By the time she was twelve, Vergie had them headaches once or twice a *week* and Granny said you could hear her screaming as you were going past the house. Said she was pitiful when they was on her bad. She couldn't stand no light to hit her eyes and no loud noises and sometimes she'd beg somebody, anybody to cut her head off. By the time she was fourteen she was the very center of her little world and I am not faulting her people one little bit. No, I am not. It makes me mad as the devil when people get all high and mighty and say *If it was me I would do this or I would do that.* You don't know *what* you would do if you was faced with the same thing.

Vergie figured it out, but I can't even blame her for it either. Who don't want to make things a little easier for themselves, is what I would like to know. She never struck a lick at nothing from then on as far as I can tell.

Granny said by the time she was fifteen Vergie was her mommie's cross to bear and her daddy's darling. Her daddy made her a rocking chair and she'd set out on the porch all day long just rocking back and forth and waving at folks that went past the house. She was a real pretty thing with the fairest skin and thick hair the color of a rubbed buckeye, and she talked so soft that you had to lean in close to hear what she was saying. It was from the porch that she got her first glimpse of Wade Hensley.

She set great store by her teeth and she cleaned them religiously with a birch twig twice a day and was going after them with such a vengeance that she hadn't even seen him come from the road to the house. As I heard it she liked to have fell out of her chair when Wade spoke to her from the yard saying he had something in his bag that would work better than the twig. She first thought he was the biggest man she'd ever seen because he had a big pack on his back. Wade was a big man and was a pretty thing, too, even when he was old, and he always went about dressed up in a suit with a vest and everything. I just loved the way they said he introduced himself to her and I have to say that if some man had done that to me I might not have married Zeke Wallin. They said he swept off his big floppy hat and said, "Wade Hensley, missy—blacksmithy, mule trader, bear trapper, liquor maker, watch repairer, log splitter, hog killer, 'coon hunter, banjor picker, and drummer, at your service." Don't you just love that?

He dug around in his pack for a minute and whipped out a fancy tooth-brushing contraption and handed it to Vergie. He talked and talked that first day about this being the first time he'd ever come up this far and how he usually follered the river between Asheville and Greenville, South Carolina, and how he was born and raised over in Hendersonville and how on that particular day he'd just decided to foller this road to see where it wound up.

Maggie told me that Vergie had asked him if the road had ended up there at her house and then she'd asked him which end of that tooth contraption to put in her mouth and Wade felt sorry for her. And then her daddy might as well have been one of the tribes of Israel for he was just as lost. From then on everybody felt sorry for *him*.

From out in the yard I bet he had thought she was a young'un not more than ten year old. She was little and had the smallest feet I've ever seen on a woman grown. But she had great big pretty bosoms and when he got a look at them I know he did not still think her a child. Right up till the last time I laid eyes on her she could look at you with them eyes all big and round and as empty of care and trouble just like a young'un. But I bet you a nickel to a quarter it was the eye of a woman that looked Wade up and down that day and decided to have him as her own. Granny said she had culled every boy in this part of the country. Just about every one of them had tried to spark her, but she showed no interest in any of them. But once she set her mind to it, Granny said it were a sight to behold how fast she whipped out her needle and sewed Wade up.

At the end of two headache-free months, she married him, and ten months after that she had Maggie.

Everybody said Wade was a fool over Vergie, and I know that for a fact. Why, even when I was a girl and they lived right below us, he'd round that curve and be almost running for the house, he'd be so glad to see her. And she'd be right there waiting for him too. Maggie said her mommie was somebody who dearly loved the part of being married that she called a woman's duty. We used to laugh about that 'cause me and her loved it too. Mommie had told me—and these are her own words—"Lay still, Arty, and, God willing, it will be over quick." Well, let me tell you they was nothing quick about Zeke Wallin's hands, nor could I be still when he took hold of me that first night. And praise be about *that*. Being a woman is hard work and the man that manages to get him a good one ought to have sense enough to use his hands gentle and slow. My friends, you cannot catch flies by pouring a big platter of vinegar but, oh, how many will flock to just a little dab of honey. They is a real passion in most women—even a cold and selfish one like Vergie—and if you can tap into that you can stand most anything life throws at your head. Study on that for a minute or two all you men.

MAGGIE HAD TO GROW up quick. Bless her heart, she was a good little thing and had nothing in her to fight against her mommie's workings. She was well trained by the time she was six year old. She could cook a full meal, milk the cow, churn butter, keep the house clean, and, most important, Lord, she could change diapers with the best of them. Vergie rocked on, and about the only time she left her chair was to give birth and add yet another burden to Maggie's scrawny shoulders. Maggie started hipping young'uns even earlier than me. She had one on each hip when I was hipping Larkin. And where I had the choice with Larkin, Maggie did not.

But Maggie slowly began to put the puzzle pieces that was her little mommie together. She couldn't help but notice how them headaches hit hardest just as Wade's wagon was rounding the curve on its way out of sight. Or when one of the young'uns fell sick and needed tending. Or when it was clothes-washing day that we always called blue Monday. Or at hog-killing time. Or when the heifer calved.

Yes, sir, I can tell you that under the knife of Vergie's complete and total selfishness Maggie's good nature was peeled away and her raw heart got hard as a rock. She had one of the sweetest voices as a child, but as she aged her tongue got sharp as a straight razor. She got used to giving orders and made them young'uns mind like ringing a bell.

When she was thirteen she married a boy from off Shelton Laurel. Now that was a show. When she told Wade and Vergie she aimed to marry you'd have thought she'd come in and allowed as how she was going to chop off all their heads with an ax. The young'uns cried and Wade carried on for days. But Vergie went to bed with the worst headache of her life. Or so she said.

And I said to her, "Do not let your mommie keep you from marrying Dedrick. She'll come of it."

I do think that if Wade had not told her that her mommie was going to have another baby she would have stayed home. But, boy, that fixed the deal for Maggie. She told her daddy that she would not stay there and raise any more of their young'uns. "I aim to mommie my own," she said. But that was to never be. Maggie proved barren and carried no children in her body. But being the woman she was, she carried several of the heart.

Eight months later, Dedrick stepped on a rusty nail and died of the lockjaw. Three days after putting her man in the ground, here come her daddy carrying the rocking chair up the path with Vergie slowly picking her way behind him, the children strung out behind her, with Laurie Bett carrying baby Kelvin bringing up the rear. She moved in front of the chair before Vergie could settle into it. Vergie had decided she needed to be with her at this awful time, but Maggie didn't put up with that for a minute. She put them all back out into the road. Things were not going back to the way they were.

Maggie had been on her own ever since. And she did like the men, but to my knowledge, she had never messed with another woman's husband. So by my way of figuring they was not nothing wrong with that.

BUT THERE SET LARKIN, so what did I think now? Hackley was not married to nobody and neither was Maggie. She was three year older than me, so therefore older than him, but so what to that as well. I looked at Larkin studying about all this. It was not right that they had run him off from his own place. I told him so and told him I would tell Maggie and Hackley that. He turned real red in the face then and said, "No, don't do that. They didn't make me leave. It don't matter to them one way or the other." And I was just struck dumb at that. All sorts of things went to flying about in my head and I finally just out and said plime blank, "Did they do it in front of you?" And you might be thinking, now, what kind of wicked woman is that Arty anyhow? Well, I was and still am a curious woman, and though it might have killed the cat, it did not kill me. And then it all come rushing out from his mouth, and though it made me feel funny I listened hard anyway.

HACKLEY HAD BROUGHT SOME liquor to the house and all three of them had been drinking. Larkin not as much, or at least that is what he said, although you can take that with a grain of salt. He could lay right in there with the best of them. For all of Hackley's bragging and swaggering he could never hold his liquor and wound up passing out. Larkin and Maggie messed around with the fiddle for a while. He had always wanted to play since he was little and he said Maggie was actually getting to where she could play a few tunes. Maggie finally said she had to go outdoors. While she was gone he said he banked the fire and got in the bed. The next thing he knowed it was morning and there was Maggie straddling Hackley on the pallet in front of the fire. He said she was naked as the day she was born, and though he wanted to look away he could not. I knowed how he must've felt. I wanted to tell him to hush but could not. And he said that Maggie knew he was watching too and I said, "How do you know?" And he said, "Because the whole time she was riding him she was looking me right in the eye."

I did not know what to say about that. You can believe I studied about it a lot over the next few days. I thought about talking to Zeke about it, but I already knew he'd just say *Goodness* or *They law* or something like that. Or he might have surprised me and been real interested in that little tale. I was not real sure how I would have liked him being in such a big way to know about that so I just didn't mention it. And I caught myself wondering what Granny would have said. But then I already knew. *Bullshit.*

I saw Maggie at the store the day that the big cat had been at my chickens. She'd killed two, leaving feathers and blood all over the snow off the end of the porch. She eat one and carried the other off to her kittens I reckon. Zeke said the cat would have to be hunted down and killed, but I said, "She does not have to be killed, she is just hungry and trying to see to her young'uns just like us. We just need to put the chickens up where she can't get to them." His eyes got all darkish blue like they do sometimes when he looked at me. "I love you, Arty," he said. I said to him, "Why, I love you, too." Men are funny creatures, and I will never figure them out if I live to be a hundred, and ain't that a grand thing? They is some things that needs to remain a mystery in this world and the love between a man and a woman is one of them things.

So I had gone to the store to get some nails and there was Maggie buying some cheese. I sidled right up to her and was hoping she was in the mood for talking, but she did not say much while she was running Cassie's big old tomcat off of the cheese wheel and cutting herself a wedge. We just talked about this and that, and I could not get her to talk about the this or that of which I most wanted to hear. I felt like I was going to start hopping from one foot to the other if I didn't ask her. Finally I just blurted out, "Well, have you seen Hackley or Larkin lately?" And she come right back at me with, "Well, damn, Arty, why don't you just come right out and ask me?" And though I felt awfully sheepish I looked her eyeball to eyeball and said, "Well, I reckon I just did."

We walked home together and she talked and talked. Mostly about Hackley, and I could tell that Maggie had done give her heart away. She denied it to me, though. I told her I hoped she had not because my brother was a lover boy with all the women, but he would wind up marrying just the one—and that would be Mary Chandler because she was the only one that was not letting him have what all the other women did. Maggie turned red as blood when I said that, and I could tell it sort of made her mad. But they is one thing about me, and that is that I will call a spade a spade. She denied all about Larkin and that kind of made me mad. She said, "I don't know nothing about Larkin Stanton, Arty." And I told her I believed that he might be a little bit sweet on her, and she said, "I would not hurt that boy for nothing in this world." And though I wanted to believe her, I thought to myself that Maggie just might bear watching where it concerned Larkin. She got right fiesty when I mentioned Mary again. She said, "Well, the virgin Mary might need to set up and take notice of Miss Maggie." And I looked at her standing there with her head up and her shoulders thrown back and her blue eyes just flashing, and I have to say she was a good-looking woman. But she would not take Hackley from Mary. I knew that as good as I knew my own name. I felt sorry for her but I did not have the heart to tell her what I knew.

• • •

IT WAS GETTING UP towards four o'clock that evening when Larkin come by the house bringing me a mess of deer meat that him and Hackley had killed that morning. As I was washing it, he said they had been in the woods all day. I did not tell him that I had talked to Maggie. I just let him talk and to be honest with you, I only about half listened. They is only so much interest I can keep up for a boy talking about hunting deer all day long. But of a sudden he had all my attention because I heard him say this: "So I told him to marry, then." And I said, "What?" He looked at me with his eyes as dark as the sky on a new moon and said, "I told him to go ahead and marry Mary." And though I knew he was hurt and I was trying to pet him a little, my mind went to wondering what if Mary was to find out about all this business about Maggie. Wouldn't that change a tune or two?

But at that time I was not remembering that my brother was nobody's fool.

BIG JOHN AND DAISY Stanton had their big frolic right at Christmastime. I was having a big time that night and I must admit to drinking of Sol's liquor. I was even flirting a little with some of the men just to get Zeke's attention. Me and him both knew I would never do anything other than some harmless flirting, but he liked to know that other men still noticed me and, oh, they did. So I didn't even know that Larkin was on the place until I saw him standing in front of the door looking mad as hell with little Julie Chandler looking up at him all serious.

That night when we was going home, Zeke told me that Hackley had told most everybody there that Maggie had been walking out with Larkin. I allowed as how nobody had told me that and Zeke

laughed and said, "Honey, they would not have dared to tell you."
No wonder Larkin looked so mad and I can't believe that he didn't
slap the hell out of Hackley for the lying dog that he was. Poor Larkin.
Getting all the talking about but getting none of the goody.

I remember he danced a lot with Julie that night. Maggie come but
barely spoke to me and kept herself right in the middle of a big crowd
of men laughing too loud with her eyes way too bright. And Hackley never laid that fiddle down a single time. He come by and give me
a big kiss on the cheek and told me I was the prettiest girl there, and
even though I knew he was full of himself and told him as much, it
still pleased me. He was on fire with that fiddle and played some of
the best music I'd ever heard him play.

If they was any doubt before as to who he loved and aimed to
marry they would not be after. My pretty little brother broke a hundred hearts that night.

They'd just finished a Virginia reel when Hackley went to playing
"The True Lover's Farewell," and while he was playing, he went
across that floor and stood right in front of Mary. Her face was red
as a beet and Hackley was looking her right in the eye. And she
looked right back at him too. Rosa Wallin come up to me then and
said, "That Hackley could charm the birds right out of the trees,
Arty," and I said, "It is not him that is doing the charming." And it
was not. Mary Chandler was the charmer, if you want to know the
truth. He stood there and sung every word right to her.

> A-rovin' on one winter's night
> And a-drinkin' good old wine,
> A-thinkin' about that pretty little girl
> That broke this heart of mine.

Oh, she is like some pink-a rose
That blooms in the month of June.
She's like a musical instrument
Just late-lie put in tune.

Oh, fare you well, my own true love,
So fare you well for a while.
I'm going away but I'm coming back
If I go ten thousand miles.

And it's who will shoe your pretty little feet?
Oh, who will glove your hand?
Oh, who will kiss them red rosy lips
When I'm in some foreign land?

The crow is black, my love,
It will surely turn to white
If ever I forsaken you,
Bright day will turn to night.

Bright day will turn to night, my love,
And the elements will move
If ever I forsaken you,
The seas shall rage and burn.

So fare you well, my old true love,
So fare you well for a while.
If I go I will come again
If I should go ten thousand miles.

Every girl in that room give up hope right then. But even with the
giving up, they was still wishing he was singing to them. Oh, Lord, I

wished I'd not even looked at Larkin's face. He was staring at Mary like he was just going to die, and I thought to myself, *Don't show everybody here where your affections lay.* And Julie was staring just the same way at Larkin. But it was Maggie's look that caused that cold finger to lay itself at the bottom of my spine. They was a longing in her, too, but there was way more pure old mad. They was the eyes of a woman what has been scorned, and I thought, *Oh, Hackley, what a mess you have made for somebody to get to clean up,* because that is just the way my brother was.

THEY WAS NOTHING I could do about any of what was going on, so I did not worry about it. I just kept dancing and dancing. Sometime after everybody had come back in from hollering and shooting in the Christmas day I realized that Maggie and Larkin were both gone, and Julie was setting off by herself looking like a dying calf in a hailstorm. Somebody hollered out that it had started to snow and since I purely love to watch it snow I went back out on the porch. It was plumb hot in the cabin and the cold air on the porch felt good. I was just standing there taking in some of that sweet air when I heard Maggie's voice from out in the yard. "Talk was worse than we thought," she said. I weren't a bit surprised when Larkin answered her, "Does Mary know?" and my heart squeezed at the foolish hope I could hear in his voice. What little bit was there was dashed I am sure by her reply. "She knows but is acting like she don't. She'd have to quit him if she let on like she knew. So, the virgin Mary won't say nothing." I knew right then that Maggie was exactly right. Mary did know but would never say it. And then she said, "You want to walk an old widder woman home?" And there was a world full of promise in them words. I wanted to holler out and remind her what she had said to me about not hurting him, but I did not. About then Julie opened the door and called out, "Are you out here, Larkin? They're starting up the next dance." She didn't see me standing there at the end of the porch 'cause the light didn't reach that far. But I could see her face and I want you to know that she might not have been the looker that her sister was, but she was not bad looking either. They was not a sound from the yard and she stood there just a minute then closed the door.

By the time my eyes had lost the light from the door, they was nobody out there but me.

## 8

THERE WOULD BE NO broom jumping for Mary Chandler. She let on that it was on account of her religion, but I believe she figured that if she finally had Hackley hemmed up and headed in the right direction she was going to make sure that everything was done right. She did not even want much drinking to go on, but I told her she might as well put that to rest. I had seen it where the man what was getting married had to be held up on either side and poked in the ribs when it was time for him to take the vow. They was nobody what got married that didn't do it in front of folks what had been drinking. That is just the way it was done. She did raise enough hell with her daddy and brothers and with Hackley to where nobody got really drunk until after the church service, which I told her was four steps beyond what I would have thought Hackley would agree to anyway.

I have never in all my life seen such a crowd as come out for their marrying. Hackley had been all around playing the fiddle and it seemed like everybody that he'd ever played with, or for, come that day. The church was full and people stood all around out in the yard. It is a good thing we was having a weather breeder that day and it was fairly warm. To show you how little Hackley knew about things, he went and asked Larkin to be his best man. Mary asked Julie to stand up with her, and you have never seen a happier bridesmaid. I was very proud of Larkin. At least for this one day he managed to bury his feelings way down deep. I was probably the only one that noticed that muscle that kept jumping about knotting up in his jaw.

Maggie was *not* invited.

It come a big snow that next day but that did not slow us down one bit. It actually made for a real good time. We loaded up on sleds and went all around and about singing and cutting up and there was a frolic at somebody's house every night for a solid week.

Maggie had a big dance at her place, and Hackley and Mary were *not* invited. Poor Maggie. I didn't want to make a big deal out of how this was probably the only night those two had had by themselves since they'd married.

Larkin had a big time and got pretty drunk and danced every dance with Maggie. If they was a single solitary soul who had not known about them before all this, they was not one now. Some folks called it a scandal because she was so much older than him. I did not think it so, but I surely did feel sorry for the lot of them. Everything was all mixed up with everybody wanting somebody else and having to make do with what they could get, and that is not a good way to do business of the heart.

NOW YOU MIGHT BE saying, What is wrong with this here woman Arty? Did Hackley and Mary not marry in the beginning of the year 1861? Is this Arty a blithering idiot? How could she not know what was going on down off the mountain in South Carolina and Georgia and all points south? Is she just a simple-minded person who only knowed how to gossip and pick in everybody's business and not mind her own? And to all that I will say this: No, I was not blind then, or deaf, and we all knowed what was happening all around us. But you must understand it had not come for us yet. We were just people living a hard life and getting by. The men would knot up together and talk. But that was all it was then. Just talk, and some little words on a piece of newspaper somebody would bring in from Warm Springs or Marshall. Why, to us Charleston might as well have been up on the moon. Our biggest sin, I reckon, was being innocent, but we would get well over that. South Carolina proved a whole lot closer to us than we ever thought it would.

AND JUST IN CASE you're interested, I did find myself in the family way for the seventh time. And I knew somehow that this one was a girl and I allowed that I would name her Pearl.

SO THAT WINTER PASSED just like every other one we'd ever lived through. I was not sick a single day, and Zeke said I had never been prettier in my life than I was then. That is how I recall that spring. I felt so good and was strong as a mule.

Mommie was pleased as could be with her new daughter-in-law, which I must say might have in itself been reason enough for me to be hard on Mary. These are Mommie's own words: "I am so glad Hackley did not get trapped up with one of them old road whores in spite of all them what was after him." I flew mad at that because though she did not mention any names I knew she was meaning Maggie. But I just felt too good to argue with her so I did not. I did, however, pick just that time to tell her I was breeding again and must admit I went to feeling even better when that big grin dropped off and she went back to looking all pinched up with that smell-something-bad look.

So I was not at all ready for my feelings about Mary to start softening up when I went over there to help her cook when Hackley had his barn raising toward the end of March. But soften up they did. Her little place was as neat as a pin, and you could tell she was really trying to be a good wife and she seemed as happy as a little girl with red shoes on. It did not hurt one bit that she was courting my affections either. She asked my advice a dozen times in that one day, and I could not help it if that went to my head and by the time supper was on the table me and her was laughing and talking like old pals. While we was washing up I told her I was expecting, and, oh, how wistful her face got with the news. She said, "I want to have Hackley's babies more than anything in this world, Arty." And I laughed and said, "You ought to be enjoying the time you have with just him, honey. The babies will start and then they'll just keep coming and coming." Later in mine and her life we would talk about that conversation and each and every time her face would carry that same look. I would reckon she thought about it right up till when she died. They would be just the one child born to her that was my brother's. And that would end like so much in life what turns out to be sweet as honey and bitter as gall at the same time.

But during that spring I decided that whatever had come before might as well be forgiven and forgotten, and me and her put together a good friendship that weathered well the rest of our lives. I cannot help but believe that if things had just been allowed to go their natural course and times had not changed for us in the awful way they did, I would surely not be telling this tale. But telling it I am, for the times they did change.

It come a big wet snow right about the time the sarvice trees were blooming, and some of it was still on the ground when Larkin come by the house. He was on his way over to help Hackley do some fencing. He was looking fine as snuff and twice as dusty, which means he was a big pretty man. I couldn't keep the grin off my face when I said, "And how is Miss Maggie getting on?" And he blushed plumb to the roots of his hair and mumbled that she was fine. I had high hopes then that maybe he was moving beyond his old feelings for Mary and I felt a debt of gratitude in my heart for Maggie. As soon as the sun climbed high enough, I told Larkin I had to go let the cows out and he said he'd walk that far with me and then he probably needed to get on over the hill. I linked my arm through his and we strolled along looking at how green everything was. I found the first violets peeping out of the grass along the path to the barn, and we talked about how he used to pick them for me and put them in the water bucket where I'd be sure to see them.

Up in the day I took my littlest young'uns and crossed the ridge myself to see Mary. We set on the porch talking, and I thought, *It does not get much better than this.* There was a little breeze playing about the yard and the sun felt so warm and the young'uns were just drunk with it all. Larkin and Hackley come in and we all set for a while just watching the young'uns. Then Larkin asked if we'd heard they was having a big politicking over at Laurel on Thursday. I allowed that me and Zeke were aiming to go and Mary said her and Hackley was too. I said we ought to go camping and stay all night and they all allowed what a fine idea that was. We flew to making us some plans and by the time I got up to go home, I was looking forward to a big time. I wished Zeke Jr. had not come running to me crying with a skinned elbow. Then I would not have reached over in that water bucket for a handful to wash it off with. But things happen for a reason, even if we do not know what it might be. All I know is that when I brought my hand out, it was covered with violets and I did not even have to think twice't about who might have put them there.

I COULD NOT BELIEVE how many people were on the roads that Thursday and every one of them heading for Shelton Laurel. By the time we got there the big cleared field beside the store was already full of wagons, horses, and mules. And the whole place was just throbbing with hundreds and hundreds of people. And this was a rare thing in the spring of the year. Any other year would have found us at the house working in the fields, so they was a right festive air with everybody wanting to visit. Men was standing around clumped up in little groups, talking and waving their arms around while they did it. Us women left them to it and clumped up ourselves. And a thousand sweating young'uns was wild as bucks running and winding their way through what must've looked like a forest of legs. Carolina's eyes was as bright as new pennies, and when she found Sophie Rice she squealed and grabbed her hand and said "Let's pretend we're two blind girls" and they went staggering off like two drunks. I hollered after them that they'd better keep their eyes wide open if they knowed what was good for them. She was the only one of my bunch that took off but then she always was one that could not be still. Abigail flew right into helping me set up camp while the little ones stood looking about with great big eyes. I said, "John Wesley, quit standing there like you've took root and help your sister." I guess my voice must have got that tone to it that makes Zeke nervous because he said, "Arty, honey, why don't you go get what all we need at the store."

It took me forever to finally get down there because they was so many folks I knew. I could not go any more than a step or two when somebody would holler out, "Arty, Arty, come over here a minute."

When I finally made it, who did I meet coming through the door but Larkin. Him being way taller than me, I was asking him to look out there and tell me who he could see. Of a sudden this big, red-faced man come jostling his way up onto the top step, elbowing everybody out of the way. It was only when he nodded at me and I saw his big round bald head that I knew him to be the great preacher Lester Lydell. Back when he was young and more slender he would take a run-a-go and jump clear over the pulpit, but he was not so young now nor was he slender, so I reckon his jumping days was over. He could still talk a good preaching though. "Brothers and sisters, God spoke to me in a dream. He said to me, 'Preacher, you get out yonder and deliver my message. I didn't call you to set around and say nothing. I called you to preach.' Clear as a bell I heard Him say what I'm saying now. He says we are to leave the Union, separate ourselves from the heathens in the North. God would be on our side if we leave. If we stay in it'd be a sin and disobedience. They'll be punishments heaped upon us if we don't heed his wishes."

Just then a great flood of people come pouring out of the store and he got caught up in them, and the last I saw of him he was waving his Bible in the air still preaching while being carried along by the tide.

Larkin laughed and I did, too. Oh, it was a wonderful day we was having. I turned around still laughing and come smack up against Vergie Hensley. She was as round as could be and had on an orange dress and what went through my mind was, *Oh, how much like a punkin she looks,* but what come out my mouth was, "Why, howdy, Vergie."

Her eyes was all glassy-looking and they sort of slid over my face and then they fastened themselves right onto the front of Larkin's britches and they did not move the whole time we stood there talking. I swear to you that this is no lie, and I thought to my never that I was going to bust wide open I wanted to laugh so bad. I just kept on talking asking her questions about her young'uns, if Maggie was there, when was the last time she'd seen Mommie. I was talking about anything just to see how long she would stand there staring right at Larkin. Finally I said, "Larkin and me have to go, Vergie," and I took him by the arm and pulled him off the porch.

When we got around the corner, I fell against him just dying and all he could do was shake his head. "What do you reckon that was all about?" I said, "I reckon she's heard you like them older women, honey." And he said, "Not that damn old," which set me off to laughing again. We was standing there laughing so hard we was crying when Mommie come around the corner. She come bustling up calling out, "Arty, you, Arty," and she looked and sounded so much like Granny it come near to taking my breath away. I could not help myself, I started to just bawling. "Don't pay me no never mind," I said to Larkin. "I am just some woman who is bigged."

You would have thought I had stuck Mommie with a hot poker the way she sucked in her breath. "Arty Wallin, don't talk about such to him."

I said, "Why not? Is this not a grown man here that has seen me in the family way before?"

I will spare you further details. Suffice to say it was like a thousand other arguments that me and Mommie somehow managed to get into every time we caught a whiff of one another.

• • •

AFTER WE'D EATEN I wandered over to where Mary was talking to Gracie Franklin and Patsy Bowman. And for all of you that thinks Arty's big nose must be stuck in everybody's business, I must tell you that I had not heard the story what was being told.

"Clemmons just up and left," Gracie was saying. I reckoned they must be talking about Red Boyce's son since he was the only Clemmons I knew. "He come in one evening and throwed a big fit. Lindy had been to the barn and already done the milking. Had her buckets setting on the table and he took his arm and swiped bucket, milk, and all right off into the floor. They ain't seen hide nor hair of him since. Lindy's having an awful time of it, they say."

"I reckon she would be having it hard! Her and them two little babies." Patsy was red-faced and mad. "Tell you one thing, if it was me he'd done that-a-way he'd better never come back around me again. He'd better just keep going!"

There was that saying I mentioned before, *If it was me.*

Mary patted Patsy's arm. "I swan. And nobody has seen him since?"

"A man like that ain't worth the powder it would take to kill him." Patsy said.

Hackley popped up where he'd been stretched out on a pallet of quilts laid out on the wagon bed. "Sound like you girls has done got poor old Clemmons tried by jury and hung."

"You better watch it, Hackley Norton, you rogue," Gracie said. "You keep running that mouth and I'll have to come over there and straighten you out."

Butter would not have melted in her mouth and I thought to myself, *You had your chance a long time ago, honey, and you didn't do it then.*

"Ah, Miss Gracie. How you make my head spin with all them pretty words." Hackley swept his old flop hat off and laid it over his heart.

And I said, "I'll loan you my gun if you want it, Mary, just don't aim for his head. Shooting him in the head wouldn't even addle him, let alone kill him."

Mary stood and shook out her skirt as she studied him. "I don't know if I want to waste a perfectly good bullet."

"Oh, God!" Gracie whooped. "I'll bet you folks would give money to hire it done. I'll go to collecting it right now!" She went off looking back over her shoulder at Hackley and went twisting right up to these two men what was propped up on another wagon.

I looked back at Hackley, and them lazy eyes that never missed a trick was watching Gracie. He had his thumbs hooked in the waist of his britches, and for the first time in my life I wanted to see him as a man and not my own brother.

He was not much taller than me but his shoulders was wide for a man his size and for all that he was blond, he had what Granny called a good high color. His eyes were the prettiest shade of blue I have ever seen. Standing there beside that wagon, I believe I come awfully close to seeing what it was that turned the head of most every woman. Some of it was just in how he held himself sort of slouchy-like. But they was a coiled-up something in him, something that was not tame, and when he fixed them eyes on you, it felt like he was just going to spring on you and eat you up.

And then with a little smile he picked up his fiddle and bow and started to play.

I've played cards in England, I've gambled in Spain,
I'm going back to Rhode Island, gonna play my last game.

Jack a diamonds, Jack a diamonds, I know ye from old.
You've robbed my poor pockets of silver and gold.

I'll tune up my fiddle and rosin up my bow
And I'll make myself welcome wherever I go.
Jack a diamonds, Jack a diamonds, I know ye from old,
You've robbed my poor pockets of silver and gold.

I'm gonna drink, I'm gonna gamble, my money's my own,
And them that don't like me can leave me alone.
Jack a diamonds, Jack a diamonds, I know ye from old
You've robbed my poor pockets of silver and gold.

If the ocean was whiskey and I was a duck,
I'd dive to the bottom and I'd never come up.
Jack a diamonds, Jack a diamonds, I know ye from old.
You've robbed my poor pockets of silver and gold.

But the ocean ain't whiskey and I ain't no duck,
So I'll play them "Drunken Hiccups" and trust to my luck.
Jack a diamonds, Jack a diamonds, I know ye from old
You've robbed my poor pockets of silver and gold.

Rye whiskey and pretty women have been my downfall,
They beat me and they bang me but I love them 'fore all.
Jack a diamonds, Jack a diamonds, I know you from old.
You've robbed my poor pockets of silver and gold.

I'll eat when I'm hungry, I'll drink when I'm dry.
If I git to feelin much better gonna sprout wings and fly.
Jack a diamonds, Jack a diamonds, I know you from old.
You've robbed my poor pockets of silver and gold.

As he gave a long stroke of the bow to end the tune, I thought to myself, *Now, Arty, what woman would not trade her soul for all of that?*

Hackley nodded to the crowd that was clapping and hollering, bowed to Gracie, placed his fiddle on the quilt, and said "I know you folks didn't just come to hear me and looks like the speech making is fixing to start."

Larkin took me by the elbow and we made our way through the crowd that had gathered around a little stage of a thing that they'd built up for the speakers. I wanted to get as close to the front as I could because I wanted to see this Zeb Vance person. Zeke talked about him like he was God's gift, and his name had been all over the papers for months. Daddy said he had given twelve speeches in fourteen days begging for us to stay in the Union. He was only six years older than me, which would've made him thirty-one. My eyes was scanning the crowd looking for somebody who looked to fit that bill and I must say I was surprised when Larkin poked me in the ribs and nodded at this tall man standing across from us. He looked like he was carrying the weight of the world and was wore out from it. Looking back, I reckon he was carrying it. Much later he said that he knowed that all his speech making was doing little to change people's minds, and that nothing he could say would stop what he called the rush to secede. But he done it anyway. And if what he said to us was any proof, he done everything he could.

I pulled on Larkin's arm and said, "Who is that standing with him?"

"That's Nick Woodfin, one of the biggest slaveholders in Buncombe County. He's come to give us the other side of things," Larkin said.

Oh, I had read about him in the papers. He had wrote this big long piece about how the South was guaranteed the right to pull out of the Union by the Constitution. Him and Vance had argued back and forth about all this down in Raleigh and finally Woodfin had hollered out, "You know the Constitution of the United States, don't you, Mr. Vance?" And Vance had fired right back, "Yes, Mr. Woodfin, I know of the Constitution. Right now I feel like I helped write the damn thing. Whether we have the right is not the issue," he said. "If we're making our political bed, then I want to be certain we can sleep in it." Now that is my kind of man that can talk about sleeping in the bed you have made.

I looked hard at this Woodfin, because to my knowledge I had never seen nobody what owned slaves. He had on a white linen suit and looked like what I had always thought somebody like him would look, which is to say all proper and sort of citified.

"I like Vance the best," I whispered to Larkin.

"How do you know, Amma? You ain't heard them talk yet." He whispered back.

"I just do," I said. And I did. I could see what Zeke saw in Vance. He looked like he could walk right in the store over home and not draw attention to himself. He had big rough-looking hands and Woodfin's hands looked smooth as a woman's. I made fists of my own and hid them in my skirt because his hands did not look like mine.

*Go it, Vance,* I thought just as he stepped up on the stage. The crowd quieted right down, and he took a deep breath and sort of bowed to us and then he started to talk. I had never heard the likes of that in all my life and do not much expect to hear it again before I die.

• • •

"MY FRIENDS." HE TURNED to the local big shots. "Honored servants of these good folks." He nodded at Woodfin. "My esteemed colleague. I've not come to inform you that these are serious times. You already know that. Our sister state has left the Union, practicing a right given her by the great men that founded this beloved country in which we live. This country that many of our ancestors went to Kings Mountain and fought for during the Revolutionary War. Some of them didn't come back. They died for a purpose. Has it been so long ago that we've forgotten?" He looked out at us with his dark brows all bunched up above his eyes and give a little shake of his head. "I say no, we have not forgotten. Think of them, my friends. Those mountain men that stood and fought with such tenacity against the English. They could look off in the distance and see the mountains." He give a big sweep of his arm that could have took in the whole world.

"Now we are faced with a grim and somber decision. Will we tear asunder that which we have struggled to form? We might. But must we rush forward with ruinous and indecent haste? Mr. Woodfin will no doubt tell you that we must act now. To hesitate would cause the states that have cast their lot in with that of South Carolina to think badly of us, to think us a rider of the fence. I have heard this argument time and time again." Vance looked at Woodfin for a long time, and I can tell you that I would not have wanted him to fix me with that kind of gaze. When he looked back at us his eyes was shiny bright. "I am convinced that this is a decision that must be made by the people. Good, God-fearing, everyday people like you. This decision *cannot, should not* be made for you by politicians! The leaders in the disunion move are scorning every suggestion of compromise and rushing forward with such speed that it appears that they are absolute fools. Yet don't you be deceived. They are rushing the people into a revolution without giving them time to think. They fear lest the people shall think!"

"Damn them what wants to bust up this country, Zeb!" one man hollered.

And they was a bunch of men that hollered *amen* to that. But they was just as many that stood there with their arms crossed and did not say one single solitary word. It was hearing that big silence that caused the first little ripple of fear to run through me. Zeke had come to stand next to me and I reached out and linked my arm through his. He was as stiff as a board and I knew that he was afraid, too. That was the first of many times that I would know he was afraid, but it did not make me love him any less. It made me love him more.

Vance raised his hands patting the air.

"I understand your anger. But, again, I remind you of the need to proceed through these perilous times with caution. We can't afford to rush in the other direction either. The people must think, and when they are given the time they will begin to think and hear the matter properly discussed." He pointed a long finger at us. "Then and only then will we be able to consider long and soberly before we tear down this noble fabric and invite carnage, civil war, financial ruin, and anarchy. I beg you to think, think, my friends. I implore you to think! Neighbors, we have everything to gain and nothing on earth to lose by delay, but by too hasty action we may take a fatal step that we never can retrace. We may lose a heritage that we can never recover, though we seek it earnestly and with tears." He brought up his hand and pointed a finger straight up at the sky.

I was so caught up in listening to him talk that I did not even see that white-suited Woodfin had climbed on the stage with him until he was close enough to lay his hand on Vance's arm. I even know what he said to him though his voice was low and gruff. He said, "I am so sorry, Zeb." I believe he meant it, too, because you could see it in his eyes. But when he faced us the sorry was gone and his eyes was hot as fire.

"My fine friends and neighbors, I have just received word that South Carolina has fired on Fort Sumter. Lincoln has called for seventy-five thousand volunteers."

And that big crowd that had been so quiet just went to blowing up all around me. Everybody was hollering and cussing, but I was standing there numb as a stump. Vance stood right where he'd been and looked right foolish because he still had his finger pointing and I watched him bring it down to shake the hand Woodfin was offering him. I heard years later that Vance said he raised his hand that day a unionist and brought it down a secessionist. He really did just that. Hell, if you had said them words to me on that day I would have looked at you as dumb as a cow. I would not have knowed what either one of them meant. But, oh, you can believe I know what they both mean now.

Woodfin stepped down off the stage and men literally swarmed around and about him and he was quick swallowed up and gone. I done something then that I look back on today and shake my head about. Of a sudden I had to talk to that Zeb Vance and I had to do it eyeball to eyeball. I pulled my arm loose from Zeke, jerked my skirt up, and rushed that stage, catching him just before he stepped down. I climbed right up there with him too. "Wait, wait," I said. "What does this mean for me?"

Now, I have knowed some what I would call men in my time, but when this one looked down at me, I knowed I was looking at a great man. He had looked tired before, but Lord, now he looked absolutely killed. His voice sounded as sad as any sad I have ever heard.

"This means there will be war."

"But not for us," I said. "The war won't come here."

Oh, how cold his next words left me, even though he was trying to be so kind. "It is here already, madam." And then he said, "I must apologize and excuse myself. There's much I need to do." He was telling the truth about that and he had no way of knowing when he said it how true it would turn out to be. His own troubles was just around the corner—in nineteen days he would be made Confederate captain and would form up his own company and would go marching off to fight. They called themselves the Rough and Ready Guards. He did not know as he stood right there talking to me, Arty Wallin, in Shelton Laurel on that pretty day in April, that he would finish out them long and bloody years far off from his home.

I did not know that I was looking in the face of the man that would be elected governor in a little more than a year. But I would remember him the rest of my life, because in that little minute he opened up a world of worry for me. He handed it to me in a box without a lid and it come swirling up right in my face. Of a sudden I knew in my heart that the war was here as sure as I was a foot high because all around me hollering and cussing was men what was foolish enough to fight in it. Oh, God, and what would Zeke do? He was a good man, a decent man, but a man nonetheless. And good and decent men had a bigger dose of honor than them what was not so good or decent. I thought I would fall up when I knew that yes, he would go. And Larkin? Oh, what would happen to the first child I had not carried in my body but snugged up tight against my heart? I looked at him standing right there, and though he was big as a skinned mule and living on his own and already bedded a woman, he was still a boy. A million memories crowded into my mind and went to racing back and forth. The time he'd had the whooping cough and couldn't breathe and I'd sucked the thick snot out of him with my own mouth. The squeals he'd make when he was learning to crawl. How his little face would get all dreamy when he was listening to them old love songs. And in with all them feelings come the words to an old song I hadn't thought of in years.

> "The warfare is a-ragin' and Johnny you must fight.
> I want to be with you from morning to night.
> I want to be with you, that grieves my heart so.
> Won't you let me go with you?" Oh, no, my love, no."

> "Oh, Johnny, Oh, Johnny, I think it's you're unkind
> When I love you much better than all other mankind.
> I'll roach back my hair and men's clothing I'll put on
> And I'll act as your servant as you go marching along.

> "I'll go to your general and get down upon my knees,
> Five hundred bright guineas I'll give for your release."
> "When you're standing on the picket some cold winter day
> Them red rosy cheeks, love, will all fade away."

As for what happened next, I can only say God bless my brother Hackley, because right then he give an ear-splitting whoop and a holler and said, "Well, would you looky here if it ain't Willis and Columbus." I knowed right then that we was in for some fine music, seeing as how them brothers could play banjo and fiddle like nobody's business.

You might wonder why I did not think of Hackley having to go off to the war, but you should not. If you had known him then, you would have knowed too that the very thought of him in a war with people bossing him around would have made you laugh your head off. My brother was not the sort to give much thought to something that was not right in front of him unless it was in a jug or wearing a dress. Oh, do not get me wrong; Hackley had to come of it. Just not on this night. For him this was just one more excuse for a big frolic.

I went to dancing like a fool the minute they swung up in a tune, and if I had not been in the family way, I would have got as drunk as one too. I could not drink one drop when I was that way because it made me have the heartburn so bad. But they was lots of drinking being done. Hackley was as happy with it as I would ever see him. He always loved that mix of Sol's liquor and playing the fiddle. And when you throwed him in with other musicianers like Lum — which is what they all called Columbus — and Willis, you could figure that one tune would follow another, and you could dance all night if your feet and legs could stand it. Between them boys they probably knowed every fiddle tune they was to know.

There are many other things I recall about that one night. It is funny how our mind works that-a-way. For that night I can remember the exact words people said or the clothes they had on and now I can't remember something that somebody said to me just last week. Hackley's face was red and his eyes was so bright they looked like they could burn you. And I remember him laughing and saying, "Why, iffen I'd have knowed how the whiskey flowed at these speech makins and such I reckon I'd have took to politicking a long time ago. I might just run for sheriff." Bless his heart. He didn't have much time left to him and would never live to vote for a sheriff, let alone run for one.

I had to quit dancing for a bit while I made the young'uns lay down. They all went to sleep pretty quick except for Carolina. I knowed she was up and gone before my back was good and turned. That girl has always told me what she figured I wanted to hear and then done what she wanted to start with. I reckon there has to be one that we pay for our raising with, and that would be Carolina for me. I guess I was Mommie's, although I cannot for the like of me figure out what it was my poor little Mommie was having to pay for. She was always such a good thing.

I can still see how it looked as I was coming back. Things has changed so much from what they used to be. Everybody's wagon was now their bedroom and you could hear all sorts of things. Some things I might not ought to have heard right out in the open that way, but I must say I took my time and meandered along trying to determine who was in what wagon. By the time I got back to that little stage a right smart of time had gone by. They was a great big fire that had been built up against the cool of the spring evening, and you could see folks standing black against the orange light. The musicianers was up on the little stage that Vance had talked from and Hackley looked like some kind of haint. I just had to stand there and look at him for a minute. His hair had flopped down over his forehead and he was bowing that fiddle like he meant to saw it in two. He was lost in that music making.

Larkin was not hard to find. He was so much taller than everybody else that he stood right out. And I could tell he was talking to Mary because her hair was all aglow from the fire. Before I got to them she'd turned away. I went to stand beside him. He slid his arm around me and give me a side-armed hug. His breath smelled pretty strong with liquor. I asked him if he was drunk and he said, "Not near enough." And about that time here come Maggie. Me and her talked for a minute, but I could tell she was after Larkin so I just kept talking and talking and she kept raising her eyebrows and giving me these little nods in Larkin's direction. I kept letting on like I didn't know what she was wanting, and she got to the point where her eyes were just about rolling around in her head. So I took pity on her and said, "Oh, there's Zeke. I need to talk to him," and left her and Larkin standing there together. But I didn't go far enough that I didn't hear every word and see everything that happened.

Larkin had his eyes closed and was patting his leg in time to the music.

"Howdy, Larkin," she said, and I wished you could have heard how her voice sounded. Our Maggie could really be something when she set her head to it.

But Larkin had learned a thing or three and said right back to her in a voice *I* had certainly never heard him use on me, "Howdy, Miss Maggie."

"What are you grinning about?" she said as she walked right up in his face as bold as you please.

"Me to know and you to find out."

I couldn't help it. I eased over a little closer where I could see, and I want you to know I blushed plumb to the roots of my hair when I saw the way she was looking him up and down, letting her eyes stare at certain parts which were much easier to see now than they was when he was talking to his Amma just a minute ago. "I love how I keep getting reminded what a pretty boy you are, Larkin Stanton."

"You don't have to forget it, honey. My door is always open to you and you know that." They was not a thing in his voice that would make you think he was anything other than a man grown, and I finally got it through my thick head that they was things about Larkin that I did not know. And that they was things I did not need to know. I made to leave just as she leaned up close against him and whispered something in his ear. I was still close enough to hear what he said back to her.

"Right here in front of God and everybody?" I knew as sure as the world what they was talking about and, with a face as red as that fire, I swear to you I was trying to get my big nosy self out of their way, when all of a sudden there was Hackley standing right next to them. I wished I had just gone on about my rat killing and not heard or saw nothing because this is one time that I would have been better off not knowing. I was friends with both of them women, and I put myself right smack between the devil and the deep blue sea. I had not noticed nor had Maggie and Larkin that the music had stopped. But it had and when they turned toward the woods, there stood my brother with a great big sloppy grin on his face.

"Why, looky here. Two of my favorite folks passing the time of day," he said. And though his words was light and teasing like, his tone was not. They was an edge to his voice that made me think, *Oh, no, Hackley is drunk and wanting to fight.* I stepped right up close then because I meant to put myself between them if I had to. One look at Maggie's face told me she was not missing a thing and was pleased as could be about what was happening and I silently cursed her for this.

"Why, Hackley Norton, if I did not know you was a happy married man, I might think you was flirting with me."

My brother got right up in her face like me and Larkin was not even there and said, "Being married does not mean I died, nor has it caused me to go blind neither. And you do look mighty good, Maggie."

I could not help it. I said his name and I know my voice had to have sounded my dismay to both of them. "Damn it, Hackley Norton, do not even think of doing such a thing."

Him and Maggie barely glanced at me and both of them might as well have said out loud, "You shut your mouth, Arty." Neither one of them give me or Larkin another thought, and they was no way to tell who was leading who toward the woods. It looked to me like they was racing.

Though you might think I am lying, I am not when I tell you that my very first thought was of Mary. I looked around trying to see where she was. I guess I would have wanted somebody to do the same for me, unless they was planning on telling me about it, which I already knew I would not do. For just a minute I forgot it was not just my secret to keep. But one look at Larkin's face cured me of that. He was mad as fire, they was no doubt about that, but there was another look about him too, and as you have probably figured I am not one for the big words, but the only one that works here is *triumphant.* His eyes was plumb hot looking, and they was such an awful thing to look at that I had to turn my face from his. And he said, "Damn his soul," and he slammed his fist into the palm of his other hand. And quick-like I said, "Don't damn nobody's soul, Larkin." And he said, "I'll tell her now, Amma. You just wait and see if I don't." And I said, "Oh, honey, you cannot be the one that tells her this thing. She would hate you for the bearing of this." So once again I was right in the middle of them all.

When people gets old we have at least one or two moments in our lives that we can look back on and say to ourselves, *If I had done thus and such right here, my whole life would have been different.* It might not even look like it would be no big life-changing thing, but it is. Or if we ain't big thinkers, of which I am sometimes sorry to say I am, then we will say *I wish't I had* or *I wish't I'd never have,* and at the end of that you can put just about anything. *I wish't I had looked the other way* or *I wish't I'd never have seen his face* or *I wish't I had been somewhere else that day.* Or *I wish't somebody would've just picked up a rock and knocked my brains out right then.* Or *I wish't I had turned right around and told Mary right then and let them all go to hell in a handbag.* Well, I wished all them things on that night. But it was a long time later when I wished it the hardest. And that is the worst kind of wishing.

Who should come up to us right then but Mary. I swear, it was like she was put on this earth to try them two boys. The bad thing was that I could not hate her for it, for she did not know. I tell you it even tugged at my heart—and it could be hard as a rock sometimes—to see her standing there holding that pie tin. She held it up to Larkin, and her eyes were great big and held the light from the fire like a looking glass.

"I can't find Hack nowhere," she said, and I thought, *Thank God for small favors,* and give a nervous look back over my shoulders but could not see neither one of them as they had already cleared the trees. "I made him a stack cake because he loves it better than anything in this world." And I thought, *Not better than anything, honey.*

I looked at Larkin then, because I knowed it was do-the-business-or-git-off-the-pot time. He would either tell her or not. I watched it run every which way across his face and there was that muscle bunching in his jaw.

"Larkin," I said. And with that one word Mary must've known something because she turned her little face to me.

"What, Arty?" she said, and her voice was soft as down.

But I was looking at him and did not even shift my eyes. And I knew by the way his shoulders slumped that he would take what I had told him a while ago as the bitter truth. He could not tell her.

I spoke up and was amazed at how light my voice sounded but I guess it ought to have since I was so relieved. "Maybe he went to shit and the hogs eat him."

Mary looked at me and her eyes were just dancing and she said, "Oh, Arty, you just won't do," then she laughed and it was such a pretty sound that I could not help but laugh back. Larkin laughed too, but his voice held a trace of bitterness that I knew went all the way to his soul. Mary must have heard it, because she stopped laughing and looked up at him. But he did not stand for her to look at for long. He turned and went off toward where Lum and Willis was tuning up and drinking up. We watched him turn up the jug and Mary said, "Oh, he is drinking. I thought I smelled it on his breath," and for her that was the end of it.

But my hurt went right on. Even so I stood right there and talked to her until Hackley come waltzing up pretty as you please and took that pie pan from her and wolfed it down. The whole time he did not even look at me. I was staring at him as like to burn a hole plumb through him. When he finished his cake he made this big deal of licking his fingers real slow, staring me right in the eyes, and it was like I could read his mind: *See here, Arty, think where my fingers has been.* And I could not stand it. I had to leave them standing there. I did not say a single word to Mary but she called out to me, "Arty?"

But I acted like I did not hear her and what I carried off with me was the sound of Hackley laughing.

• • •

THE FIRE WAS DOWN to red embers when I got up from beside my sleeping husband later. Zeke could sleep through Gabriel blowing his horn. I never could and I believe it had to do with laying half awake listening for Larkin when I was a girl and then my own coming so quick. Every woman knows that all it takes to wake us quick as lightning even in the dead of night is that one word, *Mommie*. And though not one of my young'uns had called to me out loud—I went round and looked—I still could not sleep. All I had to do was see Larkin's big self setting on that little stage to know that he'd been calling to my heart. I set down with him and right then a shooting star went diving through the sky.

"Make a wish quick, honey," I said.

He said, "What would I wish for, Amma? Anything I can think of that I'd want would mean the ruination of somebody's life and probably mine, too."

"Ah," was all I said, because I knew he was telling the truth.

I put my arm through his and hugged it against my side and we set there for a while and neither one of us said a word. Then I thought of something that we could both wish for. "Let's wish that there won't be no war."

"That would be a waste of a wish, Amma."

He sounded so finished, like they was no doubt in his mind. I said, "Why, I don't reckon this war is wrote in stone, Larkin."

He looked over at me and his face was part dark and part red from the fire. His eyes looked like black holes in his head. "I believe they ain't nothing that will stop this war. Did you not hear what that Zeb Vance said?"

I got all puffed up about that because I knew I did not have an educated mind, but I had a decent head on my shoulders. "I was listening and I heard every word. He was a fine speech-giver."

"He was, Amma. But everything he said was culled when Lincoln called out them troops."

Like a fool I said, "Why, what has that got to do with us, honey? It don't make no matter-mind to us. We'll just go on with our day-to-day."

He glanced at me and said, "No. Things are way different for us now than they was just this morning. It is going to be a pure-D mess."

"But we ain't got no slaves nor nothing. And ain't none of us rich."

He sighed and his voice got this real patient sound to it and I must say I felt my temper flare up because it sounded like he was talking to a child. "This here is not about slaves nor being rich, Amma. It is about *South* Carolina."

Oh, and then it all come washing over me. "And we are *North* Carolina," I whispered.

"Exactly," he said back. Then after a while, "But he did have a fine way of speaking."

From out of the dark beyond the fire I heard Maggie give a little bark of a laugh. And Larkin heard it, too, because his shoulders slumped a little more and he give a great big sigh. I patted him on the arm. "You done right there, Larkin."

"Probably. But doing right don't always make it feel right."

I had to admit that was the truth.

"I will not understand Maggie if I live to be a hundred years old. After that business between all of you back at Christmas, how could she go right back to the trough for more?"

Though he laughed, he sounded awful sad. "Ah, she can't help it. She loves Hack. How can I hold that against her when I love him, too?"

I took to spluttering on that note, and he went to laughing and did not sound so sad. "You can't stay mad at him, neither, and you know it."

I thought about him licking his fingers and didn't know so much about that. My voice sounded more hateful than it ought to have. "Well, what about Mary?"

"Poor little Mary."

"Poor little Mary?" I mocked him. "Don't poor-little-Mary me. It ain't as if she did not know my brother before she married him."

"She knowed him. But I wonder, did she really know him?"

"She knowed what she wanted to know and that is the way of most of us. I have learned twice as much about Zeke Wallin since I married him, but if he had turned out to be a runner of women I would have killed him." You note I did not say *If it was me.* "Are you all right about Maggie?"

"Why, yes," he said. "I liked her all right but I would be lying like a dog if I was to say I loved her. To be honest with you, this has sort of made me sick to my stomach with her. I won't never have nothing else to do with her and that's a fact."

And you know he never did have a thing to do with her in that way. The way it ended up, I wished he had. Again Arty was not in charge. But oh, how she would wish she had been.

## 9

I HAVE THOUGHT ON that spring night often over the years and it has laid ever sweet in my heart. I know now that it would be one of the last innocent times any of us was to have. In my mind I can just see me and him setting there talking with the dawn coming on all around us. We was right on the edge of a great change and, bless us, we did not know it. We might have thought we did but we did not. The change was not long in the coming either.

IT WAS THE MIDDLE of May when Larkin come by the house way before daylight. Zeke had told me the night before that he aimed to go to Marshall with Daddy to vote and that Larkin and Hackley was going with them even though they could not vote. I allowed that I would just go too, but Zeke had said, "No, Arty, it will not be such a place for women on this day. They will be all manner of rough characters milling about and I do not want to have to worry about you." So I was more than a little miffed that morning but got up and fixed breakfast anyway. I could not bear the thoughts of Zeke leaving home hungry but was not a bit happy about having to do it, so I made a great racket with slamming things around. Larkin could tell I was mad and cut a wide berth around me until I set a plate for him at the table. Neither one of them said much and it was only when Zeke was going off the porch that I run to him and give him my list. He pulled me to him then and I let him. I did not want him going off thinking I was mad.

Mary come by that day and we set out under the trees for a bit. The leaves had feathered out really pretty, and the apple tree over our head was just covered up in blooms. She asked me if Hackley had been with Larkin this morning and I said no, that it was just Larkin that had come by. She said nothing for a long time. Carolina come running up and said she'd seen the first hummingbird and I told her she could expect to see them the very same time next year, too. Granny always said you could set your calendar by the coming of the birds. Carolina ran back to the house and I looked at Mary. She'd pulled up some grass and was working it with her hands and was staring down at it.

"What's the matter?" I asked her, though I had a good mind already what it was.

"Did Larkin say anything to you this morning about him and Hack going hunting last night?"

I sighed to myself. "No he didn't, but that don't mean nothing. They might have and Hackley went on to Mommie and Daddy's."

She looked at me and just busted out crying. "You know better. Why is he doing this? Oh, Arty, I am trying the very best I know how. What am I doing wrong?"

I put my arms around her and she just sobbed and sobbed, and I set there cussing my brother to myself. After she'd got through the biggest of the crying I said, "Mary, you knowed how he was when you married him. Surely you didn't think to change him?"

Her chin come up and her eyes was still bright with tears. "I thought he would want to change."

"Why?" I asked her.

She turned bright red but her eyes stayed right on mine. "Well, you know why."

"Because you held him off till after you were married." I knew that was what she was trying to say, so I just saved her the trouble.

She nodded and then her face sort of crumpled up and she started crying again. "I was afraid I wouldn't be enough for him and now my worst dreams has come true. He don't love me." Now she was just wailing.

"Mary, honey, it ain't that. Hackley loves you or he wouldn't have married you. Some men just runs women. It's just how they are." Meanwhile I am fuming inside.

"But it was me he was running this time last year."

*Yes it was,* I thought, *but then he caught you and now you are all bagged up and he's got you.*

But I did not say any of this. I just set there and let her cry it out. Then we went in the house and she helped me fix supper. She stayed on while I put the young'uns in the bed and was sitting on the porch watching the moon come up when I went out and set down on the step next to her.

"Are you all right, honey?" I asked her.

"Oh, Arty, I'll be fine. I've decided what I'm going to do." Her face was lit all aglow by that soft moon.

"What?" I said fully expecting her to say she was going to leave him or kill him one.

"I'll tough it out till I can get pregnant. Then he'll straighten out."

I felt so sorry for her. I finally had to tell her how that wouldn't change a thing. I told her that I knew women all up and down the cove that had done the same and all that had happened was when their old man come in drunk and raising hell and shooting things up, they would just be young'uns in the way. You cannot make a decent man out of one that is not.

"Arty, he is your brother. How can you say he is not a decent man?"

See what I got for telling her the truth as I saw it? I swan some folks cannot stand the truth even when it is looking them right in the eye.

I WAS STILL SETTING there long after she'd left for home when Zeke come up the path. The moon was almost setting over across the way but I was not about to go to bed until I heard what all had happened on their trip. And I was surely glad I had stayed up, for he had a big tale to tell.

He said they'd gone over the Sim Mountain heading for Marshall. They'd stood around waiting on Hackley at Mommie's, and I said, "Oh, so he was there, then," and he shot me a look and said he'd got there a little before them and took his own sweet time getting ready to go. They had finally walked on and Hack had caught up with them at the top of the mountain. I made some comment about how I reckon he was probably wore out from all the hunting he'd done the night before, and Zeke said, "Now, Arty, do you want to hear my tale or not?" so I hushed. They'd gone down into Marshall right as the sun was burning off the fog that always come in off the French Broad, and he said it looked like everybody and his brother was there. I could not imagine that there would be more than on court days but he said indeed there was. He said, "They was way more of us than they was them what was for pulling out of the Union," and this was the very first time I'd heard my man put into real words that he counted himself for one side. So I said nothing else while he talked but only listened, and my heart grew heavier and heavier.

Sheriff Walter Woods was already drunk and was out roaming about. I had seen him over at Shelton Laurel that day and he was drinking then, too. He had spent that whole day going about praising them what had already left the Union. He did not have a gun over there but Zeke said he had one in Marshall and it was tucked down in the waist of his britches for everybody to see. Right where the men was voting he hollered out, "Huzzah for Jeff Davis and the Confederacy," and somebody hollered right back at him, "Hurrah for Washington and the Union." I would not have been a bit surprised if he had told me it was Daddy that had hollered it. He had told me that we had just managed to wrassle this country away from the English, and he could not for the life of him figure why some folks now wanted to bust this country up.

But it was not Daddy. It was Hense Shelton. The sheriff come staggering up to him and drawed his gun on Hense asking if he was the one what hollered and Hense said he was and that he reckoned this was still a country where you could say what you believed in. And the sheriff cocked back the hammer and come right on. And that was when Daddy stepped out and said for him to hold up a minute, that they was no need in this. I felt like somebody had dashed cold water on my back, but I did not say a word. Zeke said, "Now, don't worry, it turned out all right." The sheriff recognized who Daddy was and said, "Why, William Norton, you old cur dog," and Daddy managed to get him walking back down the street away from the voting place. All would have maybe been saved had the sheriff not seen Virgil

Capps standing there with a gun tucked down in his own britches. Why do men have to do such things is what I want to know, although I did not ask. Zeke was bad to tote his own gun around and about, even if the only thing I've known him to kill with it was my big pretty black snake that lived down at the barn. Men and guns is not a good mix, is what I think.

According to what Virgil told Zeke, he had forgot he even had it, but that made no matter mind to that drunk sheriff. He jerked loose from Daddy and went over to Virgil, but Zeke said he lost interest in him when he seen who was standing right beside him, 'cause he hollered out "Charles Tweed, you black-hearted Tory" and pointed his gun at him. Zeke said he hit the ground right then because he saw the sheriff meant to shoot Charles, but Charles seed it too and he dove for the ground as well. So the bullet did not hit the one it was intended for. It hit Charles's boy Jack. And I thought, *Oh, no, poor Belvie.* Jack was her baby and she thought the sun rose and set on his fifteen-year-old head. I knowed it was bad, too, because Zeke said by the time that boy went down, he was already breathing a bloody froth. The crowd got quiet then and the sheriff must've decided he had stepped in a big pile because Zeke said he turned and run. And Charles come up off that ground looking completely wild out of his eyes. He pulled his own gun out and took off after the sheriff. Zeke said a door slammed somewhere up the street, and then the sheriff come out on the upstairs porch and hollered, "Come up here, all you damned Black Republicans and take a shot about with me." I reckon Charles did just that and one better. He busted into that house and went right up the steps after him and shot him dead right then and there. And I said to Zeke, "Oh, my God, they'll be trouble for sure now."

By then the pretty light of a silvery spring dawn had found its way into the cove and Zeke's eyes was as gray as a goose when he looked at me. "Arty, they was already more trouble than we knowed what to do with and this will make it even worser." He said that a big fight started there in the streets after that, and he turned the other side of his face to me and I saw a big bruise already blooming on his cheekbone. When I jumped up to see to him he only laughed and said I ought to see the other feller and waved me off. He went back to his tale telling but I paid him no mind. I had my own thoughts to study on and I kept hearing what he'd said before, "This will make it even worser."

He was right. This was only one of many things that happened to us here in this part of the world during that damn war. They was so many bad things that took place here that we come to be called Bloody Madison. And oh, God, it were a bloody place even after the damn war. The sheriff's family brought charges against Charles Tweed's family and they fought it out in the courthouse years later. That always seemed funny to me since the sheriff was dead and so was Charles. He got killed up in Kentucky when he was up there fighting. As a matter of fact he went down right beside Zeke. And God forgive me, but all I can say is if a bullet had to take somebody on that day I am glad it was not Zeke.

In case you're interested the vote that day in Marshall went 28 for leaving out and 144 for staying in. I reckon I do not need to tell you that Daddy and Zeke was two of that 144. I reckon I do need to tell you that if us women had been able to cast a vote they would have had to rewrote that ballot. It would have had to read For, Against, and No War A'tall. Do I need to tell you where Arty would have put her X? No, I did not think so.

THE WAR COME RIDING in for us on the hot breath of an early summer and the men went pouring out of Sodom like water through a sieve.

Mary's daddy Andrew and her brother Andy rode off for Asheville the day after we caught wind that North Carolina was leaving the Union. Fools went with big grins and shooting off their guns. They went to join up with the South and Zeke never said a word as we stood on the porch and watched them go.

He did say something when his brother Shadrack went with the same intent a week later. He said, "Well, there goes my brother, Arty," and his voice broke at the end. I would not say nothing. I did not care which way Shadrack Wallin went. For somebody who had not spent much time worrying in the past I was making up for it now. The worry that laid in my breast was much bigger than the baby I was five months gone with.

My own brother Robert left and never even told Mommie he was going. Oh, how that broke her heart.

Mary's other brother Jonah that was Hackley's friend went one evening and nobody never heard from him again. Poor Lucindy. She lost all of her boys in that damn war and was not worth killing from then on. She died when she were fifty-four, an old wore-out woman.

You could hear Big John Stanton's ax thwacking for a solid week. He split more wood than I have ever seen in my life before he rode off. Daisy noted it down in her Bible: *this 6th day of July 1861 is one on which my pur hart has brok. John has gone to the war.*

I KNEW IT WOULD come home to roost with me as well, and I vowed to myself that I would not throw a big fit when it come. I spent a lot of time hiding around from Zeke so he would not know how much I was crying. I swear I was just like a young'un apt to go to crying at the least little thing anyway. But this was like I was standing under a big hammer just waiting for it to fall right on my head. And even though I had tried to ready myself for the blow, when it finally fell on me it almost drove me to my knees.

I was out on the porch trying to catch a breeze when he come up behind me. The young'uns were asleep and it was so peaceful and quiet except for the sound of the night bugs out in the trees. My name come from him on a sigh and all the hair stood up on the back of my neck at the word. "Arty," he said and that was all. But I knew what it meant. The child within me gave a great knock and was still. I laid my hand over my belly and it seemed like we stayed like we was for a long time. Finally I said, "Well, tell me what to fix for you to take with you," and he told me later that night as we was laying next to each other in our bed that he had never loved me more than he did right then.

But I did not cry.

The next day he plowed the upper field and all of us went to planting late corn. I kept looking at him wanting to fill my sight with him standing there stripped to the waist and his lean body glowing with sweat. John Wesley, Carolina, and Abigail was out with me covering the last hills. Sylvaney, Ingabo, and Zeke Jr. was playing out under the big poplar at the edge of the field.

"Sylvaney, honey, go get us a bucket of water," he called out and her little head popped up and she was off toward the house at a run. I watched her go and thought again how much she favored me. That is one thing I will have to admit about me and Zeke. We had the prettiest young'uns. And of the whole bunch Carolina was the only one dark like the Wallins.

I looked back at Zeke and found his eyes on me. They was as purple as the lilacs that bloomed down by the house. I felt the tears starting and got really busy covering up that corn.

When I looked back at him he had turned and the plow point was parting the dirt digging a straight dark furrow that looked like water streaming out behind him.


IT WAS IN THE cool dark of the next morning that I grabbed onto him as like to never let him go. I kissed his face all over and his breath smelled like biscuits and gravy. I put my face into the hollow of his throat, but I did not cry. "Don't worry about John Wesley running off. He done that so you would not see him cry," I said, and the face I offered to him was as dry as dust. "How'll you manage?" And his eyes seemed like they was digging around inside of me trying to see my very heart. "Hush," I said and put my palm flat against his mouth. "Don't say no more. If you're going, go on. Larkin said he'll help me and he will. Now go on." I nodded out toward the road where Hugh set his horse. His fingers dug into my arm and he said, "I love you, Arty." I thought then I was going to break down, but I did not. "I know that," I said. "And I never have knowed love with nobody but you." And I tried one more time to memorize his face by the light of the stars. "Don't be no hero, Zeke," I said. And he said "I ain't no hero, Arty," and then he pulled away from me and a space ain't never been as empty as the one he stepped out of. He got up on his horse and I started to turn back toward the house. I could not stand to look at him anymore, and I balled my hands into fists and went almost running. And then I thought, "Arty, you cannot let him go like this," and I made myself stop and watched him go until I couldn't make out his shape anymore.

Then I cried and them tears I had been so stingy with come in such a flood that I thought I would surely drown.

ON THE DAY PEARL was born I was as restless and cagey as an old sow bear. I had gone up on the ridge above the house and was allowing my eyes to feast on the colors of that fall to see if that would calm me down. I loved watching the change come on and my eyes picked out the red maples that were always the first to change. On down the slope was the deep gold of the striped maples and the bright orange of the sugars. Mixed all in was the bloodred of the dogwoods. And way up on the very top of the ridges was the soft yellow of the chestnuts. It was almost as though the mountains knowed somehow of what hardships was waiting for us and was trying to put on a big show now. I leaned down to pick up a chestnut burr and the pain grabbed me low in my back. You can just imagine what I thought when I went to straighten up and could not do it. I knew right then that this baby was going to come and come quick. I hollered for John Wesley and he come running with his eyes big as saucers. It is a good thing he come fast as he did, for if he had not I would have had her right out on the mountain. I just barely got back to the house and she was born. Let me tell you, this is surely the way to have a young'un. Abigail was all that was there to help me and all she really did was catch her when she come out. And as I looked at her little round head covered up with all that black hair, I thought, "Well, they will be no doubt as to who daddied this one, Lige Blackett, thank you very much," because it was just like looking at a little bitty Zeke Wallin.

But Lige Blackett never got to see my precious Pearl. He fell dead as a doorknob two weeks later.

Larkin and Hackley had been all day stripping cane when Julie run to get them. Hackley wanted to have a molasses making which as usual was just him an excuse for a big drinking and a frolic. But I must say since he'd mentioned it my mouth had been pouring water at the thought of a big mess of 'lasses. They was nothing better in the winter time than a chunk of cornbread smothered in butter and warm 'lasses.

They was hot and quarreling like two old women when they stopped by the house on their way down to the Blacketts'. Larkin had been stung by a hornet and Hackley was giving him down the road about it. "You still favoring that sweat bee sting, Larkin?" he said. And Larkin said, "Sweat bee, hell, it was big as a damn crow." I fed them and sent them on their way and was glad to see the back of them.

Pearl started to fret and I picked her up and held her while she nursed. She was a good baby and had kept that big thick mat of hair. I smiled at the little bows Abigail had tied all through it and kissed the top of her head. They is nothing in this world that makes your heart go all peaceful like kissing the downy top of your young'un's head. I was not even sore these two weeks after her birth. I reckon what your body has done six times before it has no trouble remembering on the seventh time around. And I was glad of it.

I fixed a big pot of stewed taters to take to the setting up and by the time I got over there the house was standing full. My young'uns scattered and Mary met me on the porch but her eyes were all on Pearl. She took her and I could see the want on her face like some-body had painted *I want me one, too* on it. I went on in the house to speak to the family, and who should I see but Andrew Chandler big as you please standing right by the cooling board where they had Lige already laid out.

"Why, howdy, Arty," he said. And I howdied him right back. It was no secret that my man and Hugh was fighting for the Union. And they was no secret that the Chandlers had casted their lot with the South. But we was still neighbors, and through Mary we was family. I could be as polite as the next one. I had nothing to say when Shadrack come slinking around like the yeller dog that he was, though. As far as I was concerned, he was not family for all that he was Zeke's brother.

Late up in the night Andrew cornered Hackley and set in on him about when he was going to join up. "Ride back with me tomorrow morning. I'll get you in without a bit of trouble."

"I ain't about to go off and leave Mary till I have to," Hackley said. "They's some of us around here starting to wonder who's going to look about our own."

I could tell by how red Andrew's face was that he was getting mad. "That's what I mean. I can get you in with them that's staying around here."

And I could tell Hackley was getting hot, too. "I ain't leaving Mary till I have to."

"You sure it's not that now everybody's leaving you'd hate to give up being the only rooster in the henhouse?"

It went quiet as a tomb in that house, and Hackley sounded sort of strangled-like when he said "You accusing me of something?"

And I thought, *Andrew Chandler, you better hush right now or you will have my brother to kill.*

Thank God for cooler heads, because Sol Bullman stepped right in between them and said, "Why, Hack, Andrew, what is the matter with younse? Acting like two little boys, I say. And us here trying to bury poor old Lige. It always proves an amazement to me how you never know when the angel of death is going to come swooping out of the sky and cut you down." He looked from one to the other.

And you know me. I piped right in with, "Why, what are you talking about, Sol? Lige was ninety year old."

Andrew popped a shaking finger right under Hackley's nose and said big and loud, "You mark my words, Hackley Norton. Time's coming when you won't be able to set on your fence. You'll have to jump one way or the other. So you ought to decide whether you are with us or against us."

"Why, I reckon I'll ride that fence for now. I'm for me and mine, and if you need reminding, mine just happens to be yours, too!" Hackley said, and his voice was just as big and loud.

Andrew flipped the back of his hand at Hack and went on out the door. And I was even gladder to see the back of him.

Sometimes, especially if the person is old, a setting up can be right jolly, but this one was not. It seemed like them harsh words that had been flung back and forth cast a pall over everybody and it was a quiet night spent round poor old Lige. As we was walking home the next morning a big wind come up and it turned off cold. I told Abigail that it was blowing straight out of the north and she said, "Ain't that where Daddy is?" I could not even answer her.

When I went to bed that night the wind had laid down and I knew they would be a big frost come morning. I laid there listening to my young'uns sleep and my eyes just poured water that I could not let leak when they were awake. I missed Zeke so bad that I finally scooched up next to Pearl and held on to what felt like all I had in this world left of him.

It looked like it had snowed the next morning and I had to break a rim of ice to get water from the spring.

We buried Lige that day and I had never seen a bluer sky in all my life.

WE LET OURSELVES BE lulled along that fall. I must say that there is a certain peace in knowing that nature will move things in the direction they've been going for generation after generation. For me they was comfort in knowing that I went along doing the very same things that Mommie had done and that Granny had done before her and so on. The war was still roaring all around us but there in Sodom it was still out of our sight, and as they say, out of sight, out of mind. You couldn't help but notice it when we all got together for a frolic since they was no men to dance with and us women would dance together with one of us taking the man part. I will have to say it was not near as much fun, but Hackley made sure the music was good even though Lum was gone off to the fight.

When we killed our hog it was up to me and Larkin to do the biggest of the work. Bless his heart, he stayed all night with me and we ground sausage till almost daylight. I told him I'd come help cut cane when it was ready, and he said that would be good and if the frosts held true they would be cutting it in a week.

That was some of the biggest cane I've ever seen. It was just full of juice and I was sticky all over with it on the day we cut. That was a good day. Mary looked after all the young'uns, and me, Larkin, Julie, Hackley, Abigail, John Wesley, and Carolina had a big time. I got to telling tales about Granny and we laughed. Daddy showed up about quitting time and we deviled him about coming right when the work was all done. He helped us carry it to the barn and as we was stacking it, he asked Hackley if he knowed how to witch the boilers like Granny used to. She used to have the biggest 'lassie boilings ever was and to my knowledge never lost a single run to scorching, which is an amazement. Daddy used to tell it was because she cast some sort of spell. Everybody in Sodom would come toting every pot and jug they had. One year the color of every run looked like spun gold and it was just as thick. Now them was some of the best I ever put in my mouth.

They was a big crowd that showed up that year too.

That first morning I'd gotten there before the sun was up and Larkin was just hooking old Dock up to the grinder pole. I patted him on the nose and remembered how I used to ride his back turned around so I could talk to Pap while he plowed. Lord, them was the good old days. I wondered if mules had memories and if old Dock missed Granny as much as I did.

"You'll walk twenty miles today, Dock," I said, "even if it is just round and round in a big circle."

"It'll be good for him," Larkin grinned as he give one last tug on the cinch under his belly. "He don't do nothing all the day long but pick."

Daddy was setting out on the chopping block with all my young'uns gathered around him. He had his pocketknife out and was cutting them off some sopping sticks and they was all standing around big-eyed, waiting. He was laughing and cutting up with them, saying how these was the best sticks in the world. Years later I took that same knife out of his pocket on the day he fell dead at the milk gap, and it was sharp as a razor. I carried it myself until Zeke Jr. got up big enough to give to because Daddy always said a pocketknife was a thing to use.

Up in the day as we were taking off the first run Carolina got stung by a yellow jacket and carried on like you would not believe. Somebody was always getting stung, because once the bees found the fermented leavings they would get drunk as hoot owls and would sting you as quick as look at you. I reckon they would fall into that mean drunk category.

It was such a pretty day and by three o'clock it was hot. Larkin stripped off his shirt and he was sure a pretty creature standing there feeding the grinder. I was nursing Pearl, and Mary went over to get a bucket of juice and stood talking to him.

"Ain't you afraid your back will blister?" she asked him.

And I said, "Why, he ain't blistered in his life."

"If I was to stand here five minutes without a shirt, I'd have water blisters as big as your hand."

Now some women would have said that sort of sly-like, trying to get attention, but Mary said it as easy as she would have said, "I believe it might rain this evening." One look at Larkin's face told me that his mind was painting all kinds of pictures.

Julie hollered out wanting to know what she ought to do with the seed heads and Mary said, "Just a minute, I've got a sack I'm putting them in." As she turned the neck of her dress slipped down and for just a thought her round white shoulder popped into view. She went pulling it back up.

Larkin was watching her so hard he forgot to duck as that pole came back around and it give him a pretty good knock on the head. Good enough for him. If I'd been close enough I'd have give him a knock myself. I could not help noticing that Julie made a point of being at the ready each time that bucket needed emptying the rest of that evening.

By the time the night fell, the smell was almost too much for me. It felt like the inside of my mouth had a thick, sweet coat on it, although

I had not helped sop a single boiler. I had sent Abigail on to the house with Ingabo and Sylvaney, both of which had eat so much sweetening they had took to throwing up. Another run had just come to a boil and the women was skimming off the scum when I had finally had enough and eased off with the excuse of feeding Pearl again. She was not really hungry and fell asleep pretty quick. I was dozing a little myself and was not really paying no attention when I heard Julie say to Larkin, "I just get so tired of being Andrew and Lucindy's other girl. Not the pretty one, the other one."

I studied about her saying that the rest of the night. I would have hated to have had to go through life that way, longing to be something I could never be. I don't reckon I was never anything other than just Arty. I vowed right then and there to make it a point to try real hard to never show a preference with my own young'uns. And as you know, that can be hard, for some young'uns is easier to love than others for one reason or another. But I figure life is tough enough to live through as it is.

LATER ON THAT MONTH Mommie and Daddy had a big frolic at their house. We carried every stick of their furniture out and piled it up in a big pile so there would be more room to dance. We danced and danced and it got hot as fire in the house. I went out to catch my breath and while I was standing there I looked back through the open door. We had danced so hard that we'd kicked up a layer of dust that was level with everybody's knees. It looked like they was all floating on a cloud and I was full struck by it.

As was the custom when Hackley and them got tired of playing, we all set into singing the old songs. Them was such good times when we'd be ganged up and all of us would sing. I can still recall the thrill

I'd get when I would hear somebody sing something I did not know. That night Rosa Wallin sung the prettiest version I would ever hear of "The Little Farmer Boy."

> "Well met, well met, my own true love,
> Well met, well met," cried he,
> "For I've lately returned from the saltwater sea
> And it's all for the love of thee."

That song has got Zeke's favorite verse of any song in it and it goes like this:

> "Oh, take me back, oh, take me back
> Oh, take me back," cried she,
> "For I'm too young and lovely by far
> To rot in the saltwater sea."

Seeing as how she'd traipsed off and left her little babe setting in the floor, I can only say, Whatever did she think? She got no more than what she richly deserved.

I had seen Larkin and Carolina with their two black heads together right before we started singing but had no idea of the surprise they was cooking up for me. My mouth hung open like a gate when she stood up right in front of everybody and allowed that she wanted to sing. When she shut her eyes and started, I could not believe the sweet sound that come from her mouth. My girl sung "My Dearest Dear" just like it was meant to be sung and even throwed in a verse she would have had to learn from Hackley since I had never heard nobody but him sing it.

> Oh my old mother's hard to leave, my father's on my mind,
> But for your sake I'll go with you and leave them all behind.

But for your sake I'll go with you, I'll bid them fare-thee-well
For fear I'll ne'er see you no more while here on earth we dwell.

Folks made such a do about her singing that her and Larkin sung a back-and-forth and it were one of the sweetest things in this world. Larkin started it out.

I'll give to you a paper of pins and that's the way our love begins
If you will marry me, me, me, if you will marry me.

> I won't accept your paper of pins if that's the way our love begins
> And I'll not marry you, you, you, and I'll not marry you.

I'll give to you a dress of red skipped all 'round with a golden thread
If you will marry me, me, me, if you will marry me.

> I won't accept your dress of red skipped 'round with a golden thread
> And I'll not marry you, you, you, and I'll not marry you.

I'll give to you a dress of green and you'll be dressed fit as a queen
If you will marry me, me, me, if you will marry me.

> I won't accept your dress of green for I don't care to dress fit like a queen
> And I'll not marry you, you, you, and I'll not marry you.

I'll give to you a key to my desk and you can have money at your request
If you will marry me, me, me, if you will marry me.

If you'll give to me a key to your desk and I can have money at
    my request
Then I shall marry you, you, you, then I shall marry you.

Oh, I'll take back the key to my desk and you can't have money
    at your request
And I'll not marry you, you, you, no I won't marry you.

They about tore the house down over that one and I could not help
it, I started to bawl like a baby. I cried because I was proud of her and
because I would have give anything in this world if her daddy had been
there to hear it. The saddest part was I did not know if he would *ever*
get to hear her and that was almost more than my heart could stand.

When I went outside later I realized it was the night of the hunter's
moon. My mind flew back to this time last year. I was not the only
one remembering. Larkin was out in that strange light standing with
his arms out in front of him and I knew in his heart he was holding
Granny as she'd breathed her last.

God bless her sweet soul. I hope they're having a frolic wherever
she is.

BEYOND THE MOUNTAINS, THE beast of war was literally
roaring. We was starting to hear it too. We read in the paper how Tennessee had barely scraped up enough votes to secede. But right over
the line in the eastern part, the vote had been two-to-one to stay in the
Union. When the Confederacy moved troops over there, they really
stirred up a hornets' nest. I can understand it, because most of them
saw that as nothing more or less than that they was being invaded.
And that pot that had been just sort of simmering boiled plumb over.

Mommie got a letter from her cousin Davina over in Greeneville that said her husband Ross had fell in with a gang that had meant to burn all the railroads that the Rebels controlled. It didn't work out but the Confederates come through anyways and arrested a bunch of men. They tried them and hung every one of them. Davina wrote and these are her words: "They's mor sojers than you can shak a stik at. We aim to mov frum here Nance. We air cumin home." And it was not long before an absolute flood of people come pouring over the border into Madison County. Among them that crossed over was one John Kirk and one David Fry. John Kirk was the brother of the as yet unheard of George Washington Kirk, and David Fry was the ring-leader of them would-be bridge burners. None of them was famous when they first come but, oh, they would be soon enough. It was not long at all till word was going around that they was recruiting for the Union army.

Finally the letters started to roll into Sodom, and in January Daisy got one from Big John. He had hooked up with some like-minded men from over in Mitchell and Yancey Counties, and they had made their way north to Kentucky. He was with the Union army up in the Cumberland Gap. "I'll not mak it hom in tim to plow," he wrote. "Tell Larkin I said to hep you."

Do you know what a happy woman I was when my Zeke's letter come through? I had not knowed where he was or if he'd been killed or nothing for the longest seven months that had ever rolled over my head. I had tried and tried to go along, but Lord, it had been an ever present pure-D torment not knowing where he was or if he'd made it through, but praise be, make it he had. Him and Hugh was also in the Cumberland Gap and he mentioned nothing about no fighting up there, though he did send me twenty dollars. He only talked about how pretty it was and that if he stood just in the right spot, he believed he could see plumb to North Carolina. He was homesick and I could tell it. I was Zeke-sick and he closed his letter out with this and these are his own words: "May God bless and keep you my dear wife and if we never meet any mur on urth Arty let us so live that we may meet abuv."

I cried the whole time I was writing him back but I did not let on to him. I did say to him that we now had a precious Pearl.

Andrew, Andy, and Shadrack were in and out of Sodom so much you'd have thought they was swinging doors set up down at the forks of the road. They called themselves the Madison Rangers, a Confederate company raised up by Lawrence Allen who was the clerk of court over in Marshall. Now reckon who comes up with the names for these outfits and why did all of them sound so high and fancy?

And you could not have blowed Hackley off his fence with a keg of dynamite.

LORD HAVE MERCY, I thought that winter was just going to go on forever. It was cold and snowy right up through the middle of April. When it finally thawed out enough to plow, us women had to go it alone. There was just not enough of Larkin, Fee, and Hackley to go around, although I will say Hackley tried to be *everywhere* at once, if you know what I mean. I had never plowed in my life and to tell you the truth had thought myself to be above it, but by Ned and God I did come of it. But that was not the worst of it. I had to drag the ground with the spiked harrow to bust up the big clods and then come the scrubbing with the big log. Every night it seemed like something else pained me to the point of distraction. Except for my arms. For that first three weeks or so they *always* felt like they was being jerked out of their sockets. After that though they quit hurting, and I swear I was strong as most men. Though I had never been soft-bodied like a lot of women, now I was lean and did not have one bit of fat on me. I want you to know it was with the most satisfaction and no small amount of pride I carried in my heart as I walked through them fields and seen the first shoots of corn and wheat coming up.

When it first started to rain I was so thankful, but after a week my heart went heavy as a rock. Day after day it poured and my spirits sunk even more as I watched the water run and run and keep running. I swear the fields seemed to just melt right before my eyes. It looked like a river of mud coming down the road out from the house and all my seedlings looked like merry little green boats as they went bobbing by.

They had what they called a bust-out on further north of us. I had never heard of such a thing. They said this woman was in her house cooking supper with two of her young'uns and all at once it come the biggest clap of thunder she'd ever heard but it did not come from the natural place. It come from under her *feet* and everything went perfect black and then everything started to slide. They found the house at the bottom of the mountain and it took them over an hour to dig them out. It was a pure and simple miracle that she lived to tell the story as they said every bone in her was broke. The only thing they could figure was that it had rained so much that the ground held as much as it could and then what it could not just busted out. As if I did not have enough to worry about, I laid awake night after night worrying about us having one of them bust-outs here.

Yes, I was getting to be a pretty decent worrier.

But the rain finally slacked off and quit way up toward the first of May and I could hardly stand to wait for it to dry off enough before I hit them fields with a vengeance. Things was no more than up and tender green when it come a hard freeze on the second day of June that killed most everything I had.

I don't know what I would have done without Larkin and John Wesley. I guess we would have starved to death that winter for sure, though we come damn near to it as it was. But I'm trying to get ahead of myself here.

The time come for Hackley to jump off that fence but he didn't jump. They had to push him off.

LARKIN AND ME WAS in the field behind the house planting what few rows of corn I had left when here come Julie just tearing up stumps. She was hollering the whole time saying, "Larkin, Arty, Larkin, Arty, Larkin, Arty." I thought she was going to fall up before she finally managed to say, "Mary wants you to come. A bunch of soldiers has come and took Hackley and a whole passel of others with them. They was just going past Jim Leake's store when I went by down there." And I said as if it really made some sort of difference—but in my own defense I was sort of addle-brained—"What kind of soldiers?" And she looked at me like I was a fool before she went back down the hill at a dead run, "Gun-toting soldiers is all I know." A look went between me and Larkin and then both of us broke to run too.

I dashed by the house and grabbed Pearl and screamed out for Abigail to mind the others and fix them supper. I swear it is a thousand wonders that my young'uns had not took to calling her Mommie. I was truly blessed to have had such a fine oldest child. She, however, might not have thought she had been thusly blessed with her mommie.

I done the milking for Mary and by that time it was dark in their cabin. Mary had not lit so much as a candle, and I had to feel around on the fireboard till I found one. As it sputtered to light, I saw Larkin squatted down by her stool and he had his arm up around her shoulders and she was sort of leaning into him. It rose up in me that this was not right, but what could I say? Holler out big and loud, "You get away from there, Larkin?" I think not, even though one look at Julie's poor stricken face surely made me want to. But I did mean for them to take note that they was not in this house alone, as much as they might want to act that way so I spoke up and my voice was big and loud. "Mary, tell me again what they said." Larkin looked at me and said, "She's already told us once," and I jutted my chin out at him. He knowed better than to mess with me when my chin was out like that so he told me himself.

"Something about them being with the Buncombe County militia. They was a big-mouthed feller that kept saying something about rounding up anti-Confederates, and though Hack kept saying he weren't against nobody they grabbed him up anyways. Said she saw Sol and Greenberry and your brother David and a bunch more and that she even saw Fee and it looked like they'd hit him in the head with something."

As I said a while ago I had already heard this, but him repeating it had served its purpose. He got up from Mary and was just standing there with his hands hanging down.

And it is a good thing, as right about then I heard feet come pounding across the porch and Mommie come flying through the door with her hair out of its bun and I knowed she'd been caught just as her and Daddy was fixing to go to bed.

"Lord have mercy, Mary." Mommie went to her and grabbed up the very same hand Larkin had just been holding. "Oh, honey. Your poor hands are cold as ice." She rubbed them between hers.

"Damn them all to hell in a handcart!" Daddy said and went to pacing back and forth. "What do they mean coming in here and pulling such a trick as this here? It's that damn bunch from Tennessee what's caused this."

"Don't blame them for this. They can't help it." Mommie said.

"Damned if they can't!" Daddy was just this side of screaming. "That bunch over on Shelton Laurel has brought the whole damn southern army down on us, sure as I'm standing here."

Mommie rose and her back was stiff as a poker. "You hush, William Norton. Raring and raising hell ain't going to do nobody a bit a good. You go to the spring and git me a bucket of water, and I need you to have a cool head when you come back."

Now they had never been no doubt in my mind who was really the boss with Mommie and Daddy, but this was the very first time I had ever in my life seen it so out in the open. Mommie always took care to make sure Daddy thought he was in charge, and she could play him like a fine-tuned fiddle. I waited for a blow that never happened. Daddy's eyes was red as blood and he was blinking and blinking and then he finally just grabbed the bucket and went storming out the door.

Mommie's voice was calm as could be. "He'll be all right when he gets back. He's just hidebound as to what to do. He gets that way sometimes, bless his heart." She handed me another candle. "Light this, Arty. It's dark as pitch in here."

And from then on I did not have to worry who was in charge.

Mommie turned to my baby brother Tete. "I want you to go to the house and gather up some of your things. I hoped to wait but it appears the time for waiting is over."

It is funny how I never even paid any attention to that one of my brothers. I was already married and gone long before he'd even been born, and I was thunderstruck to have just seen how big he had got.

"I'm sending him to Knoxville," Mommie said. "A man that Granny Nance is friends with is taking him to Greeneville. He'll be working with a captain in the Union army. Only way I could figure to keep him safe during this mess." She looked Larkin right in the face. "I can send you too, if you want to go."

Oh, how I wish I had throwed the awfulest fit in the world right then and just made him go. That is one of them moments we all look back down our lives at and know that we could've changed everything that was to come.

"I can't, Aunt Nancy." His eyes were dark and I could read nothing in them by the dim light of the candle. "I've got too many folks depending on me—Daisy, Arty. I can't."

And my heart cried out and said, *Not me, but Mary.* I looked at Mary to see if she was setting there all full of herself and felt sorry in an instant. Her poor little face looked like it had caved in on itself and bore such a look of suffering that I felt scalding tears flood my eyes. We was rowing the same boat now, Mary and me was, and I was ashamed of my feelings of a minute before.

I said nothing and simply went to peeling some shriveled up taters because that is what Mommie told me to do.

I HAD LAID DOWN with Pearl way up in the night just to try to rest as I knew I would not sleep, and it was just getting daylight when we heard footsteps on the porch.

Mary come up out of that chair like she'd been scalded and jerked open the door. "Oh, Hack, Oh, Hack!" she kept saying over and over. But the way he acted you'd have thought he'd just been out hunting. For once I think he was really trying to put our minds at ease, and especially Mary's. "Hell, honey. I ought to git rounded up and took off more often, if this is how I'll be treated when I get back."

"Are you all right, son?" You could tell Daddy was just worried to death.

"Finer than frog hair." And he grinned at all of us but I noted how pinched he looked around his eyes and then knowed for certain it was all just a big show.

"Come and eat," Mommie said, holding his arm and all but dragging him to the table.

"All right, all right. Let me get untangled from Mary and I'll eat. I am plumb starved, sure enough."

It was while he was eating that he told his tale. He said they'd went along rounding up men until they had joined up with another group coming down from Shelton Laurel. They had been asked a bunch of questions, and then they had made some of them join up with the Confederacy on the spot. When it come his turn, one of the fellers had asked him if he was Andrew Chandler's son-in-law. They had asked him to sign his name on a paper and let him come home.

I could see Daddy had went white as a sheet and he said, "Oh, God, son, what did you sign your name to?"

"And that was all?" Larkin asked.

"Well, pretty much." Hackley would not look at Daddy. "I told them I had been planning to join up as soon as I got my crops in anyhow. They reminded me that the Conscription Act had took effect back last month and that it was the law that I sign up, so I did. Then they let me go."

"Oh, God, help us." Mary's voice was barely a whisper.

"So you'll go now?" Daddy asked.

"Nah. I won't have to go right now. Won't have to leave till the end of this month." He give such a big yawn that his jaw popped. "But for right now I'm going to bed. I am wore out."

Larkin followed him all the way to the bed.

"Hack, what about Fee?"

Hackley set down on the edge of the bed and went to pulling off his boots before he fell sideways on the bed. "They took him on. He didn't go quiet neither. Took three of them to drag him off and that damn dog of his was absolutely trying to eat them up. They aimed to shoot it but didn't. Finally just whistled it up and took it off, too."

"But Fee won't fight! Did you tell them that?"

I could tell by how cloudy his voice was that he was already half asleep. "I was having a hard enough time trying to save my own hide, Larkin. Git on, now. I'm wore slap out."

But Larkin would not hush. "Where did they take Fee? Do you know?"

A soft snore was his only answer. Larkin made a move toward the bed, but I laid my hand on his arm. "Let him be. It don't matter where they took Fee. He won't stay long wherever they got him."

AT DAWN ON THE last day of June, thunder shook the very house as a big storm come tearing its way over from Tennessee. Great black clouds boiled up over the highest peaks and lightning streaked down and hit a big oak tree up on the ridge. It caught fire and the flaming limbs was whipping back and forth in the wind. Fat drops of rain soon followed and the fire cracked and popped like something alive and mad as hell before it sputtered and died in the downpour. The storm moaned and howled and then went screaming on across the ridge. By daylight it was as if it had never been, except for the water that was standing a good three inches deep on top of the ground. This was how it was on the day my brother went for the war.

I WOULD NOT HAVE gone over there for the world if Hackley had not come by the night before and asked me to. I said, "Are you sure, honey? Mary might want you to herself." And he looked at me and said, "She's why I'm asking you to come, Arty." Now how could I refuse him that?

By the time I got over there him and Larkin was standing in the yard and he reached out and loved me. I loved him right back and we wound up standing with our arms around each other for a long time. He had on a fine white shirt that Mary had worked on for the past two weeks and he smelled good and clean. When he finally let go of me and I looked at his face, they was not one bit of foolishness nor devilment in the blue sky of his eyes.

"I'd rather eat shit with a splinter than to have to do this," he said to us. "I don't even know when I'll be able to git back." He give a wave all around the place. "The corn out yonder will need hoeing in two weeks or so."

He hushed then and covered up his eyes with his hand. When he looked back at us his eyes was standing full of tears. "I got to go and ain't no other way around it," and then his eyes went to overflowing and I started crying, too, and of course when I done that my milk let down. You could always tell Arty in a bad situation because she'd be the one standing there with the front of her dress wet as water.

And then he looked at Larkin. "You promise me that you'll look about Mary, and you, Arty, have her help you with the young'uns. She loves your little Pearl and we was hoping she was—"and then he hushed again, but I knowed what he'd meant. She had told me she thought she might be expecting but I knowed now she was not.

I said I could always use help with my litter of hellions and he laughed at that, and I was proud to hear it. I did not know if I could have stood seeing him this way much longer. The tears were gone from his eyes now, but he was still talking as serious as a judge.

"Don't let no harm come to her. Somebody come here and tries to bother her, you kill them, Larkin," he said and did not even blink an eye.

And I said, "Why, Lord, Hackley, surely it won't come to that."

He looked at me. "Arty, them was some of the roughest characters I ever seen riding with them fellers last month. And that bunch that's been hiding out on Shelton Laurel from over in Tennessee ain't no better. You could throw every one of them in a sack, Union, Confederate, don't make no matter mind, and you wouldn't be able to tell which one would fall out first. They'll be robbing, pillaging, plundering, murdering—" He looked back over his shoulder at the cabin. "And raping too. You women'll be left to root hog or die. You'll need to watch yourself, too, sister, and I wouldn't let them biggest girls of yours out much neither. That's where I'm counting on you, Larkin. I think I'll be able to go on down that road and leave if I have your word."

I had never even thought of that. In my heart there bloomed a new respect for Hackley Norton.

"You've got my word that I'll do the best I can," Larkin said.

"And you'll take care of yourself, Hack?" I blurted. "Don't you be taking no bullets."

He laughed at me then and seemed more like his old self.

"Hell, Arty. Don't you worry none about me." He looked up at Larkin with a big grin. "Course I'll miss you covering my back. Remember how we used to do that? Fight back to back? Weren't nobody could whup neither one of us if the other was within hollering distance."

Oh, how fast the years had passed us by. Of a sudden I could just see them as boys and my heart squeezed up in my chest.

But the moment went by and there he stood cocky as a little banty rooster.

"Anyhow," he said, "I figure it won't take me but a little while to get this whole mess straightened out and headed in the right direction."

And Larkin said something I will never forget. "Since I ain't going to be there fighting at your back is all the more reason to watch it closer. If you believe what the papers is saying, then both sides is winning. And me and you knows that can't be right. Somebody's got to lose. And it won't be too much longer afore they ain't no men left around here. All of them's being sent off to Virginy."

"Like I said, it'll get a lot worse through here," my brother said. He looked me right in the eye. "Take care of things, Arty." Then at Larkin, "Mind what I asked you to do."

And then he turned and left us standing there in the path.

We watched him go for a minute and then Larkin hollered out. "Hackley!"

He stopped and turned back to us.

"Sing me something I don't know."

Though in the dark shade, I saw the grin that split his face.

Hackley's voice floated back to us on the breeze, strong at first, but faded as he went on down the road.

A soldier traveling from the north
While the moon shined bright and clearly,
The lady knew the gentleman's horse
Because she loved him dearly.

She took the horse by the bridle reins
And led him to the stable.
"They's hay and oats for your horse, my love
Go feed him, you are able."

She reached and took him by the hand,
She led him to the table.
"They's cake and wine for you, my love
Go eat and drink your welcome."

Hit's she pulled off her blue silk gown
And laid it across't the table,
He pulled off his uniform suit
And he hopped in the bed with the lady.

Larkin seemed to be straining to listen as the words became faint and fainter still, and then disappeared altogether. When all we could hear was birdsong and the loud burring of the katydids we turned back towards the cabin and Larkin said real low, "I already know that one."

I did not answer him for I knowed he was not talking to me.

## 10

THAT SUMMER WAS HOT as hell and dry as a bone. It was a constant fight to save our gardens, while the corn patches in the upper fields just withered up and died. We toted bucket after bucket of water from the streams until they dried plumb up. They was not enough water to wash clothes and everybody went nasty and dirty smelling. We couldn't even wash the dishes, we just wiped them clean and used them again for the next meal. Oh, how I dreaded them white-hot dog days to come that rendered snakes blind and mean. Sores would get all caked up with a yellow scab and would not heal and then would come that red line streaking toward your heart. Dog days—when skunks, coons, bats, and dogs went mad, and the creeks would be standing pools of sickness.

And this year brought the most dreaded of all to us, and that was the fever.

I SAT AT THE table watching a wasp bumble across the cabin. It bumped against the ceiling, dove down, and bumped the ceiling again. It slapped its body several times against the walls trying to find a way out. But it found none so it turned and started the journey back. When I rubbed my eyes it felt like they was full of grit.

Two days ago I'd had to send Abigail, Carolina, Zeke Jr., and my precious Pearl to stay with Mommie when Sylvaney got the headache. Though it was hotter than the hinges of hell, she was saying she was cold. I kept Ingabo at home too because she was warm to the touch. I sent John Wesley to get Larkin and told him to go on to Mommie's after that. My bosoms felt like they were going to bust wide open, but they was nothing to be done about it. I couldn't even get my mind to wrap around how Mommie was managing with Pearl. Pearl had a few teeth and had been eating some mashed-up food but was still nursing regular. She would be weaned for sure when this was all over. The steady thwack of an ax outside offered me some comfort even though I had not allowed Larkin any nearer to the house than the edge of the yard. He was bedding in the barn and allowed as how he'd slept in worse places. Just knowing he was here had at least knocked the sharp edges off this hellish fear that had been working inside of me like a bunch of worms. Lord, I was tired. I had been up all night bathing first one girl and then the other. Poor little lambs with their skin so hot I could only wonder as to how they was not being baked from the inside out. Every time my mind tried to go down that dark path of what I already knew deep in my bones, my heart would jump up and say, *No, no, it is not.*

I know now that when we really know something we can never not know it. But I was not that way then. I thought that if we believed something hard enough, that we could make it so. When we are young we really believe that all it takes is grit and determination, and it is only with the living of life that we come to wisdom. Well, I say that wisdom is wasted on the old. But maybe not. Mayhap if we knew how tough life was going to be when we was just starting out, it would prove more than we could stand. Maybe nature runs its course just as it does for a reason. That is not to say I do not ball my fists up and shake them in the face of life even now, and me an old woman. I am still a hardheaded person and will not take nothing laying down. I will stick my chin out and take it right there, thank you very much. But I have learned what I have come to believe is the most important thing and do not fight against it no more. And that is that we cannot change the way a single hair grows in another person's head. We all have our own row to hoe and nobody can hoe it for us. It is just a heartbreaking thing when somebody we love has such a hard row. But it was right there in that little cabin that I had to learn the hardest lesson of all, which was that some of us are given short rows.

I did not know that I was fixing to get a big dose of life's seasoning. All I knew to do was fight on, so I did.

That day was so white it hurt my eyes, and I propped my arm on the door facing and put my head in the crook of my elbow. Then such a longing went through me that it made my knees weak, and before I could stop myself I said out loud, "Granny," and you could never know how bad I wanted to see her dear old face right then. I would have traded my soul for just ten minutes.

Right next to my head the wasp give a final slap against the ceiling and dove out into the bright sunlight. I watched it go until I could no longer see its little dark shape against the faded green of the mountain.

That night Sylvaney set straight up in the bed and cried out, "Mommie," and the blood just come gushing out of her nose and her fever went sky high. I done everything I knowed to do trying to stop the blood, but it just kept pouring out to where we all three looked like I had slaughtered a hog right there on the bed. Finally I grabbed the nearest thing which just happened to be the ladle Zeke had carved for me and I snapped the handle off and mashed it as hard as I could against her upper lip. I kept saying over and over, "Granny, don't let this happen, please," and finally the blood stopped.

I have the bowl of that ladle on my dresser and oft times I take it up. And though I cannot see it I rub my hands over it and remember what he said to me when he give it to me. "Here, Arty, it is like you, warm to the touch." So that ladle is like just about everything else in this world that is sweet and bitter at the same time.

Toward morning I stretched out on the bed next to the girls and fell into a deep sleep. I didn't even hear Larkin when he hollered for me from the yard at dawn. But when I opened my eyes, there he was, quietly stacking firewood in a neat pile. I was so wooly-headed that I didn't even say nothing to him and he come to stand at the foot of the bed looking at me and the wasted forms of my girls. I saw in his eyes what I could not carry in my heart, and somehow seeing it there helped me to bear it. He come to my side of the bed and said "Amma," and I said to him, "Git out, git out, Larkin. The girls has got the fever," and he just shook his head. Before I could stop him he reached over me and picked Sylvaney up in his arms and carried her to the table and started washing the dried blood off her face. Though his hands was gentle as could be she started to fight him and he went to singing to her low and soothing-like.

> They'll be no night in that bright land,
> No clouds to blight the sun.
> Like little children we shall play
> Oh, how we'll sing and run.

I could not find my tongue to tell him nay.

It was a few days later when the rosy spots bloomed on their scrawny chests and what little doubt I might have held onto was put to rest. I bathed and sung and cried and could not eat a bite. I was running on nothing but pure will and Larkin's strength. Poor thing. If he made one trip to the spring he made a hundred. He did not say much and I did not have to line out for him a single thing to do. He did whatever he saw needed to be done, even down to taking the blood- and shit-soaked rags out behind the barn to burn.

TWO WEEKS BLURRED BY as we battled against that unrelenting foe. One morning before dawn of the third week, Ingabo bled from her guts so bad that the blood went all the way through the corn-shuck mattress and pooled up under the bed. After I changed her I set down and just held her. She died there in my arms and I laid her on the table. I did not even cry. You might wonder at that, but you should not. You see, I did not have time for the dead. I went right back to bathing Sylvaney. Sometimes you have to set grief down and not carry it right then, but do not fret. It will squat right there and wait for you to pick it back up.

Sylvaney went to sleep down in the evening, and I had to get out of that house or take to screaming like a mad person, so I went out on the porch and set down. I heard Larkin come out behind me but he never said nothing.

And then the strangest thing in this world happened to me. In the blink of an eye they was two Artys setting there with Larkin. One was very stout and clear as a bell and able to think even better than usual. The other one was crazy as hell and wanted to jump up and go to running and clawing at her throat because all the pain known to mankind had balled up and lodged itself there to where she could barely breathe around it. So I said, *You, Arty with the clear head, do this thing, because something must be done with Ingabo, for we cannot leave her long in this heat.* So I opened my mouth and to my amazement I found that this Arty could talk though it come out cracked and brickle.

"Put her in the root cellar."

He waited for me to say something else and when I didn't he asked me, "Do you want me to go git somebody?"

It flashed hot as fire through me that somewhere else people was going about their day-to-day and did not have to bury their little red headed girl down in a cold black hole. And them two Artys was one again.

I started shaking all over and could not stop and my mouth opened and the awfullest sound come out, and I began to keen for that little part of me and Zeke that had left from this world.

I did not even know Larkin had moved but of a sudden he was there. He done nothing more than lay his hand on my shoulder and we stayed that way until a near to full moon showed itself above Picked Shirt Mountain. Then we got up together and went back in the house. We stood for a while by the table and then with the gentlest hands ever was, he gathered my baby up and carried her out the door.

Sylvaney died the next day.

They is no way in this world to make losing a child real to folks what has never lost one. You might think you could imagine it, but friend, you cannot. I have lived a long life and I have forgot more than most folks will ever know, but I have never lost a minute of them awful days. And as you know I can lay right in there with the best of them when it comes to talking and telling tales. But watching them two little girls leave this world and then laying them in the ground done something to me, and I was not the same ever again. From that day on when somebody asked me how many young'uns I had I always said seven living two dead because to have done anything else would have been like they'd never been here a'tall, and I could not stand that. They are your young'uns and they remain so until you are laid in the ground. The wound you tote with you, and though it never closes up, it does get to where it does not feel like you are pouring salt in it. Nature helps you in that way at least.

LARKIN AND DADDY HOLLOWED and charred out a coffin log big enough to hold both girls and we buried them up on the ridge next to Granny. I went half foolish when they started covering them up and Mommie had to hold me up. When I was leaning against her I could feel her flesh trembling, but each time I met her eyes they was as clear and still as a blue pool of water. I stayed until they mounded the dirt over them because I knew I had to. But to tell you the truth I just wanted to jump in the hole with them, and Mommie said to me, "Scream, Arty, scream as loud as you can, if you want to," and I could not. It was a pitiful little crowd that gathered that day. Just me, Larkin, Mommie and Daddy, Mary, Julie, and Maggie. Larkin had to half carry me back to the house.

It says a lot for Mary and Maggie, I think. They might not have said nothing to each other, but by God them two set all their differences aside and come that day for me. Women are not like men in that way.

IT WAS JUST ME and Larkin went back to that empty house. We spent the next two days scrubbing it down. Mommie's brother had died of the fever and she had almost died herself, and she said Granny washed everything with lye soap after. I went at it with a vengeance and by the next day, all the skin on my hands was cracked and bleeding. I did not even so much as pay that no mind. The pain in my hands was good because it made me know that at least on the outside I was still alive.

On the second night, Larkin went to the barn and got a jug of liquor that Sol had give him. I got as drunk as a hooty owl, and I will say that is exactly what I set out to do. Granny told me one time that pitching a big drunk is the best cleaning out we can offer to ourselves, so I took her at her word. I do not remember much about that night nor the next day. I got up on the fourth day weak and shaking but clearheaded and knowing I had to get on with things now. I had buried two of my babies but I still had five in the world of the living.

They come in like little scared rabbits. Even Carolina was quiet and big-eyed. Pearl had growed but she reached for me like I was a long-lost friend and I grabbed a hold of her and held her so tight in my arms that I could feel her little heart beating next to mine. When I finally set her down she come right back up off that floor and walked. Abigail give a little grin, like she didn't know whether she ought to or not, and said she started walking about a week ago. And I was struck by something right then that I have never forgot. All my other young'uns would grow and change and all that, but Sylvaney and Ingabo would always stay my little girls.

Somehow that made it a little easier to bear.

It was just then that a soft little hint of a breeze blowed its way in through the door and the sweet smell of lilacs come sighing into the room. Larkin's head come up and he sniffed the air and the corners of his mouth curled up in a smile. Pearl set into laughing and she went to reaching out her little arms just like somebody was standing there to pick her up. My hair was damp with sweat and of a sudden, it felt like a hand had laid itself on my forehead to push it back. And then it seemed like it went to moving about the room stirring around and about all of them, and then it settled on Larkin. His hair blowed about for a little bit and then it was gone. Abigail scooped up Pearl and all the young'uns went running out. And I stood there for a minute with my mouth hanging open and then I started to cry, and it were not a half-crazy crying neither. It was a good cleansing cry.

Larkin put his hand on me and I turned into him and buried my face in the front of his shirt.

"It felt like she moved through me," I said, and I pushed my face into his shirt again and breathed in.

"The smell is all over you," he said.

I had never had such a feeling of peace in my life as when that happened. Nothing will ever make me believe anything other than that Granny come to let me know that my girls was with her and that they was all right.

And though I have missed them and wondered about them, I have never worried about them since.

## 11

THE FIRST CONFEDERATE BUNCH come foraging five days later, and damn them for the blackguards they was. We were expecting them too. They was talk all through this part of the world then as to how they would come prancing right onto a body's land demanding part of what little food there was without so much as a fare-thee-well, talking their big talk as to how a law had been passed giving them the right to take 10 percent of everything we had managed to coax up out of the ground. Well, to hell with them and their laws, and I told them that. I asked them if they somehow thought I had took them to raise, but it done no good. They took it anyhow and we come damn near to starving that winter. I still get mad as fire just thinking about how they all treated us back during their big fine war.

They went to Mary's the day after they come to my place and this is how she told it to me. And she left nothing out, bless her.

She didn't have much and she allowed if they got it they was going to have to fight her for it. I can just see her little slender frame standing up to all them big rough men. But stand up to them she did. She said the horses was all spattered with mud, and the men was covered with a silvery coat of fine dust. Ain't it funny what your mind latches onto to remember in times like that? Before she could open her mouth one of them kicked his horse out a little further than the others and he touched the brim of his hat.

"Afternoon, ma'am," he said in a slow drawl that fingered him as being from further south than North Carolina.

Mary was not about to let them know how scared she was, but her knees was knocking under her dress. "Howdy."

Then he give a little smile and Mary said that flew all over her, and before she could catch it that redheaded temper popped out and of a sudden she was no longer scared. She was mad as hell.

"Is they something you think is funny here?"

And he sobered right up and said, "No ma'am. I've not found humor in much these last few days. Is your husband around?"

"My husband is off fighting in this damn war, mister, and he's on the same side as you."

Mary said there was a little flicker of something that went across his face, but that did not stop him from saying, "My men are thirsty and hungry," as if that had anything a'tall to do with her.

She answered them better than I would have. "The spring's out yonder. Ye can help yourself. Don't take the horses down in it. They can drink from the branch out yonder behind the barn."

He looked her right in the face then and said, "And we'll be needing food, too, ma'am."

She looked right back and said, "They ain't no food to spare for you, mister," which was the total truth.

His voice was awful quiet then. "Ma'am, I am authorized by the government to collect ten percent of all food growed on your land."

And Mary put it right back to him. "Well, the government ain't setting here in Sodom trying to figure out how it's going to make it through the coming months without starving to death. And besides that, ten percent of nothing is still nothing."

You know what I have to say about that, don't you? I say, "Go it, Mary." I told her that then, too.

But it done no good, because all he said was, "I'll take all that into consideration while we look about. Men, see what you can find."

The men all got down and set into roaming free about the place and Mary said she was so dismayed that she just stood there like she'd took root. The sound of a pistol shot out back of the house unrooted her, though, and she come off that porch like a screeching hellcat. "Don't you kill my chickens. You stop." Wailing like a banshee she launched herself at one of the men what come carrying a chicken and a sack of salt, and they both went down in a flurry.

She had no way of knowing that Larkin had just topped the ridge heading from my place to hers and he was just in time to hear her scream.

He told me later that all he saw was her setting on the ground with this feller looming up over her so he acted before he even had time to think. He went in low and caught the soldier unaware and hit him full force. The next thing he knowed he was flat on his back and the soldier was setting astraddle of his chest with a knife blade at his throat. That was awfully hard for me to believe because they come no tougher than Larkin Stanton, but Mary and Larkin both swore it as the truth. Larkin said this feller's eyes was mild as mud pies as he studied him for a minute.

Then he said, "Catch your breath, son, then you can tell me why you come tearing in here intent on knocking the infernal hell out of me."

Mary had crawled over to them by then and said, "Don't you hurt him. Take everything I got but don't hurt him."

The soldier looked at them and then said in the tiredest voice ever was, "Oh, honey, I'm not going to take everything. I'm just going to take what the government says I can." And then he hollered out for them other soldiers to put their guns away, and Larkin said that was when he noticed that they was about fifteen guns pointed right at his head.

Once the rest of them had gone back to their pillaging and plundering, the soldier got up off Larkin and offered his hand to Mary. "Now I'll get back to what I was doing awhile ago," and he helped her get up. Larkin said he felt pretty damn foolish then.

Mary said while she was knocking the salt and dirt off herself, the soldier stuck his hand out to Larkin and said, "Major Silas McMahan," and him and Larkin shook hands. Men are the funniest creatures. Fighting like dogs one minute then shaking hands and grab-assing the next.

He then turned to Mary and held out his hand, and when she give him hers he bowed over it. I wished I could have seen all that as it would have surely been a sight to see. "Please accept my sincerest apologies," he said.

And Mary said he was the sweetest man ever was. I did not believe it at the time but once I myself got to know Silas, I have to say he was one of the most decent humans I would ever know. He'd been a soldier all his life and had come close to losing his leg down in Mexico. That's why he weren't off fighting up where the big fighting was. He was from down in Central, South Carolina, and his family had been there since God's dog was just a pup and he told me us mountain folks was as foreign to him as anybody he'd ever seen and he had traveled all over. But I'll tell you this much. I don't know what we would have done during that damn war without Silas McMahan.

He took only a little that day from Mary and said he was sorry for having to take that.

Poor little Mary said to me later that she had studied about it and come to where it was all right since it might help them feed Hackley, wherever he was.

Knowing my brother she didn't need to worry about that.

Larkin said that Silas told him before he rode off that no woman was safe living by herself. Well, don't that take all. What do you reckon they was thinking when they started their merry little war and took off all our menfolk, is what I'd like to know.

But the one thing Silas done that day without even meaning to was to give Larkin and Mary the go-ahead to get closer to the line than ever before.

And what happened next put them over it.

It was long after when Larkin told me the whole of what happened a few weeks later, the day the Union soldiers rode up to the house.

Larkin was out watering what corn they had managed to save when he heard horses coming up the road. He didn't want to draw notice to the corn so he went slipping out of the field and into the barn, thankful that Hackley had butted it up against some trees because he was able to get the cow out and tied up back in the woods without being seen. He eased back and peeped between the logs. He said what he saw caused his blood to run cold as ice. He said it was all in the way them men got off their horses at the same time and started meandering toward the house that caused him alarm. He said he was desperate for a weapon of some sort when his eyes fell on Hackley's big mowing scythe. What he aimed to do with a scythe against guns is well beyond my way of figuring, but then I reckon at least it made him feel like he was fixing to do *something* other than just stand there with his teeth in his mouth. I shudder to think what might have happened had it not been for one of Daddy's razorback shoats. Larkin said he heard a snuffling sound and from out of the stall nearest him come this pig just sauntering along like it had not a care in the world, and I don't reckon it did. Them hogs was as mean as old billy hell and feared neither man nor beast. It must've thought kingdom come when Larkin slapped it on the hind end with the flat of that blade. He said it went squealing for all its might out of the barn and went hell bent for leather straight at them soldiers. One pulled his gun and shot it right between the eyes. Larkin said they loaded it up and went riding off.

That was how the story went for years. Later I got to hear the rest of it.

AFTER THEM MEN LEFT, Mary went to pieces and Larkin done what he always did. He went to comforting her and they wound up in each other's arms. He said when they kissed he felt like he'd been struck by lightning, and it was like his skin was on fire. He said when he come to his senses he tried to shift away from her, but she'd moved with him and pushed against him even closer. And that she'd whispered his name and he was lost. Had it not been for Granny's little hen flying out from under the house, they is no telling what would've happened, but fly out she did, and it scared the livelong hell out of them. He had tried to say he was sorry then, but she would not let him. "Hush," she had said and then run into the house. He said he'd gone to the barn then and cried like a big baby. And he said to me then, "Amma, I am shamed by it still and I am sorry from the bottom of my heart."

When we are young we might have a bushel of sense but we ain't got a lick of reasoning. We have feelings and yearnings, and to deny them is not natural. I will even go so far as to say we cannot deny them. Even you old people can surely recall what it felt like to wake up in the morning next to the one you love with your skin buzzing and sizzling like fatback in a hot skillet and your heart feeling like it would bust wide open with the wants and longings that is ours when we're in the bloom of youth. Recall how it dropped itself in your gut and went to rippling all through you in the blink of an eye? It washed over me with Zeke and I have never knowed it with any other man, and I was a lucky woman because he felt it for me, too. He give as good as he got. And let me tell you right now, he got a lot. We had many years of strong nature between us and when it began to wane, we still had the memory of it and every once in a while it would flare between us and we would act like young'uns again, if only for a little while. Let me say here how much I thought of that man who was my great love and my best friend. He was my heart's desire until the day he died and remains so even now that he is gone. This is so.

Now to think that strong nature is only between a man and his wife is a foolish, foolish thing. Larkin Stanton had no more reasoning when it come to Mary than any other man-creature on God's green earth. He was seventeen year old and had a healthy dose of man nature and them Stantons was hot-natured men, if you know what I mean. She was a nineteen-year-old vision of pure loveliness with a healthy dose of the woman nature. And then you have to throw in that pot the fact that Larkin had loved her most of his life in one way or another. It seemed like he'd climbed on a bullet when he was born and his whole life was headed in her direction like he'd been shot out of a gun.

The only trouble was that Mary was my brother's wife and to get to where that bullet was heading, it first had to go through him.

I WAS PROUD TO mark the end of summer that year and felt a slight easing in my heart when the first cool rain fell up toward the middle of September. For the first time since burying my girls, I really felt like I might live. I have never cared for the end of summer since and figure I will go to my grave that way.

Me and Mary put our heads together and our gardens as well. Thank God there was a bunch of apples and pears that year. We figured if we was *real* careful with a wing and a prayer and everybody going a little hungry, we might just have enough to make it through the winter.

We talked about where to put the crocks of food to keep them away from the soldiers that was in and out of Sodom in a constant stream, and Larkin come up with the best idea. He got a maddock and shovel and crawled way back under the house and hacked out a root cellar that you could not see until you was right on it. Me and Mary and the young'uns worked every day and night putting stuff up, and it was almost like old times. Carolina worried Larkin to death dancing on the floor over his head. The only way he could get her to quit was by singing to her, as she was as foolish over them old songs as he'd been, and she would quit with the stomping to listen. Them was some good old times.

We built a holding pen back in the woods for our cows. Mary said this would not work because the big cats would get them. I allowed I would rather the panthers kill and eat them than for them to be killed to feed a single solitary soldier. I was sick unto death of all them foolish men that we now had to contend with. What the damn Home

Guards weren't ten-percenting, the damn Yankees was raiding, and what little was left, the deserters was plime-blank stealing. To give you an inkling of how it was with us, I will tell you this. Larkin spent one whole day harnessed like a mule to the sled with me and Mary loading it up with hay. We'd no more than got it off and put in the hayloft than the Home Guard come through and took most of it. All you Yankee lovers don't need to get your drawers in too big a self-righteous wad, neither. Your fine boys in blue come through later that evening and took the damn sled itself.

Larkin had give up all thought of staying at home. He stayed a night or two at Mary's just the two of them, and when that was made known to me I throwed three fits and a quare spell. I told them they would be too much talk and that I would not have it. I was trying my best to protect them and was glad when Julie come to stay. I guess my reasoning was that now at least folks might think he was took up with her and that was the better of the two evils, if they is such a thing.

THEY HAS NEVER BEEN no love lost in me for them high-browed folks up in Asheville. They have always thought themselves above us and I have no use for such. That feeling was only shored up in October when that man that I named Little Shitting Colonel come riding up to Mary's when her and Larkin was getting in the last of the squash. Larkin said they'd already been seen so they was no need to even try to hide the squash, so he picked up the full basket and went to meet them. They was five of them and all of them dressed up in their little Confederate uniforms like that made them God's gift. Now, people, I want to tell you that some men is not kind nor decent and they was looking one right in the face. He was the sort of man what is perfect cut out for this business of war and as far as I'm concerned, every last one of them needs to be consigned to the deepest, hottest hole in hell. And I hope they all wind up in that hole with their backs broke. I will not even say I am sorry for the wishing of such an awful thing.

When Larkin told them they was looking at what food that was left, Little Shitting Colonel blared his eyes and said that was not why they was there. He jerked some papers out of his pocket and sort of waved them at Mary and asked if she was the wife of Hackley Norton.

Well, Lord have mercy, of course poor little Mary's mind went to the worst place and her knees buckled under her. She sort of leaned over against Larkin and he had to hold her up for a minute to keep her from falling. But then that chin come up and she stepped out to meet it head on, bless her little heart. "I am his wife," she said. "Where was he killed?" Little Shitting Colonel said, "Oh, no, madam. Nothing quite so noble as that. He is a traitor, Mrs. Norton. I cannot tell you whether your cowardly husband lives or has been murdered by one of his fiendish friends. All I carry are the papers that identify him as a deserter from the army of the Confederate States of America as of September 23, 1862." Can you believe that somebody would use that word *fiendish*? Well, that is them people from Asheville for you.

"Why, that's been over a month," Larkin said. "How come now is the first we heard of it?"

Little Shitting Colonel made this big show of looking off in the distance and sighing big and loud. I guess he was trying to be a big shot and make sure everybody knowed what a high opinion he had of hisself. "I'm certain the government has much better ways to waste the time of its men without rushing about madly to notify the likes of you folks of the goings and comings of men like this here Hackley Norton." As far as he was concerned, he said, it was good riddance to bad rubbish.

Then he must've took a good look at Larkin, because he asked why it was he had not been conscripted. Larkin answered him with the truth, which was that he'd just turned seventeen back in the summer. You can rest assured that this was not the first time that boy had answered that question. But this was the first time he'd been asked to prove it. Larkin allowed as to how he had no way of doing that except the saying of it and that he did not lie.

Little Shitting Colonel had rared back in the saddle and said he wished he had a ten-cent piece for every time he'd heard that little tale. Then with eyes as flat as a snake's he'd asked for Larkin's name and he got a ugly look on his face and his thin little lips got even thinner. I have always said you should not trust a man that has no lips. And then he said to the rest of them men, "What do you think, gentlemen? Is this hulking giant the child he claims to be? Or is he lying to us so he can remain about to diddle this pretty little trick here?" Larkin said if he'd had a gun that would have been one dead son of a bitch. But he did not, and then Little Shitting Colonel said, "I repeat, can you prove your age?"

Larkin said Julie hollering from the porch was all that kept him from getting into it with them men. All I can say is thank the Lord somebody was thinking on that day.

"I can prove it," she said as she come off the porch and marched her little self right up to them. She was carrying a Bible in her arms and talking a mile a minute. Mary might have been the pretty one, but they was no flies on Julie Chandler. "This here is his granny's Bible," she said in a big loud voice. "The date's wrote down when she married and when all of her young'uns was borned. Larkin's in here too," and she went to giggling like a foolish girl, and it was so unlike her that Larkin said all him and Mary could do was stand there and stare. "Though Lord knows," Julie went on, "Larkin couldn't of been her young'un. Why, she'd a been way too old to of birthed a young'un by the time Larkin come along. See, his mommie died giving birth and his granny wrote his name right next to her daughter's name. It was the durndest thing. When he was born they surely didn't 'spect him to live, though you'd never know it now, would ye? He sure is a big ole thing, ain't he?" She made a beeline for Larkin then and locked her fingers around his upper arm and went to batting her eyes at him and looking up at him like she was going to take a bite out of him. "And, why, you know what they done? His Aunt Nancy, I mean. I don't think his granny was for it, or least ways I don't think she was, course I couldn't swear to it since I weren't there. Anyhow, they let Hackley name him." She giggled some more. "Bless his heart! Hackley's, I mean. He weren't but a young'un hisself and, why, he named Larkin after one of his mommie's brother's coonhounds."

I still get tickled thinking about it. She might still be standing there talking that bunch of foolishness if Little Shitting Colonel hadn't hollered out, "Silence!"

Them other men took to laughing and one of them muttered, "They God."

Julie drawed a great wind as though she was going to start in again.

But the little man had heard enough. "Oh, for heaven's sakes, child, be quiet! I am not interested in all this prattle!" He looked at the Bible she was holding up to him and give a snort and allowed he'd take her word for it. He lost all interest in Larkin and turned back to

Mary. "Mrs. Norton, I am here to officially inform you that your husband is considered by the Confederate States of America to be a criminal and as such may be shot on sight, arrested, and hanged, or placed in prison for the rest of his natural life. Many of these men try to return home. Should he do this, it is your duty to your country to persuade him to turn himself in, or you must take it upon yourself to notify the authorities. We will be patrolling this area and will continue searching for your husband. Do you understand what I'm saying, madam?"

Larkin said Mary's back got stiffer and stiffer the longer he talked to where she was ramrod straight by the time he finished and her eyes was blazing mad. "I am not deaf, mister, and I understand ever word. Give me them papers."

Little Shitting Colonel was right taken aback with our Mary. But he still managed to say he'd told her because he'd assumed she wouldn't be able to read.

"Give me your damned papers. I can probably read better than you can." And she grabbed them papers right out of his hand and then she said, "Now git your Rebel asses off my land!"

They left then but not before Little Shitting Colonel had ordered one of his men to take the squash. That aside, I got the biggest laugh when they all three come by the house that evening and told me that tale.

I had only one question for Julie. "Where in the world did you get Granny's Bible?" And with a grin she said, "It weren't your granny's, it were Mary's."

It done my heart good to know that a proper-mouthed Little Shitting Colonel from the big fine town of Asheville could be outfoxed by a skinny little mountain girl.

Some things is just too rich for words.

## 12

As the days of that year came to an end, Sodom got buried under a big heavy quilt of the first snow. The Home Guard come through just every little whipstitch taking what it wanted, and looking for what was now a crowd of men what had deserted from the army. They was all kinds of God-awful stories being tossed about. This one I know was the truth because Clarissa told me herself.

She was at home with her little baby that was just setting up good when the Home Guard come riding up wanting to know where her husband Craven was. She knew he was hiding out somewheres but did not know the exact spot. They would not believe her and drug her out fighting like a wildcat the whole way and tied her to a tree. Then they set her baby boy in the doorway where she knowed if he fell over he would fall onto the big flat rock they used as a step and bust his brains out. When she still couldn't tell them where Craven was, they rode off and left her tied to that tree. Who knows what would've happened if Little Bob hadn't come along. He'd been blinded by the fever when just a boy, but he was able to follow the sound of that baby crying and then helped her get untied. Poor old Little Bob. He got bit by a mad dog two years later and went mad hisself and died.

They was all manner of stories every bit as bad as Clarissa's, but the worst one I ever heard was the one Pete McCoy told us one evening when Larkin, Mary, and Julie had come by the house and we'd fixed supper. It was way up in the evening and all my little ones was asleep except for Abigail and Carolina.

When Zeke's old dog went to barking something fierce, Larkin got up and went to the door. Old Shag would defend his people like ringing a bell, and I was sort of surprised when he quit barking right off and went to whining like he did when he knowed you. You could have knocked me over with a feather when Larkin come leading Pete McCoy to the table.

"You're a long way from home," I said. "Surely to goodness you ain't out hunting on such a night." He was an old hunting buddy of Larkin and Hackley's.

"Lord, Arty, I wished I was hunting. I hate to bother younse, but I need help." The top of his head barely reached Larkin's shoulder. "They's been some trouble over on Shelton Laurel," he said in a low-pitched voice.

"We've heard some of it." I said. "Come in and eat."

"I'm obliged. My belly's been trying to eat my backbone all day."

I ain't never seen nobody eat like poor old Pete did that night.

After his second glass of buttermilk he closed his eyes and sort of slumped back in his chair. "Nothing never tasted better," he said.

"What all has happened?" Mary said.

He opened his eyes and studied her. "They's been a slaughter over home."

"What do you mean a slaughter?" I said with a look at Abigail and Carolina. I made up my mind right then that they was old enough to hear it. They might have to face a like thing one of these days, and this might help them ready for it.

Pete rubbed his eyes and then rested his forehead on one hand.

"We been having a hell of a time. Like everbody else I reckon. They's a constant flow outen Tennessee. They're having a worse time of it than us, if you can believe it." He looked at me. "How did you manage when it come hog-killing time?"

"We never had no hog to kill, damn them stealing Yankees to hell." I said.

"Oh." Pete said. "Reckon that took care of that. Well, my crowd was in a bad way 'cause we never had no salt. Not even a good handful. Know now what scraping the bottom of the barrel means. Mommie had not only scraped the bottom of her salting barrel, she'd scraped the sides. But word come to us that they was hoards of salt being kept in Marshall. For the soldiers, see. Plenty of it just setting down there in a warehouse. So John Kirk talked up a salt raid. Big gang of us got together and headed toward Marshall. Wednesday—no, Thursday, two weeks ago, the eighth of January. Reason I remember the day was 'cause I remembered that was the name of a fiddle tune Hack used to play for frolics." His face fell in grim lines. "But this weren't no frolic, not a'tall. We crossed through the Tater Gap about midday. Stayed around down in Walnut Creek till dark laid down, then headed out. We made good time. We aimed to get a raft at Macintosh's Ford and make our way down the river, get the salt, and head back." He barked out a laugh. "Hell, weren't no need of a raft. River was froze solid as a rock. We *walked* down the river on the ice to the warehouse. Why, hit were easy as pie. One old man guarding all that salt. He laid o'er quick, even told us they was a wagon hitched up and ready to go right outside. We took as much as we could pile on that wagon. Some of us was even carrying a sack or two. They was some other stuff we took, too, blankets, bales of cloth, and so on. Then as we's going out of Marshall some of the townpeople come out of their houses and started hollering at us. This feller what was named Peek, Captain Peek, dressed up in his uniform come out and hollered fer us to halt. Then all hell broke loose. Peek drawed his gun and fired, and John Kirk shot back and hit him in the right arm. They was a lot of hollering and screaming. Then this one man slapped Johnny Norton. You know Little Johnny. He rared back and hit that fellow right there in the road. Them folks scattered like a bunch of yeller dogs then.

"I don't know who started the plundering. Mayhap it was on all our minds. Anyways, we started going in the houses and taking stuff. Me and Little Johnny went in this big white house and this little woman commenced to screaming like a hellcat. We paid her no attention 'cept to tell her to shut up. Then Ned Woods come in with five or six of them boys off of No-Fat and he hollered that this was Lawrence Allen's house. I told him I didn't give a good goddamn whose house it was. We went upstairs and they was a little nigger girl setting on the floor right at the top of the steps. Little Johnny had never seen one, I reckon. He knelt down in front of her and she sort of shied back from him. He licked his finger then reached out and rubbed her face and she squealed like a stuck hog. We could hear young'uns crying at the back of the house. We started down the hall and here come that woman and them boys from No-Fat right behind her sort of herding her up the steps." He glanced at us. "Her dress was tore at the front. I reached out and took her by the arm and she commenced to fighting me. I shoved her in behind me and told them boys to leave her alone." He shrugged. "We searched about upstairs and took some stuff, clothes, some more blankets. Then we left."

He looked at me. "Reckon I could have another glass of buttermilk?"

Carolina was already up and crossing the floor before I could even move. She fetched the crock and set it on the table. None of us said a word as he tipped it to his mouth and drained the whole thing.

"They's a little something stronger if you want it," Larkin offered.

"Maybe after a while." He dropped his face into his hands and scrubbed as though trying to get the blood flowing. "We hightailed it out of there, heading hell-bent for the Walnut Gap. We crossed through picking our way by starlight since they weren't no moon to speak of. But, hell, we've hunted all through there so I knowed the placement of every rock and chug-hole. We got back to Shelton Laurel afore daylight, and you could hear hunting horns blowing all up and down the creek.

Pete signed. "I wished you could've seen the look on Mommie's face when I give her that salt and blankets and stuff," he said.

Here Pete was telling us this big tale and I was setting there having to swallow one big mouthful of hot water after another. Just at the mention of a damn sack of salt and I was almost drooling. That's what we had come to, friends. I had to make myself go back to listening.

"It snowed for three days and everybody stayed in. You folks got more than we did, I believe. Anyway day 'fore yesterday it turned off cold as hell, and the snow was really coming down good and hard so it was starting to pile up purty good. I was out hauling Mommie in some wood when I heard the horns blowing. I knowed they was bound to be trouble, and I reckon I ought to have left home right after we got back. But I was trying to help Mommie a little, you know what I mean? Since Daddy died she hadn't had really anybody but me and Edison.

"Word got passed along that it was Lawrence Allen's bunch. His blackguard cousin, that James Keith, had crossed over Sugar Loaf and was coming down the other side. All up and down the creek we hid out in the laurel hells. They was out in the open and started shooting blind. I thought fer a while that we was gonna run them out. Then they hit us with the cavalry, and it was just a matter of time afore we had to break and run. They weren't shooting blind no more, 'cause they shot and killed six of us. He rode out with a few of his men. The rest of them stayed on. At the time, we thought they was fixing to quit and go somewheres else. But that weren't what happened." He give a great heaving sigh. "I'll take some of that whiskey now, if you don't care, Lark."

He took a long long pull from the crock before he set it back down real careful-like. "You might want to take a drink. It ain't been pretty up to now and it's fixing to get worse." He looked at me, and what I saw on his face I hoped to never see again. "You might want these young'uns to go to bed, Arty."

And Carolina spoke up and said, "We ain't young'uns no more, Mommie."

I did not argue with her and let them stay.

Mary went to the sideboard to get cups and he waited till she was back in her place.

"Allen got back the next day. We knowed by then about his sick young'uns, and that his little girl had died. Some of our number had been took already. Morris Franklin, his brother Paul, and Mermon Shelton went to Marshall and give themselves up. They sent all of them on to Asheville. It were like Allen and Keith went crazy after that. They's going up and down the creek ordering people to tell them where we was. Why, they weren't about to tell Allen ner his men where we's hiding out. So Allen started whupping people, hanging 'em up by the neck till they turned blue and was almost dead, then they'd let them down and ask them again where we was. They whupped Mary Shelton acrost the back till it busted open."

"Lord have mercy." Mary whispered as she lifted the cup to her mouth.

Pete swung in Mary's direction. "Mercy?" he said and his voice was bitter as gall. "They was no mercy this day."

"They held Ott Tweed's girl, Hannah, down and—" he looked sideways at my girls. "She's about the same age as you, Abigail. They took turns at her.

"We followed 'em down the creek shooting at 'em, trying to kill as many as we could. But they was too many of them. By the time they caught me, Edison, and Little Johnny there at Paul's place, they had took ten other prisoners." He snorted. "Prisoners! They had old man Joe Woods, who was seventy year old if he was a day, and little David Shelton who was but a boy! They did have six er seven of us what was in Marshall that night. Rest of 'em, though, was innocent as Julie here. They made camp that night on Paul's place, and I told Edison and Little Johnny that I aimed to try to make a run for it. Now, they'd told us that evening afore they put us in Paul's shed that they's gonna take us into Asheville for a trial. But I saw the look in Allen's eyes that evening. They was red and flat as a snake's during dog days. Edison allowed as to how I'd get myself killed or maimed, and I told him I figured that was better than what Allen aimed to do to us."

I thought Pete was going to set into crying then, but he did not.

"I let on like I needed to go to the woods. Finally made such a ruckus that one of the soldiers let me out and took me to where the trees started at the edge of the barn lot. I squatted down like I aimed to take a shit and felt around under me till I found me a good-sized rock. Hit him in the head with it and run. I knew if I could make it up to the laurel thicket, they's no way they could catch me. Hell, they didn't even send nobody after me. I sneaked back about daylight and when they pulled out, me, John Kirk, and Hersh Cantrell counted thirteen prisoners. One of them had got away. I knew hit weren't Edison. I could see his red hair in amongst them that was being led off. We watched till they was gone and then there come Little Johnny sneaking out of that shed, purty as you please. I whistled and he come straight as a shot.

"We set out after Allen, keeping to the ridge. When they got down to the flats at Hickey's Fork, they stopped and Keith commenced to giving orders. We eased on down the mountain till we got to where we could hear him. Six of the fellers they had rounded up was jerked out into the open field and they commenced to beating them till they was all on their knees. Then Keith hollered for some of his crowd to shoot 'em. They was all right still and quiet. Then Keith hollered that if they didn't shoot, then they could join the prisoners. Old man Joe asked for time to pray if they were going to kill them. Then Keith dropped his sword and they fired. Killed five of 'em. And Edison." Pete swiped at his eyes. "Edison was begging fer them to let him go. That soldier raised his gun and shot him."

Pete reached for the crock but it was empty and he put it back down on the table. Larkin reached down beside his chair, brought up a full one, and handed it to Pete.

I knowed Abigail was crying before I even looked at her. Though she was just twelve, her and Edison had set together twice during church and we had all deviled her about it. He was the sweetest thing, and I was certain he would have been asking to walk out with Abby this coming summer. But that would never be now, and my heart just broke with the knowing of it. I reached out and took her hand in mine and was just about done in when I noticed it were as big as my own.

"Then they made the rest of them kneel down and shot them too. They gathered up and rode out then. Us there on the mountain didn't dare come off till the next morning. We loaded the dead on Nance Franklin's sled. Had a time digging the holes. The ground was like flintrock.

"After they was buried, I lit out. Struck out by myself. They won't catch me if I'm on my own."

Larkin got up and went over to the fire. He squatted down and laid on three logs and stirred up the red embers until flames caught the dry wood. Pete hunched forward and laced his fingers together on the table. "One of the reasons I stopped in here was to see if Hack was home." His voice seemed loud in the quiet room.

"No," Mary said. "He deserted from Allen's regiment back in September. We ain't heard nothing since. For all we know," she swallowed hard, "he might be dead."

"I don't reckon. Not unless he died in the last week." Pete said.

"You seen him?" me and Larkin said at the same time.

"Seen him? He was with us up till a week ago. He lit out right afore Allen and Keith showed up. I figured he was heading here." Pete rose from the table and stretched. "I'm going to sleep down in the hayloft, if you don't care. I won't sleep in the house. I'll be gone before you milk in the morning." He stopped at the door. "Thank you. I won't forget this."

"Larkin?" Mary whispered.

"I'll see what I can find out."

When Larkin come back in, all he told us was that Hackley had gone to Marshall with them and Pete hadn't seen him since. Something was just not right so I went to the barn before daylight the next morning to ask Pete myself, but he was already gone, and I never saw him again.

Later on that day, Larkin come by the house. "Hackley," he said, staring at the floor, "he's been laying out over on Shelton Laurel since September."

I did not even ask what the woman's name was. I did not want to know.

MARY WAS WORRIED TO death after that, and she was at my house more than she was at her own. Poor little thing. They was many a morning that she'd show up when I was milking the cows and she would be there when I went to milk that evening. She was still foolish over Pearl, and playing with her seemed to take her mind off her troubles.

My precious Pearl was truly a jewel. She was black-headed and black-eyed but did not have the dark skin like you might think she would. The only real pearl I had ever seen was the one that Wade Hensley had give to Vergie, and I swear to you that my Pearl's skin looked just as smooth and, well, pearly, I guess you would say. She had great big slanty eyes and little features like her daddy's people and was singing up a storm by then, even though it was all in baby talk and you could not understand a word she was saying. And she was not spoiled, though it would have been no fault of all of us. By all rights that young'un should have been rotten. She was a real friendly young'un, too, and never knowed a stranger. And Lord, she loved Mary and would go running to her the minute she saw her.

If I could have got my hands on Hackley I would have slapped him halfway to Sunday. Some men ain't worth killing, but I would have pure-D relished the chance to choke my brother senseless right about then. The least that man could have done was to have wrote to Mary and told her he was still among the land of the living. I was always watching for a line or two from Zeke, and bless him, he never let me to wonder long. I got many letters from him during that damn war and I still have every one of them today.

Mary got five letters from Hackley during that whole time.

Right after the killing over on Shelton Laurel, she asked me if it felt like to me that Hackley had just fell off the face of the earth.

She was a strong woman, Mary was. But even the strongest of us has to lay that heavy yoke down every now and again. I knowed beyond reason that she was having a struggle and comforted her the best I could, and I would have worried more about her if I had not knowed her people. They was a strong bunch of women that she was cut from. And she was young, and youth is a blessing when you are going through a hard patch. The very lack of having something to measure against can be a good thing. She would come every morning saying, "This will be the day I hear something," and when it was not she would say, "Well, mayhap tomorrow." Is that not the way of it? But she was awfully lonesome, too. And she'd had plenty of time laying with a man whose hands was not just able to bring pretty songs from a fiddle. She was missing that, just as I was and every other woman I knowed.

But the rest of us did not have a big strapping man around that looked at us with eyes as black as night and full of love. I think that had started to wear on her as much as anything.

Truth be known, it was right about this time that Mary began to harbor a different sort of affection for Larkin, too. But I, for one, knowed my brother would pop back up. And he did.

LARKIN COME TO ME late up in the evening and I knowed the minute I seen his face that something was wrong. I guess I was primed for bad news as I had got a letter from Zeke that day.

> I want you to rite to me as soon as you git this letter.
> Arty I saw you last nite very plain. O that it could
> hav been so this morning. Arty I think if I liv to git
> back we will liv and injoy ourselves better than ever.
> I will be of more use to you than ever before.

I cried my eyes out while I was writing him back. My heart was just broke. I did not have an inkling how in this world I was ever going to be able to live and stand it.

Larkin said he'd been down in the barn milking when the awfulest-looking man ever was had come up on him. Said he was nasty and had the worst smell about him you could ever wrap your nose around. I give a big sigh and said, "Where did you hide him?" because I knowed right then that my brother had come home to roost. Larkin did not even ask me how I knowed. He just said up in the cave and I said that was as good a place as any. I started gathering up quilts, an old coat of Zeke's, and snatched up what was left from supper to take up there. While I was putting it all in a sack, he said he'd had a time keeping Hack from going to the house to see Mary, but he had finally convinced him that it would put her in harm's way if she knowed where he was. I said, "Larkin, you must tell her." But I knowed he would not. He could not even look me in the eye when he muttered around saying how he would have to study about it, that he had to protect Mary.

Poor Larkin. He knowed when he told her it would take what little part of that girl he had managed to wrassle away for himself.

I cooked a little extra after that, and every evening Larkin would take it up on the mountain to my brother. And now Larkin had yet another burden to tote around on shoulders that was already plumb loaded down. It is a thousand wonders that that child did not go stark raving mad. But you know, maybe he did a little bit. And truth be told, I reckon it all probably drove Hackley mad, too. He was never one to be by himself and always wanted to be putting on a big show and having him a big time. He was lonesome up there and worried the hell out of Larkin wanting this, that, and the other. Poor old both of them, and me too, while I'm about it. I knowed it and could not tell a soul and I worried about Hack. In the bottom of my heart I knowed he would not stay hid for long. Everything Hackley wanted was just a stone's throw down the mountain. He said if the wind was blowing just right he could smell the smoke from his own chimney. But at least he was in out of the weather, and I sent all manner of stuff up there to make it more homey for him.

We had so much on our minds that we never give one thought as to what Mary might be thinking about Larkin disappearing for long periods of time. We was too caught up in trying to hide it from her to imagine where her mind might take her. She never so much as wondered that we was hiding Hackley. She just knowed that Larkin was gone a lot more than he used to be, and her mind went right where any woman's would. She decided all on her own that Larkin had him a sweetheart, and who do you think she imagined it to be? Why, of course she thought it was Maggie.

She told me years later that she would lay there in her bed pretending to be asleep with all sorts of things going through her head.

She said if Julie had not been laying right there beside her, they was no telling what she might of done and sometimes she just had to make herself keep from getting up and crossing that floor and laying down on the floor next to him. And one of the reasons she did not do this was because she thought he would have turned from her.

Now that was something that would never have happened. As bad as I hate to admit it, Larkin would have shucked Hackley's corn so quick it would've make your head spin, if only he'd knowed it could have been his for the shucking.

ONE EVENING IN MARCH me and the young'uns went over to Mary's and she fixed supper for all us. Larkin and Julie was both good hands at riddling and my Carolina was right in there with them. It felt good to be out of the house and I was laughing and carrying on too. It took me awhile to notice that Mary was looking at Larkin more often than not. Her eyes would sort of light on him and then go sliding off somewheres else. Then I caught her studying his hands with her whole heart in her face for all to see, and I thought to my-self, *Oh, no.* For a woman that goes to studying a man's hands is thinking where she'd like for him to put them, and that is the gospel truth if it was ever told.

Right before we eat Mary got real snappish with Julie, which is no wonderment when you understand that there was a real easiness that had sprung up between her and Larkin. Mary straightened from the hearth where she'd just swung the great iron pot back over the fire, and I could tell by her tone that she was aggravated.

"Git the plates out, Julie. Larkin, strain the milk. I'm tired to the bone of having to do everything."

They was a look flew between Julie and Larkin that let me know this was no new thing. Julie hitched a little shrug and went to the sideboard for plates.

Larkin said in a real easy voice, "I strained the milk, Mary, and already carried it to the spring house 'cept for the crock over yonder that I left out for buttermilk."

Mary bent over the stewpot then, and I could tell she was already sorry for being so hateful. "Reckon I'm just tired of cold weather. Tired of eating the same thing night and day. I'm so sick of cornbread I could just spit!" She bunched up a handful of apron to lift the Dutch oven and carried it to the table.

Larkin smiled and his black eyes just danced over her. "This here is some of the best cornbread in the country."

She glanced at him, then shot a look at me, and her eyes was plumb naked.

That was a long supper. I set there the whole time watching her watch him and Julie watching them and it was just a mess, I'm telling you. I was wore to a frazzle when we left.

I reckon things would've still been all right if Lucindy hadn't sent for Julie a few weeks later. Andy was home with the bad dysentery and Julie had to go help take care of him. Mary come by the house and told me that Larkin was going to stay on. I made ready to tell her what I thought about that, but before I could get a single word out she said, "Now, don't start, Arty Wallin. I have already had it out with Julie and I ain't in no mood to get into it with you, too." I just looked at her. This was the first time Mary had straightened that little back at me, but I was not about to let that slow me down. "Well, you're going to have to hear me out anyways," I said. And she said right back, "I will tell you what I told Julie, then, and save you the breath." So I just held onto my tongue and heard *her* out.

She said they was out on the porch right before Julie left and they'd sort of got into it when Mary told Julie that Larkin was going to stay. Julie had grabbed her by the arm. "Don't do nothing foolish, sister," she said, "as you will live to regret it." As I say, they was no flies on that girl. Mary looked me right in the eyes then. "I have already done it in my heart a thousand times, Arty," she said. "In your heart is not the same as in the flesh, Mary," I said. She turned beet red but raised that chin at me. "He will stay," she said, and I answered her right back, "Then God help you, for you will need it."

And right then I figured God might not watch them two near close enough, so I appointed myself the guardian of them both and that was a very tiresome job.

NOT LONG AFTER THAT Hackley finally begged Larkin into bringing him his fiddle. I figure Larkin thought that would keep Hackley on that mountain, as he was in a constant state of threatening to come down. It did seem to pacify Hack for a while.

SO THAT IS HOW we passed the rest of the cold weather, and then came the greening up of spring. And the sap began to rise, if you know what I mean, and I was in and out of Mary's house or sending my young'uns by just every little whipstitch. I went at different times so they never knew when I was coming.

Mary come by the house one afternoon with her eyes big and round and a flush on her cheeks, and I thought I had not done my job well enough. But I put that thought to rest when she said, "Arty, let me tell you that I think I heard Hackley's fiddle when I was out in the yard today." My heart was in my mouth. I knowed exactly what had happened but could not say a word to her; I had promised Larkin I would not, and I was one to keep my promises. "Now, it could have been anybody, Mary," I said in as normal a voice as I could muster. She looked at me like I had gone lame in the head. "Why, it were the tune 'Elzig's Farewell,' Arty. Do you not think I would know his hands?" And I said to myself, *I reckon you would, honey.* But what I said to her was "Well, then, you should not be out traipsing around in the woods. You should tell Larkin."

And she hied out of there allowing she would do just that.

I studied and studied about all that until well after dark. I knowed there would be no sleep for me, as I had managed to work myself up into a state. I was resolved now that she should know that it was Hackley she'd heard and be damned the consequences. After Pearl went to sleep, I told Abigail I was going to Mary's and lit out.

And so it was that I caught them.

I was not thinking of anything like that romance business when I went across the porch and pushed on through the door. I reckon in normal times I would have howdied the house, but, like I said, I was not thinking. So I can only imagine what went through their minds when they finally come to know I was standing there in the room with them. I will not embarrass you with the details. But suffice to say I saw way more than a body should see concerning the private actions between a man and woman. You could have cut the air with a dull knife when we was all standing there looking at each other. Finally Larkin said, "Amma, we was just talking about Mary thinking she'd heard Hackley playing the fiddle today." And I said, "Larkin, what you was doing was not talking," and he shut his mouth. Then Mary's chin come up and mine come out and before she could say a word that would cause hard feelings between us, I said, "Get your coat, Mary. We're going up on the mountain and you'll be there all night."

I did not even look at Larkin. He'd had all the say about this I was going to let him have.

NOW WE HAD SOME big troubles, because Mary was not the only one that had heard Hackley playing his damned fiddle, and they was folks there that was not lovers of our people. We hid him in the root cellar under the house that Larkin had dug out months ago. But after the Home Guard set fire to Granny Nance Franklin's house and it burned down on top of her three boys, we moved him out from under there. She was another one that lost every last one of her boys in that damn war, but that did not stop her from leading a Yankee charge against some Rebs one time. She was so wadded up in it that she screamed out, "Raise your fire, boys, you're hitting them in the heels."

We spent the better part of a rainy day cutting our way back into a laurel hell on the backside of Picked Shirt Mountain. That's where Hackley got to live now, and though he commenced to whining and taking on, I told him he could just dry it up. This was the best we could do right now and he might as well hurry and come of it. There would be no more foolishness now that Arty Wallin was in charge. I took the damn fiddle home with me.

But I had the awfulest feeling that seeds had been sowed and I knowed we always got to reap what we sowed, even if the harvest proved bitter.

IT WAS THE FIRST of June when I caught Mary hanging onto the porch railing waiting for the dizziness to leave her. I had suspected it and now I knew. "How long have you been breeding, honey," I said, and she said she was three weeks past her bleeding time. She must've thought she seen something in my face that was not there, because she said then, "It is nobody else's but your brother's child, Arty." I looked at her with my kindest face on. "I would never have thought anything else," I said, "and I would dare anybody to say different." "Have you told him?" I asked. "No, I have not yet, but I will as soon as he gets back to the house," she said, and then she leaned over and throwed up. I helped her back in the house and she stretched out on the bed.

It hit me as I was going home that she had meant Larkin.

WELL, LARKIN ALREADY KNEW. He'd seen me too many times not to recognize the early shine that came from the inside-out of a breeding woman. He told me later that he'd watched with a jealous heart her holding her secret close. She went about fairly skipping through those early weeks. He'd seen her lay her hand on her belly and the look that took hold of her when she did it. He'd been short and hateful with her and then immediately sorry. He couldn't stand the thought that he might have hurt her. But it was him that was hurt when he realized that his words hadn't even reached her at all. She'd never even noticed them, just as she never seemed to notice him any more.

IT WAS WHEN HE'D taken the June apples I'd poked up for Hackley that they got into it.

It had rained for a solid week, and Hack was grumpy and mean as a copperhead. Larkin had stuck around trying to cheer him up, and the talk got around to where it always wound up. Hackley wanted to see Mary as he had not seen her since she'd sneaked up there to tell him she was in the family way. Larkin said he was trying to be patient and had reminded him that he could not bring her up there again and that he could not come off the mountain since the Home Guard was all over the place now. That was when Hackley shot him this little look. "What was that look about?" Larkin said. "What look?" Hackley said, and Larkin said he knowed the answer before he asked. "Have you been off the mountain?" "Once't or twice't," he said and then, "Well, I didn't get caught." Larkin said he flew mad as hell and could barely talk. "Jesus, Hackley. Where did you go? Did anybody see you?" And Hackley could not keep the bragging from his voice: "A week ago I really made the rounds. I stopped in and saw Corrie. Then on to Dovie's. I was back here long before any rooster in Sodom crowed. Had me a time. The way they both carried on over me, you could sure tell they was glad to see me." If that was not enough, he really capped the stack with what he said to Larkin next, and he looked for all the world like a little sulled-up boy when he was saying it. "Didn't have near as much luck last night when I went to Maggie's. Somebody was already there."

"You went to Maggie's?"

"Yeah. I was really wanting to see her. Couldn't believe it when I saw the horse."

Larkin said he hit him the first time before he could catch himself. He said the second time was well planned though, and he knocked Hackley ass over apple cart down the bank.

When I went up later to see about him, Hackley was laughing about it and said when Larkin hit him, he thought the stars had come out and went to dancing all about in his head. I told him if he ever come off that mountain again, I would turn him in to the Home Guard myself. He studied me for a long time and then said "Oh, you would not do that, sister girly" and I said "Do not try me, brother boyo, for I will do as I say." He studied me a little while longer and then said, "I need you to find out where Kirk is, as I aim to join up with him as soon as Larkin turns eighteen." I left there having promised him I would find Kirk if I had to run him to ground myself for he was right. Larkin had to go somewhere and better with the Union than slinking around trying to dodge the Home Guard.

Now there was a character just made for this fine big war they was having. I had seen him once and had heard all about George Washington Kirk from Mommie's cousin Davina. Me and him was about the same age, too. He had a long and lanky frame and had a big mustache that drooped over a broad mouth with red lips. He was a good-looking sort of man and might have been called a handsome man, were it not for his eyes.

Davina said his mommie had been run from the woodpile by a panther when she was three months along with him. When he was born she went over him with a fine-toothed comb looking for any sign that he had been marked. She found nothing until his eyes started to change. I know just what she meant by that. I swear that man's eyes was the same exact tannish color as one of them big cats, and they give me a bad case of the all-overs when they settled on me that day.

But eyes or no eyes, I meant to find him. And find him I did. I set up for him to meet Hackley and Larkin there at my house the day of Larkin's birthday. They was no sense in putting it off no longer and, to be honest with you, I was just about sick of them two boys. They needed to go on.

I was not as certain of this when we were all ganged up there at the house the day they left. Mary looked pitiful standing there with her little belly just beginning to show. The night before, we had carried most of her stuff to my house, and she was going to stay with us until this damn war sorted itself and Hackley come home. That was hard on her, I know but they was really nothing else she could do except to go back to Lucindy's. As I told her when I offered at least she would be with Pearl. That seemed to bring her along as much as anything else. Hackley just loved on me and thanked me. Bless his heart. I reckon it was as Mary said, all their married life had been was one parting after another. And I allowed as how this must be some fine war that you could fight on one side for a while and get tired of that, and go to fighting on the other side. I must admit to harboring very bitter feelings. I had not seen my man in over two years; he had never seen Pearl, and she was a big girl already. Little did I know that it would be two more years before I would see his dear face. And that would prove the longest four years that would ever roll over my head.

Larkin was staring and staring at Mary and I wanted to cap my apron over my head so I would not see it. Or mayhap over his, so nobody else would see it. Finally I could not stand it no more so I went and put my arms around him, and the minute I did that he was my baby again. Some things is meant to always be, and that is one of them. I started to cry and then all my young'uns started to howl and Mary was sobbing, and we just had us a regular call to the altar right there in front of my house. I swear, sometimes I get so tired of being from a family what cannot control their feelings. At times I wish we could be more like them folks what never acts raw and what keeps their feelings all iced up. But that is like wishing to have the moon on your porch, which is not possible, so there we was running about like the crazy bunch that we was.

Finally Hackley had had enough and he hollered out, "For the love of God, hush up," and we did, but the reason we did was because we was all wore out by now. "We've got to go," he said, and he looked right at me. Well, that let me know who he was leaving to see to things, as if they was ever any doubt. I went to Mary then and stood right beside her while Hackley kissed her one last time. So I had to stand there and watch Larkin wanting to kiss her, too, and thinking he might just be bold enough to do it. Well, thank God for Carolina, is all I can say. She picked that minute to throw herself right at Larkin's head. I've never in my life seen such a thing and by the time I got her off him we was all laughing, and she was acting like they was in some play or something throwing her arm up against her head and allowing how she felt faint. What a card that young'un could be.

So what could have been a bad and trying thing turned out to be just a look between them. But, oh, what a look it was. They was more said in that little space of silence than if they'd mouthed a thousand words.

But when he turned that horse he did not look back.

## 13

I AM A KEEPER OF all manner of tales. I sometimes get tales all mixed up in my head, and they is things that I cannot for the life of me separate out and determine if they are my memories or things that have been told to me. I reckon that is a part of getting to be old. But the one thing that I did and am proud that I did it is I kept letters that folks sent to me during the wartime. And lo and behold, when Larkin come back, he come wagging home with him every letter him and Hackley got as well. So here is some of that what was sent and what I wrote myself. They are yours for the reading, and all I can say is that here is Arty laid out for all the world to view.

October 19, 1863
Dear Larkin,

It is with pleasur I am permitted this good sabbath evening to drop you a few lines to let you know that I got your last two letters on the same day which was yesterday and am pleased to hear that you are dooing well and that the army lif is not treating you vary badly. Tell my brother that I am sending him a howdey too and that he needs to rite his wif. She looks in vain for a letter every day. Tell him it would ease her mind if that means anything to him which it mite but I do not no that for sure. She is getting big now and is glad that the heat has laid oer for the cool of fall. And the colors are coming on now as I no they are there as well. You said you was in east Tennessee up around Kingsport. That seems a long way off. Does it look much like around here? When you rite me back let me know as I am curius as always about such things.

You will never guess who I seed yesterdy. I spent some time with Silas McMahan. You will not believe me when I tell you that he has been walking out with Maggie or mayhap you would believe it too for you no her as good as I do. She allows that she might even be for lovin him which is hard for me to believe.

Listen was you with Mr. Kirk when he was down to Warm Springs? We hearn he was down that way and camped out on the yard at the hotel with 800 or mor men. They said that was a sight to see. It was in the newspaper too how they was a fight with a bunch of Rebels and that Nick Woodfins brother was killed. I find it an amazement that we have took to calling one side Yanks and the other Rebels. This is as good as any I would reckon excep I might say Windbags and Bellows. I have heard from Zeke and he says they are coming down to Tennessee and that he will try to look you up and maybe even come home for a day. Oh to be able to see him again would be like a soothing salve to my sore eyes. And he longs to eyeball the younguns. Ever letter I git expresses that longing and it braks my heart every time.

Vergie has left this part of the world. She has scooted down to Hendersonville where Wades people is all frum. She has took all her young'uns and left everything for Maggie to have. I reckon that makes Miss Maggie a woman of some means and what would be called a good catch. This war has changed the face of us all has it not?

You are a sweet thing indeed to ask me about the younguns. They are all dooing well and growing like you would not believe. Pearl is talking up a storm now and sometimes I catch myself wishing this was not so. She wants to know about everthing and I do not no about some of which she asks me. I have no idee why it is that the sky is blue and so on. She gets mad when I can not answer her. Me and Mary just can not help but laf at her. Mayhap she is just like her Mommie. Carolina is getting to be a great big girl and is pretty as a picture. She says to tell you a big howdee. Mary is five months gone now and with her small frame she looks like she might have swallered a big punkin. I told her what you said and she said to tell you that you was full of squash and beans. You are rite to say she is a funny thing. She is every bit of that.

I would be vary glad to see you too honey. May it not be long before this is so. Keep yur hind end close to the ground Larkin.

Your loving Amma

October 27, 1863
Dear Amma,

I received your kind letter that was wrot me on the 19 October. You are good to writ me to tell me that all is well with you all. Things are just the same hear as they was befor. I hav just returnd frum a frolik where Hackley played with some musiciners frum up in Kantucky. Them boys nos their way around a fiddle almost as good as Hackley and for the furst time our Hack is struglin to keep all atention on hisself. Not realy as all he has to do is comence to singing and they all step back. They was no women folk at this frolik and some of us made out as girls. It was a big time and I do not no that I hav had such a big time since I left home. You would hav busted a gut laughin no doubt and might yet when you think of me as a vary big and vary ugle girl.

They jus come by and tol our regmant to cook 3 days rashings and be redy to march of at a minets warning. I no this mite cause worry to you and Mary but it is not so with us. It is the setin around that gits our goat.

Amma I must come to a clos. I will rite you more at a later day. Kiss the young'uns for me and give Mary a howdee. I tol her man he shud writ to her but have seed no sines of him dooing it yit.

Love to you Amma

Larkin

It looks the same here in one way but is diferent as well. The water is no count. I kep my tail always on the ground.

November the 22, 1863
Dear Larkin,

I am sendin this pair of britches that I made for you. I do not no if they will fit you in the lenth but I made them long and you can cut them off to wher they will fit beter. Do as you will with them. Tell Hackley that he has never seed no happyer somebody than his little wif when she got his leter last week and bles her hart she has gon into a fit of riting him back.

I am riting this in a hury as I want to send it back by Roderick as he is comin your way. I am sendin some cake as well and hope you injoy it.

Thank you for the money. Me and Mary put what you sent and what Hackley sent and bout some chickins. It was more money than ether one of us had ever seed. We fed that pore creature what fetched it to us. To see him pored the worrys over me and her both. He was sick unto death Larkin. Rite and tell me that neither you nor my brother suffers sech a way. Tell Hackley to rite Mary and ease her mind.

I love you my biggest boy. The young'uns are dooing fine as are we all. Zeke said to tell you he was back north and would not see you. He did not git home neither and I was not a bit happy with that. Keep yur hind end low to the ground.

Amma

December 28, 1863

Dear Amma,

It is with pleasure that I find the opportunity to rite a few lines to let you know I did get the cake you sent to me and tho it were mushed up it were like nectar from heaven. Thank you for figerin out a way to git it to me. I was one happy big old boy. I sliped off to eat it and wood not even let Hackley have a bit and he cussed a black streak at me but I did not care and told him as much. I am sendin you mor money and want you to use it however is best for you and the younguns. If Mary needs it give sum to her and do not fret that I do not have what I need.

They take good care of us hear and I just got me a fine big coat. Colonel Kirk has picked me to be one of his hawkeyes which is just a sharp shooter but they hav to name everthing hear so hawkeye is what I am. They hav give me a vary fine rifle and I am larning the use of it real quik.

We hav been in a few fights but none that was vary bad. One thing I can say about Colonel Kirk is that he is vary good at fighting and his men all thinks that the sun rises and sets on his head. Another thing I can say is he is one to always think of his men and that is why he is so well thot of I am sure.

Tell Mary that her man is not a easy one to liv with. He will not keep his side of the tent neat and tidy. He needs her hear to look about him. I could stand a peek at her face as well.

It was a blesed shame to hear that Roderick has been kilt. He was a good person and I will never forget how he fetched me that cake. It is soon to be a new year Amma. Let us hop this hear war will not carry over much into the year of '64.

I remain one that loves you

Larkin

January the 18, 1864

Dearest Larkin,

It is with a hevy hart that I put down these words to you. They is no way to say them that will ease the telling so I will just say it. Fee was kilt by soljers yesterdy. I know how you felt him to be your frend and I wisht I cud say hit were a quik death fer him but we know hit were not. As I told you when last I rote to you he was keerin for the horses for Lawrence Allen dam him fer his black hart over in Warm Springs. You know how good

204 ❧ SHEILA KAY ADAMS

he alus was with critters. He had come home fer a few days and when he was goin back he was set on by some Yanke soljers and they kilt him. Know that I lov you and I pray for you ever day and nite.

Your lovin Amma

It was the deepest part of the winter and John Wesley had gone out hunting and bagged a big mess of squirrels. Julie had come by and was going to stay the night with us and while the stew was cooking me, her, and Mary was setting around the table talking. I knowed Mary was in a state of pure-D misery. Her ankles and fingers was all swollen and the baby had dropped over a week ago. I had tried to offer her a little hope that it would not be much longer and knew this to be so. I had been that way myself many times and knowed just how she felt.

I fed my crowd and Mary just picked at her plate and said she was not hungry. Abigail and Julie was washing the dishes when I heard what sounded like somebody sneaking about on the porch. I reached for the cap-and-ball pistol Zeke had given me and turned toward the door just as the latch went to easing up. You can just imagine my surprise when the smoke cleared and there stood my brother looking back at me.

"Damn, sister girly. You come near to blowing my brains out."

Mary was off that bench like she'd been what was shot out of that gun.

And then Larkin come through that door and it was a race between me, Julie, and Carolina to see who could get to him first.

They was followed by a little slight man that at first I did not recognize. And then Julie hollered out "Daddy!" and my mouth hung open like a gate.

It was indeed Andrew Chandler. Now, I could not help myself, so I had to say it. "How come you all decked out in Union duds, Andrew? I thought you was took prisoner over at Strawberry Plains."

"I was but when Hackley got wind of it him and Larkin come and busted me out. I'm riding with Kirk now."

See, that is what I mean about this funny man-fighting-at-a-war thing. It seems not so much to matter which side you tote a gun for, as long as killing somebody is your intent. I said as much to them three.

"It don't matter no more, Amma," Larkin said, and he sounded so tired it broke my heart. "We just want this war over."

And I said *amen* to that and then Mary went to running back and forth setting the table and her cheeks was so flushed that she did not even look like the same girl as what had been setting at my table a little bit ago. I was not the only one watching her, neither. Larkin's black eyes followed her every step she made. *Can it be that the rest of them will finally see what is right before them?*, I thought to myself. I sneaked a peek at Hackley and he was talking to Abigail without a care in this world and had no notion whatsoever of how Larkin was watching his wife. And Julie was watching Larkin. So once again it was left to me to watch everybody watching everybody else until my eyes felt like they was run out on stems.

They was one curious thing that happened that night. Julie was washing up the last of their dishes and Larkin moved to help her. Hackley and Mary had left for their house, and Andrew had hied it for his own bed. I was laying on the bed with Pearl and had been there long enough until they probably thought I was asleep.

"How are you, Julie girl?" Larkin said.

This was said with such a tenderness that it sounded as though he was talking to a lover, so I eased my eyes open to little slits and peeped out at them. I know this was not right and though I am not proud of it, I could not help myself.

He was holding her hands and I watched as he run his hands up her arms to cup her elbows. Now I must ask you, does that not make you think they was things between them that neither had shared with me?

But this is what she said to him and her voice was low and hot as fire. "How can it be, Larkin, that you can look at me so sweet like, with your face as still as a deep hole of water? And then you turn them black eyes on my sister and it's like the same deep hole but with a fast current running right below the surface." When he did not answer her, she turned from him and went back to washing the dishes.

HACKLEY WAS STILL THERE when his son was born two weeks later, on February fourteenth. The day was warm and clear and was the perfect false spring day bearing the promise of what was to come.

Larkin come for me early that morning. It was a quick birth and over in almost no time. Up that evening I went with Larkin to milk and leaned against the side of the stall while he done the work. I was in no hurry to get home and knew Abigail and Julie would see to things just fine. The dim light of the barn was a pleasing change to how close it had been in the cabin. I shut my eyes and breathed in deep, fetching in the familiar odors of fresh milk and sweet hay. I could not help it; I grinned great big as I was right proud of myself. I'd had myself a good day's work and brought my first baby all by myself. Mary had offered herself right over and done everything I told her to do. And the baby had been fit and sound. And if the amount of liquor consumed after a birth said they was a proud papa around, then Hackley was near to busting with his son. As me and Larkin left for the barn, Hackley, Mary, and Hack Jr. had all three been piled up sound asleep in the same bed. Now in the barn, I opened my eyes and as soon as I could see good, I went to studying Larkin. His shoulders and back was even broader, and big ropey muscles rolled around in his arms while he milked. His hair was longer and I liked it better that way. There was no doubt about it, my biggest boy had growed into a handsome man.

"You thinking to draw a picture of me?" he asked.

"Do what?"

"Well, the way you're studying me I figured you was aiming to draw yourself a picture."

"No, you mister smart britches. I don't aim to draw your picture. But you keep up that smart-mouthing your Amma, and I might just turn you across my lap and give you a good whupping like I used to have to do. I was just noticing how you'd filled out since you left. They must be feeding ye pretty good."

"That's the truth. Hack and Andrew both said that's probably the main reason that the Union is winning the war."

"Are they, Larkin?"

"That's what Kirk says." He went back to milking. "Now, there's a strange feller."

"That's what you have said."

The milk hissed as it hit the side of the bucket. "All us boys likes him. He's got a way about him that you can't help but like. But when he's out raiding or we're fighting, they's a mean streak that shows itself."

"That is nothing new as I have noticed that most men has got a mean streak in them."

"You'll get no argument from me about that. I've seen it. But they's a difference in Kirk. Back in the fall we's farther west of here over toward Waynesville. We'd raided a little, set fire to a barn or two, and we happened onto this feller out in the field. Looked like he aimed to plow, though I can't see how he aimed to do any plowing. His coat sleeve was pinned up where he'd lost a arm. Kirk and a bunch of us rode up to him. Kirk drawed his gun and leveled it at this feller, and said, 'Sir, you're wearing the wrong color coat.' That was all he said 'fore he shot him right between the eyes. Killed him right then and there."

"Because of the color of his coat?"

"He's wearing a ragtag Confederate coat more holey than it was righteous."

"And nobody said nothing?"

Larkin shook his head. "That's one of the things ye learn early on, Amma. You don't say nary a word unless you're asked to."

"Sounds like the man ain't got no soul. Or the one he's got is black as pitch."

Larkin rose from the stool, picking up the bucket as he straightened. "Well, I don't reckon I've been called to preach, so I won't concern myself with his soul. I just do what he tells me to do." He gave a shrug and the corners of his mouth lifted in the saddest of little old smiles. "But, you know, I don't reckon Kirk's done no worse than what happened over the ridge in Shelton Laurel. Any way you cut this pie, it's a rotten thing."

"I have no love for neither side, Larkin, so you are preaching to the done saved." Of a sudden the good feelings of a while ago fled from me, and I recalled how I had been like a worm in a hot skillet waiting for him to ask me about Fee, but he had never done it. I knowed now was the time but I stayed propped against the door frame and he stood there with the full bucket in his hand. The wind picked up and set the empty limbs to rattling against the sides of the barn. Off in the distance, a dog went *bark bark bark* and then was quiet. My next words rode out on a big sigh. "For God's sake, Larkin. Ask me about it for you have got to want to know."

And he sighed right back and said, "I'll get that bottle I got hid in the other stall that I been saving for when I felt like I could stand to hear it. Then I'll ask about it."

We settled down in the fine dirt of the barn and leaned back against the logs. He took the cork from the narrow neck of the bottle and passed it right over to me. I took a long and slow drink, and it set me on fire as it went down in my gullet. I shuddered and wiped my mouth with my coat sleeve before handing it back to him.

"Not near as smooth going down as Sol's liquor," I said to him, and it were the truth.

"Ain't found none nowhere like Sol's." He offered me the bottle of amberish-colored liquor again. "Some of them boys from Tennessee give it to me. It surely ain't white liquor. They called it sour mash. Once't you get used to it, it ain't too bad. Hackley loves it."

"How's Hack managing?" I took a smaller drink and could not help but shudder again.

Larkin's shoulders hitched up and down in a so-so shrug. "You know Hack. Right off he found some fellers that played music. Laughs and cuts up a lot. Goes about singing purty much all the time. Everbody really likes him."

"How's it for you, Amma?" he asked, and I knowed he was just stalling me for time, but I answered him anyways.

"It's just as well that I ain't never hungry, seeing as how they ain't nothing much to eat." I wrapped my fingers around the bottle, taking note of how skinny they was. "The children is hungry all the time, though. I swear I believe we'd have starved if it hadn't been for you and Zeke sending us money." I knew right then that this liquor had a big kick to it and was already loosening up my jaw, so I got a big grip on it, as I did not want to worry him. "Most of the time I do just fine. Other times I miss Zeke, but sometimes I dread him coming back." I could not believe I had said that but it were the truth if I'd ever told it. See, I was no longer scared of nothing and had got to be tough as an old pine knot. I did not know if my dear sweetheart would like this whet-leather version of Arty or not. I was not ready to talk to anybody about this so I reached for Larkin's hand, and when I had it in mine I said, "Let me tell you about Fee."

He took another long drink, set the bottle between his feet and then he said, "Tell me, then."

My body sagged over against his and I closed my eyes like I was fixing to sing a love song. But this story would be far different than any song he'd ever learned. This one was hung with Fee's broad countenance and big sloping shoulders and gentle hands. This all went flashing through my mind so clear that tears puddled in my eyes and run down my cheeks.

"Everybody just knew that Fee wouldn't stay in the army and would prob'ly light out for home first chance he got. Well, we was all wrong, Larkin. Allen put him to tending horses down at the training camp at Warm Springs. I reckon you already knowed that, didn't you?"

He squeezed my hand and said, "Just tell me, Amma."

I squeezed back. "All right, honey."

"He had been home for a spell but I'd only seen him once't. He come by the house to see if I needed wood cut. He cut down a poplar tree at the edge of the garden and split it up for me. Took him all day and I fed him dinner and supper. He said he had to be gitting back to Warm Springs and figured to head out the next morning. I offered to let him stay at the house with all of us, but he turned me down. Last I saw of him was when he give a sharp whistle and Old White come from behind the house and down the road they went. He must've changed his mind about going back the next day or he might've just been out in the woods. You know how he'd wander about in the woods of a full moon. It were just two or three nights shy of being full.

"Marian Franklin found him next day. He was coming up from the Seward Hole and Old White barred the path barking and just carrying on. Led him right to where whoever'd killed Fee had kicked some leaves and dirt over him. Jim Leake said he'd heard a commotion out in the road in front of the house that same night and, thinking somebody might be aiming to break in the store, he'd went out just in time to see some men in Union blue ride by. We figure they's the ones what killed him. A bunch of us went down and buried him, Larkin. Lucindy said we ought to move him and bury him next to his mama, but Hoy McIntosh allowed as to how Fee would've wanted to be buried where he was. Said he always loved that part of the country so we just dug a grave and left him be. It is awful purty over there in the Gudger Tract. You can see the creek from where we buried him."

"Was he shot up, Amma? You said in your letter that he suffered."

I could have kicked myself right then and there, and my voice was sharp when I said, "I never should've wrote nothing more than that he'd been killed, Larkin. Some things is better left not said. They's nothing none of us can do about it now, anyways."

"Tell me," was all he said, but it made me mad the same as if he'd made a big speech. I jerked my hand away from him. "Why?" I said. "Ain't you seen enough of what men are doing to one another in this damn war to know? Do you need it lined out for you like a song?"

"That's why I'm asking, Amma. What I've seen . . ." and his voice died off here. I knowed he was recalling things what was too awful for me to know and I did not want to leave him conjuring about this for another minute, so I took up his hand again and locked my palm with his.

"His knee-caps was blowed off. And somebody had cut off one of his ears as clean as a whistle. You know well as me he'd have fought them to the end. They was sixteen bullet holes in him that we could count."

Neither one of us spoke for a long time. Larkin was still as the grave.

"Which ear?"

"What?" I said, though I could not believe he'd asked me that.

"Which ear was gone?"

"The left one."

Larkin nodded and then said nothing more.

"Why'd you want to know that?"

"Because you just told me who done it, Amma." He got up before I could say anything else and offered me his hand. "Let's git on back to the house. They'll maybe be awake by now and all."

When I got up blood and that damn sour mash rushed up to my head, and I was swaying like a young tree in a great wind. I grabbed hold of his arm to steady myself. And then it come over me and I could not stop myself. My fingers was like claws digging into his arm. "How much longer will this last, Larkin?"

"What? The killing?"

"You said a while ago that the Union is winning. So I'm asking, how much longer will it go on?" I shook his arm like a dog worrying a bone. "The war?"

"Hackley says only God knows, and He ain't telling."

I give a mighty snort and almost laughed at how much I sounded like Granny. "Don't you stand too close to him. He's liable to get struck by lightning right in the top of the head."

He laughed out loud and I knowed his thoughts had turned to her too. "Remember when we's little and we'd get scared when it would come one of them big thunderstorms?"

"And Granny would take us out on the porch and tell us not to be afraid. That God was just loading his taters on his wagon and the racket was them hitting the wagon bed." I busted out laughing, and things was of a sudden easy and light with us again. "I ain't a bit afraid of storms. I love them. Makes me feel all wild inside." My words was coming slow and slurry like, and I knowed I was pert near drunk. "Sort of like this sour mash has made me feel." I poked Larkin with my elbow and handed the drained bottle back to him. "A thunderstorm in a bottle."

He laughed at me and said, "Let's go and we'll see to rustling up something to eat." He took the bucket and we stepped out into a fog that had rolled in while we was milking.

We had only taken a step or two. "Look at it, Larkin," I said.

"What, Amma?"

I breathed out into the fog and my breath hung in the air right there in front of my face. "Walk on ahead of me. I want to see something."

He walked on slow out in front of me.

"That's the prettiest thing I believe I've ever seed in nature," I could only whisper because it was just that and I wanted him to see it too. "Stand still honey, and watch what happens when I pass you."

The fog just draped itself on me as I moved, frothing my hair and brows with silver, and the ice crystals in the fog parted as I moved through and left my shape behind me. It looked like I'd walked through a tunnel until it filled itself back in.

When he come to stand beside me, I leaned my shoulder into him and sighed. We stood that a way for a while.

"It held for a long time, didn't it?" he said.

"Maybe that's what living is like," I said. "Maybe Fee just moved on through and left his shape." I knowed my voice was sad but could not help it, as that is how I felt.

He never said nothing else and we went toward the house. I looked behind us and saw our shapes leaving a trail that slowly faded away.

I HAD HOPED TO my never that Hackley would straighten up now that he had a son. And he did for a little while. He behaved for a little over a week and was the perfect picture of what a good husband ought to be, but it did not last. He would just up and be out of pocket for hours at a time, and he wore his secrets like a set of loose clothes. Now you might ask me why he would be any such a way, and the only thing I can say to you is just what I had said a long time ago to Mary. Some men is just runners of women. My brother was just a runner of women, and that is all there is to say about it, really. I will have to say here that I do not understand this, as I have caught many babies in my lifetime and all of the equipment looks pretty much the same to me.

Larkin was staying pretty much with us, and it was from him that

I heard about Hackley going by Maggie's and that she'd run him off. "Well, go it, Maggie," I said. He allowed as how he'd told her them very words. He said that Hackley had let on to Maggie that he did not know about Silas being her feller. I said, "That's a damn lie, because I told him so." We both shook our heads at that. I asked him how our Maggie was getting on and Larkin said she looked really good. When I shot him a look, he grinned. "Oh, no, it were nothing like that," he said. "She let me know right off that she was very happy with Silas." Larkin got real quiet after that, and it was like I could see right into his head and read his mind. I said, "You cannot take it upon yourself to tell Mary, honey," and he got up real quick and said he knowed all about that. As he was leaving he looked at me and said something I have never forgot to this day, nor the look on his face when he said it. "Why don't you tell her, Amma?" And then he was out the door and gone.

IN MARCH, ZEKE'S BROTHER Hugh come home to see his brand-new son. Rosa had not had an easy time and I was glad that he was able to come, though I was jealous too. This would be his second time home since they'd left. He come by the house to tell me Zeke was well and fit over at Strawberry Plains and it tore me all to pieces to think of my sweetheart just across the ridge. Hugh had rode the last few miles dozing in the saddle but I could tell he was wide awake now. He was all for beating a path home. He grinned when I told him this one had come a boy and allowed how Rosa had probably had a fit since she'd wanted a girly-child so bad. I told him she'd just have to use the name she'd picked out for it, which was Cora June, the next time around. This one he'd name Douglas Eugene and call him Doug. We spoke of his other boys. Regular stair-steps they was too, Bose,

Mitch, Tom, and Jess. He made for the door then, and I let him go. But I watched his horse plumb out of sight, because from the back he surely looked like my man Zeke. It would have give me great satisfaction to have seen his dear face right then.

THE NEXT MORNING HUGH had got up just at daylight and headed for the spring. Hugh and Rosa had one of the sweetest springs in this part of the world, and they both took great care to keep it cleaned out. I know exactly what he did that morning because I'd seen him do it myself a hundred times before. He would have splashed some of the icy water on his face and cupped some water to his mouth to drink. That water was so cold it would make your teeth ache plumb to the bone. Then he would have just set back and looked out down the valley and been quiet for a little while. That's what all of them did that come from the war, all of them craved the quiet. The one thing they all said they hated most about the war was the loudness of it. Rosa said he was gone for a long time, and she finally had to send Bose for him. He'd come back all sheepish and she could tell he'd dozed off. And that was why he'd not seen the blackguard that was his brother Shadrack slinking about up on the ridge.

Hugh's brother Shadrack was not even supposed to be home. He'd left Asheville the morning before with orders from Silas McMahan to ride straight downriver to Marshall, and it were only by chance that he'd decided to take the long way around and come through Sodom. And it were only by chance that Tildy had mentioned their cow had found a calf somewhere up on the ridge, and he'd gone to look for it. But he had not found no calf. He'd found Hugh instead. Shadrack rode hard as he could go until he got to the Confederate encampment at Warm Springs, where he told upon Hugh, and they sent out some men to get him. Cassie Leake watched them go by, and when they took the right fork in the road she run to the barn calling for her boy as she went. Jimmy beat them up there, too. Hugh run out the back of the house and headed up the patch of new ground. Poor old thing had grubbed the day before clearing roots as big as his arm out of the rich dirt, and now the field offered nothing to hide or shield him from the Rebels what was coming up the road. They was already so close he could hear their horses. Rosa said he was running hell bent for leather and she saw him raise his eyes toward the trees at the edge of the clearing. She said it was funny how she'd thought earlier that the clearing was so small, and she'd aimed to ask him to clear more of it off before he left. Now she said it seemed as wide as a mile.

They were shooting at him now and he went to zigging back and forth with his eyes fastened on them trees. Rosa said bullets was hitting all about him, jerking up big clods of dirt. Hope rose in her as she realized he was going to make the trees. Just another three or four strides and he'd be there. She strained forward herself willing him on. A flash of blue caught her eye and her heart almost stopped. It was Jess! Right there straight in front of him was their boy Jess.

And she'd screamed out at him and he'd faltered, then turned and run back out into the field they'd shot him down.

THAT NIGHT HACKLEY, LARKIN, and Andrew rode out heading back to Tennessee.

IT WAS LATER THAT month that I got a letter from Larkin that ended like this:

They was a man here what had a necklace of ears that was found stabbed in his guts. He died yesterdy and was carryin on in the awfulest way about the Pharaoh of Egypt. Is it not funy what comes to us at the time we are leeving this old world?

Your bigest boy,

Larkin

I tore off that part of the letter and buried it next to Fee's grave. In my way of figuring, that's right where it needed to be.

## 14

FINALLY WE GOT US a good spring. That year of '64 they was no rain that would not stop, and I did not have to worry about one of them bust-outs happening to us. We got the corn in and we moved the garden far from the house so the soldiers could not just ride by and take it. If they got it now, they would have to work a little for it. But I will tell you I did not aim for them to get so much as one ear of my corn. I would kill them for it now as my ten-percenting days was long past.

Hack Jr. was one of the prettiest babies I had ever seen. His hair was so blond it looked white and he had Hackley's blue eyes. He was the smilingest little thing too. I reckon he looked plime-blank like his daddy, and Mary was a big fool over him. Pearl was as jealous as she could be, and we had to watch her like a hawk because I was afraid she would hurt him somehow. Mary had took to staying during the day some at her own house. I could understand that. She had her own baby now and wanted to be home, though she always come back with us around suppertime and slept with us.

I had waited till the dew had dried off of the bean patch that day in late June, and as I was picking my mouth was watering. I was not thinking about a thing other than that big mess of beans I was going to be fixing for dinner, when of a sudden all the hair on the back of my neck stood up and I raised my eyes to the end of the row and there stood Larkin. He did not say a word to me, just stood there with his big hands hanging down empty, but I swear to you I knowed it.

And I can never say what and all went through my mind. I reckon every memory I had of my little brother went to crowding up in my head till I centered on how he would stand there with his blond hair shining like gold and make that fiddle just talk. It hit me right then and there that I would never hear a single note come from his hands again. Still, I did not think it was real until I run to that mule and saw that thing what was wrapped up and throwed over its back like a sack of taters. I reached out my hand and touched it, and still it was not real to me. And then I looked down and saw shoes sticking out and the britches had rode up and I could see a pale line of flesh. They was just something so helpless and pitiful about that little stretch of white and I felt the tears coming and could not have stopped them if I had tried. And Larkin's eyes was like black holes that had been bored out in his head and they had the awfulest look out of them you have ever seen. Me and Larkin held onto one another, and we both cried. Then he said, "Amma, I've got to do the hardest thing I've ever done now," and I said, "You will not do it by yourself." I went in to tell the young'uns that their laughing and cutting-up uncle had come home throwed across the back of a strange mule.

As we went across the ridge Larkin told me Hackley was the only man killed on the Union side in the battle that was being called Winding Stairs. He made no further motions to tell me more, and I did not ask, for I was plumb numb inside and it made no real difference. We had a bad thing to do and they was no sense in making it worse.

It was getting up toward late morning when we topped the ridge and stood looking down at the house. I could see where Mary had swept the yard, and there was a curl of smoke rising out of the chimney. Even from up here I could smell that she was baking bread. "Oh, Amma," he said, "I don't know that I can do this." And I said, "You can do it because you have to."

Mary was coming up the path from the spring when she saw us. A big smile bloomed over her face and she dropped the buckets and come running toward us laughing and calling out Larkin's name in the same breath. When she got close enough to see his face, she stopped and lost her laughter and her great big eyes looked from me to him and back to him again. I don't know that I will ever feel as sorry for anybody as I felt for her right then.

"Mary," was all he had to say.

"No," she brought her hand to her mouth. "No," she said again and she started backing up and her forehead got all bunched up.

"Honey," I said.

Her heart broke then. I saw it happen as clear as day, right as she was turning to run back toward the spring. Neither one of us knowed what to do except go to running after her. From the corner of my eye, I spied Julie standing on the porch holding the baby. Larkin's legs was so much longer than mine that I thought for a minute that he was going to catch her. I knowed for a fact that there was no room for nothing else in his heart except for that little figure ahead of him, just now entering the cool, dark path that ended at the deep pool where the spring broke ground. But then he had to slow down. Mary's bare feet grabbed hold of the damp rocks going down there, but his heavy boots were slick. I was right behind him and we both heard the splash.

"Oh, God, Larkin," I hollered out and he broke to run again, boots be damned.

Mary's hair was all fanned out around her small head and she was laying face down in the water.

Larkin hit the shallow water at a run, but it was only when he touched her that she began to fight him.

"Let me be. Leave me alone!" Her fists bounced off his chest as he lifted her up out of that cold water and started toward the bank with her cradled against him like a baby.

"Mary, honey, shhh." His voice was soft and he set a long time holding her close. A bright shaft of sun found its way down through the leaves and he scooted until they were in it. They were both shivering from the icy water.

The smell of honeysuckle came to me and the sweetness of it seemed somehow out of place.

She fought him for a while longer but finally stopped. He began to rock her slowly.

I squatted beside them and went to rubbing her hair. Nobody said nothing for a long time, then finally I said, "Scream, Mary. Scream as loud as you want to."

And finally with a great wail she started to cry. I knowed she would be all right then.

We ALL PILED UP and stayed at Mary's that night. She said she wanted to stay at her own house, and I knowed I would have felt the same exact way. The young'uns right down to Hack Jr. were quiet and went off to sleep early. Mary had not wanted us to tell nobody until the next morning. I reckon she wanted some time to gather herself. She clutched onto Larkin like a drowning woman and could not stand for him to be out of her sight. We was out on the porch about all night and she wanted to hear it all over and over again until I thought if I heard how my brother had died one more time I would start screaming at the top of my voice and not quit.

"Did he tell you anything to tell me before he died, Larkin?" she asked again.

He said what he'd already told her at least ten times and his voice sounded so tired but so patient with her, that I felt so sorry plumb to the bottom of my soul. "He was dead by the time I got to him, honey."

She looked all done in, and I cast around for something that I might ask him myself. "Not even before you went to fighting?"

He looked up at me and was in such a struggle and a misery that I wished I had kept my big mouth shut. "We'd had a fuss the night before, Amma. I had not talked to him that morning."

"Oh, God. Larkin, honey, I feel the worst in the world for you," I said and went to them both and put my arms around them. We set there till it was daylight.

Poor, poor Mary. This was her first big loss in her life, and God knows I knew as much as anybody about grieving, and now she had a big mess of it to do.

AND SHE DID JUST that and I done a lot myself over that next year. I got only a few letters from Larkin after he left, and he was doing his fair share, too.

Then just like that the war was over. It had started a way off in South Carolina and it ended a way off in Virginy, and as the hot months of the summer of 1865 went by, men what had been gone off fighting in it started to come home. You can only guess at how I searched every face hoping it to be the one I loved.

In late June, Daisy Stanton was out at the chop block shaving enough splinters from a piece of firewood to use for kindling. The evening sun was slanting in at her and had throwed her shadow up against the side of the cabin. Suddenly a great big shadow popped up right beside hers there on the house. Big John had come home.

That blackguard Shadrack Wallin knowed things would probably not go well for him back here in Sodom. The hand he'd had in the death of his brother would not be forgotten, let alone forgiven. And, yeller dog coward that he was, he didn't have the heart to face neither Rosa nor his baby brother Zeke. He timed his homecoming with the new moon and he snuck in here and gathered his belongings and collected his wife and family, and they was gone by daylight, bound for Virginy. On the way he changed the spelling of his name to Wallen, and we never saw hide nor hair of him ever again. Good riddance to bad rubbish is what I have to say about that.

Brother William come up on Mommie at the spring and she hit her knees right there on the bank of the stream, praising the Almighty for delivering her oldest son back to her arms.

Soon after William Jr. showed back up, we heard from Robert, who was living in Mississippi with his new bride after having served out the war with the Confederacy.

Tete come home from Knoxville, where he'd been released from his duties as office clerk to General Hartwell Jackson.

Old Lawrence Allen and his cousin James Keith was afraid for their lives over the Shelton Laurel massacre. And well they should have been, for Pete McCoy had swore he would kill them. Them two made a beeline away from here and headed out for Arkansas.

• • •

THEN THERE WAS THEM what did not return.

Roderick Norton, Larkin's bearer of apple stack cake, was killed by the Home Guard while on a recruiting mission for Kirk.

Andy Chandler got better from the dysentery, went back to fighting, and was killed over at Strawberry Plains.

Little Johnny Norton deserted from Allen's regiment and was killed in a poker game by another deserter over on Shelton Laurel.

Pete McCoy hid out on Shelton Laurel until the war ended. After his mother died in August, he headed for the western country, but made a trip to Charlotte first, where he shot and killed a man that had been with Allen's murdering bunch on Shelton Laurel. Pete died in a dispute over a gold-mining claim in California.

But neither Zeke nor Larkin come, and I was beginning to wonder if they ever would.

ONE WARM NIGHT TOWARD the middle of July, I woke from a dead sleep by a rustling of the mattress as someone sat down on the foot of my bed. Quick as a cat I was up and running for the door when Zeke's voice stopped me right where I was standing. I come back to the bed on slow feet and could hardly believe it was really him and not his haint.

"I'm home," he said.

"I see that," I said, but was not certain until I laid my hand on him and felt him warm beneath it.

We set for a minute with our shoulders touching.

"At night sometimes I dreamed so hard that you was next to me that I would wake in the morning with my hand closed tight like this," I said and held up my clenched fist to him.

He closed his fingers around my little fist and raised it to his mouth where he kissed every one of my knuckles. "I wouldn't let myself dream, Arty," he whispered to me. "Dreaming done me no good. Only made me long for you more."

I palmed back a thick lock of hair from his wide forehead. His eyes was plumb purple in the light of the moon that was coming through the open door. "You won't never have to long for me next to you again, Zeke. You ain't never getting away from me again. I don't ever aim to be no further away from you than I am right now."

He laughed. "It'll make it hard to plow joined at the hip this way."

"There don't need to be no plowing for a while, Zeke. Except for the plowing that needs doing right here."

And he needed nothing else said when I patted the bed.

AND IN AUGUST LARKIN came home.

I WAS STUDYING HIM and he knew I was doing it. This was his third time by the house in as many weeks since he'd come home, and he was awful quiet. He'd been in the upper field with Zeke all morning, and they'd come in for dinner all hot and sweaty but easy with one another, like men can be when they've spent time working together. I followed them out onto the porch talking up a storm while they'd washed and poured water over their heads. Neither had said much, but then Zeke was always spare with his words. But it hurt me that the easy way I had always had with Larkin seemed gone. Even when Carolina had bounded onto the porch like a big puppy and went to poking him in the ribs and batting her eyes at him, flirting with him a little, Larkin had barely smiled. And it was hard not to laugh plumb out loud when Carolina was around. She was always cutting up and going on, slinging that big mane of glossy black hair, with them big blue eyes just dancing with fun. Zeke had finally sent her to the spring for buttermilk just to get her out of the way.

After supper, Zeke had give me a look that was not lost on Carolina and had announced that he had a harness that needed mending, and when Larkin started to rise, he'd placed a hand on his shoulder.

"No need for you to come. Carolina's been wanting to talk to me anyhow." They'd gone out together, leaving me and Larkin at the table.

Larkin leaned back on the bench and looked at me. "You aiming to draw a picture of me?"

I laughed and felt a little better. "No, I ain't, you smart-mouthed whelp, you."

He smiled and it almost blossomed in his eyes, but not quite. "I don't mean to worry you, Amma."

And with that he unlocked the words that had been near about choking me to death, and I let him have it. "Well now why in the world would I be worried? Just because you don't talk to me no more? That you act like you owed me money or something? That when you do come here to the house, you latch onto Zeke like you're in deep water and he's the only one about that knows how to swim? No need for me to be worried about none of that." I had to lay my hand on him then, so I brushed the hair back from his forehead and hunkered down so I could look him eyeball to eyeball. "Or that Julie left Mary's and went to stay with their aunt over at Jewel Hill. Or that Mary won't speak to her mommie since Julie left. Or that Rosa told me that they ain't been no lamps lit of an evening at your place since you come home. Or that you been seen coming from Maggie's real early in the morning." I took my hand away, but stayed close to him in case I needed to put it back. "No need for me to worry about none of that?"

His eyes were flat. He shook his head. "No."

I let out my breath in a big puff and leaned back. "Well, I won't then." And I come up off that bench like it was red hot. His hand shot out and grabbed my arm, but I was so mad I was about to cry and would not look at him.

"It's not as it might seem, Amma."

That flew all over me. "How do you even know how it might seem to me, mister? You ain't bothered to ask."

He sighed. "I'm not a boy anymore, Amma. Can't you see that?"

I jerked my arm loose. "Well, now that you ain't a boy, just don't wind up being a stupid man, Larkin." I went to washing them dishes with a vengeance and out come that chin of mine.

After a while I heard him get up from the table and go out the door.

THOUGH I HAD ROSA looking every morning for weeks after that, she never saw Larkin at Maggie's again.

But we all saw Larkin and Mary walking out together most every evening after supper. And as the tired green of summer gave way to the bright colors of fall, I knowed that Larkin had made his choice not to be a stupid man.

They took to walking up on the mountain, and I would see them go by the house with Hack Jr. riding high up on Larkin's shoulders. I could hear him laughing all the way down at the house. Larkin was a pure-D fool over that young'un, and from the very first he acted like he was his own flesh and blood. But let me say right here that this could not be. That child was the spitting image of my poor dead brother and became more like him the older he got. I swear it was just like looking at him. And you know mayhap that was the very reason why Larkin took such a shine to him. He loved Hackley, too.

They walked up to Hackley's grave a lot. Mary said they was standing next to the grave and Hack Jr. was setting right on it when Larkin asked her to marry him. When she said she would, he had grabbed up both of them and had danced all over the place. I felt like something cold went to crawling right up my spine when she told me that. Somehow, even though I cannot say the why, it did not seem right that he'd asked her there.

## 15

I OFFERED TO LET them marry in my house, but Mary allowed that she wanted it done in the church. So off we went. Do not think I did not feel happiness in my heart for them, for I did. The only reason I offered them my house was that they was some men what had come from the damn war that carried very hard feelings. I would mention here one Tyler Ray what had been up in Virginy with Mister Lee when he'd surrendered. Tyler's eyes would just fill up with water at the mention of that man's name. Some on the other side was just as bad. As I have said before, and will take this opportunity to say again, men is foolish sometimes when it comes to whether their honor might be slighted in some way. So I say to them, keep your damn honor placed somewhere that it cannot be slighted. But Tyler pulled out his pistol and shot Vernon Lewis in the hand at a poker game back in the fall just for saying that the king of spades sort of reminded him of old Marse Robert. They said the cards went every which way. 'Course in my way of figuring, Vernon Lewis ought to have been shot a long time ago for being a fool, but if we start shooting folks for being fools then we'd be shooting right up till the end of time.

So when I got to the church and it was packed with folks, I got the all-overs, but I did not get them too bad. Larkin had summed it up right as we was leaving the house and, oh, let me say that my biggest boy was as pretty a man as I had ever seed in my life. He had shrugged his big wide shoulders and said to me, "The war is done, Amma. It is time we got on."

And I had said to him something I had never said, but had meant to for a long time. "I am proud of you, son," I said. "This is a decent thing that you are doing for Hackley here on this day."

His voice was all choked up when he answered me. "I am not doing it for Hackley, Amma. This is all for me."

I had nothing to say to that and figured just as he said and so it is.

THE MARRYING THAT DAY went off without a single hitch, and it looked as though old grudges, slights, hurts, and more honor than you could shake a stick at had at least for this day been left outside the door. But do not fret all you people. It was all sorted out and picked right back up when that night ended.

LET ME TELL YOU right now that I had never give much thought to this word *beautiful*. To me people was seldom if ever beautiful. But on this day Mary was beautiful. Her hair was all down and loose and covered her shoulders for all the world like a rich wavy red shawl. There had been no need to pinch her cheeks for color, and them big brown eyes never left Larkin's face one single time while the preacher was talking.

Larkin stood straight and looked right back at her, and his voice was deep as a well when he said the words that bound his heart to hers.

They was those among us that shed tears setting on them hard wooden benches that morning. Mommie capped her hands over her face and just sobbed as the preacher said, "Till death do you part." I was bawling myself and me setting there with my lap budding yet another child. I swear to you, it seemed that every time Zeke Wallin hung his britches up on the peg on the back of the door, Arty found herself in the family way. I reached out and took Zeke's hand in mine and held onto it the whole time. I had made good as I could that threat of not letting him out of my sight. This might explain me being four months gone again. Lord, I felt so sorry for Julie, who did not sob. It would have been better if she had but only one single tear slid down her little face when Larkin said, "I do."

I had seen Maggie at the back of the church when I'd come in and my eyebrows flew straight up. She grinned at me, and I could tell she was having a big time knowing that everybody in there was watching her. Bless her, at least this would lay to rest any ugly thoughts folks might be carrying about her and Larkin. I knowed it was him that had gone and asked her to come, and I also knowed that they had been nothing between them since he'd come home. I know this because she had come by the house the week before and we'd had us a big talk. All them times he'd come to her in the early misty mornings back in the summer, it had been only to sit with her on the porch. She said sometimes they'd talked together, but most times she'd just listened. "He's got a world of horror in his heart, Arty. The things he has seen is bad enough to have killed most men." He'd told her too of how he feared he was ruined now for any woman. She'd let him talk and when he run out of words, she'd let the silence be. They never once touched, though she would have, had he asked. Then he'd stopped coming. She'd let that be as well.

She'd told me then about Silas, too.

She'd lit a fire that night so the windows would be glowing warm and welcoming in the chill of the early fall evening. He was awfully quiet as they ate supper, and Maggie said his eyes followed her everywhere she went and they were the saddest things she'd ever seen. I wanted to stop her right there and I would have a year ago, but she needed to talk to somebody and I was it. She said when he loved her that night his hands was so gentle that it jerked tears from her eyes. The fire had burned down to just red coals when he'd said the words she'd been dreading to hear fall from his lips for as long as she'd known him. "I've got to go home, Maggie."

And there they was now and she could not say nothing. When she didn't answer, he rolled his head to look at her. "I'm taking the train out the end of this week." And all she said was, "Well."

And that was it. He'd left the next morning and she'd kissed him, held him one last time and let him go. She said there'd been a little moment there on the porch when he'd have stayed if she'd asked. She had seen it in his eyes. But she had not asked him.

I asked her then why and she said she'd known, clear as anything, that if he'd left his wife and family for her, that he'd forever have held the best part of himself back from her. And she wouldn't have had him that way. So she'd had to turn from him as he'd climbed on his horse, set her back to him as he'd ridden off down the road. It had been the hardest thing she'd ever done.

I have to say that a big flower of respect bloomed in my heart on that day for Maggie. She was a good and decent person for all that she was hotter than a ginger mill. But then I had knowed that for as long as I had knowed her. I had always allowed that she had just never found the right sweetheart. I told her how sad I was that she had found him only to have to let him go, and she allowed as how it had been her experience that more often than not, life is just that way.

THAT NIGHT WE HAD such a time as it put me in the mind of the way it used to be here around home. When we left the church house we never even broke stride and went right straight to Jim Leake's and had a great big frolic in the front room of his house. I started off trying to act my age but soon got over that. They was a little bit of time right there at the beginning when Lum and Willis took up their banjo and fiddle that it got real quiet. I knowed every single soul in that place was thinking the same as me, that the best of the lot was not here with us. With my eyes burning like fire I hollered out, "Play a good fast frolic tune for my brother, boys." That broke things up and they commenced to playing a tune they'd learned off some boys over in Tennessee what was called "The Cumberland Gap," which is a fine tune with good words which we all took to singing.

Me and my wife and my wife's pap walked all the way to the
    Cumberland Gap.
Cumberland Gap ain't my home and I'm gonna leave old
    Cumberland alone.

I was singing as loud as I could and grinning at Zeke the whole time. A bunch hit the floor dancing for all they was worth, and before I could catch myself and go back to acting my age, I jumped up and was dancing every which way. When that song ended I was winded but thought I had done pretty good for an old married woman and told Zeke as much. All he could do was shake his head at me and allow how I would not do.

Me and him danced the whole livelong night, and my young'uns had themselves a great big time. Pearl played so hard her hair was plastered to her head with sweat, and she was as ill and mean as a copperhead when I finally made her go lay down. I let the biggest ones stay up and was glad I did, because Carolina wound up being the one to sing the song that sent Larkin and Mary down the road to their married bed.

We was all waiting for the musicianers to rest up when Rosa Wallin asked me if I would sing something. Lord, they was no way I could have denied that poor woman a song nor nothing else. She looked like death warmed over ever since Hugh had died, and I felt guilty as sin standing there beside my big pretty man knowing that she'd had to crawl out of her birthing bed to bury hers. I went to running songs through my head trying to figure which one would be the best to sing that would hurt her the least. You have to be careful with these old songs sometimes, for they can reach right in and twist up your heart if you ain't. Carolina give me just a minute and then whispered to me, "Can I sing one, Mommie?" And I told her to go right ahead and I was thankful for the chance to figure which to sing. But I needn't have bothered. That young'un stepped right out and sung exactly what needed to be sung. It were not too much but it were just enough.

> The heart is the fortune of all womankind.
> They're always controlled and they're always confined—
> Controlled by their parents until they are wives
> Then bound to their husbands for the rest of their lives.
>
> I am a poor girl and my fortune is sad,
> I've a long time been courted by the wagoner's lad.

He courted me truly by night and by day
And now he is loaded and driving away.

"Your parents don't like me because I am poor,
They say I'm not worthy to enter your door.
I work for my money, my money's my own,
And folks that don't like me they can leave me alone."

"Go stable your horses and feed them some hay,
Come and sit down beside me for as long as you can stay."
"My horses ain't hungry, they won't eat your hay,
So fare-thee-well, darling, I'll be on my way."

"Your horse is to saddle, your wagon to grease,
Come sit you down by me before you must leave."
"My horse it is saddled, my whip's in my hand,
So fare-thee-well, darling, I can no longer stand."

"I can love little or I can love long,
I can love an old sweetheart till a new one comes 'long.
I can hug and can kiss them and prove to them kind,
I can turn my back on them and also my mind."

I'll go to yon mountain the mountain so high,
Where the wild birds can see me as they pass me by,
Where the wild birds can see me and hear my sad song,
For I am a poor girl and my lover has gone.

When she finished it was like everybody in that room was holding
their breath. And then I looked at Zeke, and the tears was just pouring down his face and he did not even try to swipe them and make

like he was not crying for all the world to see. He grabbed her up in his arms, and it hit me then that this was the first time he had heard our girl sing.

Nobody needed to tell me what a lucky woman Arty Wallin was, because she already had a pretty good idea of that herself.

Larkin and Mary made their move to leave just then, and we all follered them out the door hollering and carrying on. I have always wondered about that sort of thing. I mean, why them men feels the need to scream out instructions is just beyond me. And some of the women is just as bad. And it was not as if Mary or Larkin either one needed instructing, if you know what I mean. But anyway, out onto the porch we went with everybody hollering the same-old same-old, and then somebody hollered that it was snowing and I crowded right up next to the front. Oh, how I loved the snow, and it were really coming down, too. The ground just barely had a little skift on it, but great big fat flakes was coming down offering us the promise of a big snow if it kept up till morning. Just then two of Edmund Chandler's big boys come toting a big sack between them and I could not believe it when they opened the door and throwed that sack right into the middle of the room. Now I am here to tell you that sack was packed full of possums, and they come out of that sack and went every which way. I have never laughed as much in my life as we spent the rest of the night collecting possums off the beams and out from behind stuff, and everywhere else you can just imagine. Boys is something else, ain't they?

While we was possum gathering, me and Maggie hung together and talked. She pulled a letter out of her sleeve and told me to read it. It was from Silas, and when I read the part that said his wife had died of a fever of some kind I looked up at her. I want you to know they was nothing in her face but sorrow. "In all my wishing I did not wish this, Arty," she said, and I know she was telling me the truth. I looked her right in the eye and said, "Maggie, honey, they will not let me or you neither one be in charge of things even for a minute, so it does not matter what we wish." I went back to reading and found that he aimed to come for her as soon as a decent time had passed. "What will you do, Maggie?" I said. And she said, "Why, I'll go raise our young'uns." And you know, that is just what she done. She turned out quite the lady down there in South Carolina.

Me and Zeke walked out for home just as it was getting daylight, and all our young'uns was stumbling along with us looking like sleepy chickens. Zeke was carrying Pearl, and seeing the two of them together looking just like each other made my heart swell near to busting.

As we come by Mary's little cabin it was closed up tight without so much as a candle lighting the window. It looked so pretty in the snow and my face got all warm when I went to thinking about what was going on just on the other side of them walls. I hoped for Larkin's sake it had been well worth the wait. My gut told me it probably had been.

When we got home I put Pearl in the bed with Abigail and Carolina, and the boys went up in the loft. Soon they was all sound asleep and me and Zeke laid there talking about this, that, and the other. That was the best thing in the world to me. During the damn war, I had learned the hard lesson that is to take nothing for granted in this world.

I got right playful then and asked Zeke what he thought Larkin and Mary were doing right now, and he looked at me like I was a crazy woman. "Why, what do you think they're doing, Arty?" And I could not help it, I just busted out laughing.

But I did not laugh too long, as just about then was when he showed me just what they might be doing. And all I have to say about that is, Lordy, I hope they was.

## 16

THERE AT THE FIRST, they was no two that was any happier than Larkin and Mary, and that's a fact. I can still see in my mind's eye how he looked when he come by the house and told me that they was pretty certain Mary was in the family way. I mean that man was plumb tickled to death. But when I said, "Well, now, son, you'll be a daddy," he looked at me all funny and said quick as a snake, "I'm already a daddy, Amma." I knowed exactly what he meant by that and knowed too just how he felt. So I held my tongue and did not say what everybody had said to me when I was carrying my own. I knowed he loved Hack Jr. like he would his own and nobody could ever tell him any different. In my way of figuring Larkin was my firstborn. I was always ready to fight anybody that allowed he was not.

As them months come and went, Mary hardly had to lift a hand to do a single thing. Larkin was like a winding blade and would fuss and carry on if she even so much as done work in her garden. She was pretty sick, though. I went by there right after my April was born and she was out on the porch throwing up. I done my best to tell her that some women was sick the whole time they was breeding, and that she was not to worry. I reckon most women cannot be like Arty and pop them out with little or no effort. April was born in about an hour, and I guess that is just as well since I aimed to call her April and if she'd waited one more hour she'd have come in May, so I was in sort of a hurry. And when I saw April's little red head, I was pleased as could be. She was the picture of her sister Ingabo and that was somehow fitting.

That summer was such a good time for all of us, I reckon. Me and Zeke got along really good, even though they was some getting used to each other again. It took me awhile to settle back into him being around all the time. I was used to doing everything for myself and had got right bullheaded. I was not as agreeable about things as I once was. Bless Zeke for having the patience of Job and letting me keep on being the person I had become. That is hard for some men, you understand. They was lots of women what had trouble with their men that first year. I think if Zeke had been like most, we would not have stayed together. Arty had done come around the fence during that damn war, and they was no way on earth she could have gone back to yes-siring all the livelong day and night.

ME AND MARY WAS setting on the porch one evening late in the summer watching the lightning bugs come up all around us. They is nothing on God's green earth to beat that. I feel sorry for folks that has never had the chance to set on the porch and watch that little miracle happen. A warm breeze was blowing and the young'uns was out catching bugs and putting them in a jar. Is that not a wonderful thing to spend your time doing?

Mary had gone all soft-eyed watching me nurse April and allowed that she could hardly wait for her own to be out in the world with us.

I laughed and said she'd better be for enjoying the rest while she could. Then Larkin started to sing down at the barn, and we just set there and listened. Lord, what a voice that man had, and it jerked the chillbumps out on me big as goose eggs. "What's that song?" Mary asked me and I said " 'Pretty Fair Miss,' honey," and I shushed the young'uns just to hear it better.

> Said a pretty fair miss all in her garden and a handsome young
> soldier come a-riding by,
> Said, "Could I impose on a fair young maiden and ask her for
> my bride to be?"

> Said, "Handsome young soldier standing by the gateway, a man
> of honor you may be.
> How could you impose on a fair young maiden who never intends
> your bride to be?"

> Said, "I've got a true love-yer that gone to the army and he's
> been gone for seven years long.
> And if he stays gone seven years longer, no man on earth could
> marry me."

> "Prayhaps your love-yer drownded in the ocean, prayhaps he's
> on some battlefield slain,
> Prayhaps he's taken another girl and married, his face you'll
> never see again."

> "Well, if he's drownded I hope he's happy, or if he's on some
> battlefield slain,
> Or if he's taken another girl and married, why, I'd love the girl
> that would marry him."

His fingers being long and slender, into his pockets they did go.
Said, "Here's the ring that you once gave me before I started for
  the war."

She threw her lily white arms around him and straight before
  him she did fall,
Said, "You're the man that used to court me before you left here
  for the war."

Said, "I been on the deep sea sailing and I been sailing for seven
  years long,
And if I'd stayed gone seven years longer no woman on earth
  could've married me."

That was the prettiest I would ever hear that sung. They was no-body could sing like Larkin Stanton, and that was all there was to it.

We set on for a while after he'd quit, and then Mary looked at me and said, "Arty, I sometimes feel like I have somehow betrayed your brother." I took a long time to answer her and what I finally said to her was this. "Life is not for the dead and gone. It is just for the living. That is the only way it can ever be. As hard as it might sound, we have to turn loose of the dead and let them go."

SOMEBODY ASKED ME ONE time if now that I was a old woman, if I had got things sorted out in my mind and was used to the idea of dying. I said to them what I will say now to you. No, I have gotten more used to living. That's just how it is.

I CAUGHT MARY'S BABY in September that year, and she was just like looking her mommie in the face. When I took her to

Larkin, he held out his big hands and I put her in them. He looked down into that little heart-shape of a face and he literally went to swaying. I reached out a hand to steady him and laughed. But then he lifted his face up and I saw his eyes. They was a great stillness in them, and my breath caught in my throat. Before I could say anything to him, he took and shoved that baby back at me, a sob tore itself loose from his throat, and he turned and went running hell bent off the porch. I took the baby back in to Mary and told her some men was profoundly touched when they see what their loins have created. But I was troubled to my very soul. As soon as I could, I lit out after him and found him down at the spring. What he was doing down there was not natural.

The deep water that had pooled for the spring was still as glass. All around us the summer bugs was churring and singing, but he didn't even seem to hear them. He was staring right down into that water like he was waiting for something to rise right up out of it. He give a little shake of his head like he was telling somebody I could not see, *no, no*. Then he slapped the water with the flat of his hand and rip- ples went to streaking out every which way. "Can't I have this thing?" he said right out loud. "Can I live it? Can I?"

My heart was feeling like it was going to bust out of my body, but I did not say a word. This was for him to figure. I watched as he put his face right down next to the water for all the world like he aimed to kiss his reflection. And then he said to himself, "They is nothing left but to live it."

I slipped off and he did not even know I was there.

OF COURSE ROXYANN OWNED her daddy's heart from the first birth cry. Larkin loved her so much that he would have walked a rotten foot-log over hell to have got to her. And he caught her heart in them big hands of his as well. I ain't never in all my days seen a young'un wean itself as quick as she did, and I believe she done it on purpose so she could go around with her daddy. And in the love he had for her, for a while at least, Larkin Stanton was a man content.

I reckon that was a good thing too, for right before Roxyann's first birthday, Mary was breeding again. Now, they was no sickness with this one and she worked like a man through that winter. I was not a bit surprised when she birthed Luke right on time. He was a great big boy and I could not help it that my mind went back to when his daddy come into this world, which seemed like a lifetime ago. They named him Luke, after Larkin's own daddy.

The older Luke got, the more he looked like his daddy. He was a quiet and serious young'un, and him and Hack Jr. was close from the very start. They was the same difference in age as what was between Larkin and Hackley. I swear for me it was just like I'd been tossed back in time watching them grow. One was sturdy, small, and blond and already taking up his daddy's fiddle and singing the old love songs. And Luke so big and dark, dogging Hack Jr.'s every step. Most of the time I called Luke Larkin and could not help it.

I reckon it was when Rosalie was born that Larkin began to change.

I GUESS SOMETIMES WE just get so caught up in the living through life that we miss the living of it. I know that is what happened them years right after Larkin and Zeke come from the war. We went along, and went along, and in what seemed no time a'tall, Abigail was getting married.

And with each year that rolled over our heads, Larkin got stiller and quieter.

I was like Mary and slow to notice. We was all so busy that we hardly had time enough to think, let alone notice how quiet Larkin had come to be. He was a lot like Zeke in that way, and I guess we'd just got used to him being about and not saying much. And he was in and out, working as hard as the rest of us. So when she come by the house with her face all pinched up with worry, I told her what had taken me a long time to figure with Zeke, that men is just different and don't always feel the need to face bark back and forth like us women do. She seemed to feel a little better by the time she left.

But I kept on studying about it and was plumb taken aback with just how long it had been since Larkin had darkened my own door. I decided right then and there that I had to catch hold of that big young'un and see what and all was churning around and about in that big head of his. A few days later I struck out for their house. But when I got over there I could not for the life of me figure out what was happening right in front of my eyes.

Mary was setting in front of the fire with a lap full of mending and Larkin was setting at the table. I went by him and dropped a big smacking kiss on the top of his head but he barely grunted at me. I never let on and started talking a blue streak with Mary, but I was sneaking looks at him every chance I could. Lord, but his eyes looked like little black chips and there was a still watchfulness in them. His mouth all thinned out and a big muscle was jumping in his jaw. Finally I couldn't stand it no more and I said just his name, "Larkin?" and my voice sounded funny even to me. The look he shot me was gone so fast my head wondered if I had seen it at all. But my heart had caught it all right, and his eyes were still holding on to some of it as well.

"What?"

Mary was watching us and her little face was looking like she was going to take to crying just any minute. I just stared at him and then said the first thing that popped into my mind. "I love you, son."

The dark thing in his eyes was gone in a flash and he smiled. "Why, I love you, too."

I did not know what had just happened, but I knew with the awfulest feeling of despair that this was not the first time whatever it was had squatted in him. And with something that felt an awful lot like fear, I knew it would not be the last.

MARY REACHED FOR THE cup of coffee in front of her, but her hand trembled so that she had to set it back down without even taking a drink. "I don't even know how long he's been this way. But, Lord have mercy, Arty, I see it everywhere now and it does nothing but get worser between us."

She had lost so much weight that her eyes looked to be sunk back in her head. "What are you seeing in him that is troubling you so?"

"With me he's quiet as the grave," Mary said. "But he talks to them boys like they are dogs. *Worse* than dogs. And they are *good* boys, Arty. You know that. They don't sass, they do what they're told." She swiped at her eyes. "For the most part they do, but they're boys and sometimes they get off to playing, you know?"

"I know, honey. Mine's the same way," I said and then, trying to soothe her, I said, "Zeke gets so mad he could spit. Hollers at them sometimes, too."

Mary folded her little hands and put them in her lap. She looked down, studying them, and when she spoke her voice was low. "Hollering ain't all he does."

I reached out and patted her hand. "Mary, hollering ain't all Zeke does. It ain't all I've done, neither."

"Has Zeke ever kicked them?" She raised eyes that seemed to carry all the pain in the world.

I felt myself go cold as ice on the inside and even my heart stilled. "Kick them? You mean kicks with his foot?" Now I knowed she meant with his foot. How else would you kick something, or worse yet someone, but I was just so shocked, you have to understand.

When I said that it was like I had reached out and uncorked a jug and turned it over as one ugly story after another come pouring out. My heart sunk lower and lower as she talked, and I kept thinking to myself, *What in this world has happened?*

Mary talked for a long time and then she just stopped. The room was quiet and a bright square of sun came through the small window that was my pride and joy. The only sound was from the clock on the fireboard and we both jumped when it chimed out the hour.

"Lord, I've got to go," Mary said. "I left Rosalie with Roxyann, and she'll be crying the house down wanting her mommie."

I followed her onto the porch. Mary looked so thin. I put my arms around her and hugged her up, and I was mad as hell and my voice was just shaking. "I have a mind to talk to Larkin Stanton, Mary, whether you want me to or not." At the look on her face I could not stay mad and softened my voice up. "But I won't if you think it'll just make it worse."

Mary swiped her hair back with both hands. "Don't say nothing to him right now."

I looked her hard right in the eyes. "All right. But all you've got to do is ask."

"Thanks so much, Arty."

She was almost to the edge of the yard when I hollered out, "Mary?"

She turned.

"He ain't hit you or the girls, has he?"

Mary shook her head. "Oh no, he's gentle as ever with them. And no, he ain't hit me neither." Her shoulders sagged. "I know it sounds crazy as hell, but sometimes I wish he would. Him hitting me would be better than this awful watching that he's doing."

MARY HAD NEVER SEEN Larkin really drunk, so the first time he come up the path singing at the top of his lungs, she really thought things might be fixing to change. She said he laughed, took her on his lap, said sweet things to her and aside from the strong smell of his breath, he seemed more like himself than he had in months. He'd sat at the table wearing a big toothy grin while she'd fixed supper. It was the first relaxed meal they'd all had together in a long while.

She said it just broke her heart when the boys come sneaking in after washing up and that they'd perched on the bench like birds ready to take flight. Luke actually flinched when Larkin dropped his knife. She had looked at Hack Jr. and caught his look of pure old relief when it dawned on him that the awful quiet would not rule this time. Larkin was actually laughing and cutting up and deviling him about this or that young girl. For all that his speech was slurred, at least he was talking to them.

She said she was feeling pretty good, but that had come to an end when they finished supper and Hack Jr. had said, "Daddy?"

Larkin had looked up from his plate with his eyes glassy and his grin on all crooked. "What, son?"

"Willis and a bunch of them are going to let their dogs run. Can me and Luke take Hummer and go with them?"

She said she'd thought to herself, *Oh, no. Don't ruin this, son. Don't.*

But her quick glance at Larkin realized it was already done.

His eyes had gone flat as a snake's and his smile was gone. "You wanting to lay out all night?"

Hack Jr. heard the change but he was already in it now. He swallowed and went on, "We'd be back before daylight, plenty of time to do our work." He glanced quick at Larkin, and even though he saw the stillness on his face, the dark knitting of his brow, he plunged ahead. "We ain't done nothing like that in so long, Daddy. Not since—" and one more look at his daddy had stopped him right there.

Mary said everybody went quiet, and even Roxyann stopped dead still on her way to the sideboard with a stack of plates.

Larkin placed both hands flat on the table. "Since what, Hack?" Of a sudden they was no slurring of words, and that happened so quick it scared the hell out of Mary. "Hack," she said, "you and Luke take the slop bucket out."

"Hush, Mary." His voice had gone soft and his eyes was holding that awful dark thing.

But when Hack Jr. lifted his chin, Mary said she'd felt something almost joyful rise up in her breast. Her son's jaw was set and they was a certain cockiness about him. His lower lip came out in a bit of a pout, and the blue eyes that he offered Larkin was not one bit afraid. I reckon his daddy popped out in him, and that was not lost on Larkin.

Them big hands what was on the table made into big fists and he brought both of them up and slammed them both down on the table so hard that the dishes bounced. "Don't you look at me that way."

But, though it was a shout, it carried no anger. His voice had held such pain it sounded almost like a plea.

Without thought Mary had put her hand out to him.

"Don't, just don't," he'd said as he'd swatted her hand away. Then he'd jumped up and went to staggering for the door. By the time Mary had gathered her wits enough to go after him, the night had swallowed him up.

That was the first night he didn't come home.

## 17

THAT FALL WAS A misery for them all. When Larkin was home, he was mean drunk. There were the few odd times when he'd come swaggering in, right playful, laughing, singing, grabbing her around the waist. Mary come to dread those times worst of all. He'd run the children off from the house and they would flee ahead of him like a bunch of scared little animals.

And then he'd turn for her.

FOR THE FIRST TIME in my life I could not reach him, though it was not for lack of trying. I done everything I knowed to do. I tried being easy with him. I rared and threatened and cussed him. I begged and cried. I even dragged Zeke into it and had him try to talk reason with him. Zeke did not want to do it and I had to beg him to. That was hard for me, as I am not a woman what begs. But Larkin would just hump up like a big log and I might as well been spinning moonbeams for all the good it done. I kept on because I could not stop. I could not stop because I loved him and it seemed like he was dying right before my eyes and by God, I would not have it. I would not.

IT WAS COLD AS a witch's ninny pies that day when Hack Jr. come by the house and said Mary was at her wits' end. Larkin had not been home for a solid week. I told him to wait and I would get Zeke to go with him to look. I watched them out of sight and then stepped to the edge of the porch to look up at the sky. It had clouded over a heavy frost that morning and the low clouds that had moved in seemed bigged with snow. I hoped they found Larkin and found him quick.

Thank the Lord, they did just that.

They had gone straight to the cave, just as I'd said for them to do. He was up there all right, and had drunk so much he'd passed out deader than a doorknob. Zeke said he was laying out in the weather on top of Buzzard Rock.

When they come carrying him in I started crying. He was so sick we loaded him on the sled and took him to Granny's old place. They was just no telling what he had, and I could not run the chance of my least ones getting it. He looked rough as a cob and had not washed off nor shaved in way too many a day.

Poor little Mary come by and it took a bunch of fast talking on my part to get her to go back home. She so wanted to help, but I told her for all I knowed he had the fever though I knowed in my heart it was not that old foe. Do not get me wrong, Larkin's body was as sick as any I'd ever seen and it might very well have been something what could be caught. But the worst of his sick could not have been caught by nobody else, for it was the greater sick of his soul. I knowed that I had to first wrassle his flesh from death's jaws and then he could at least have a shot at curing himself of the other. And they was something else I knowed though I cannot really tell you how I knowed it. Mary could not help him through this because she was a part of it.

So though she did not want to go, and I hated to let her go with a lie between us, I finally scared her enough to where she went. Oh, Lord, how sorry for her I did feel as I watched her thin little person all humped up against the cold turn down the path towards home.

Then I balled up my two fists and went to fight what I did not know. But by God, that was one battle I aimed to win. I know for a fact he would have died out there on the mountain, because it come the awfulest snow ever was over the next few days.

Hell, Larkin come damn near to dying anyways.

WHEN HE FINALLY STARTED to come around, the first thing he said was, "Oh, God, it feels like my eyes is full of broke-up glass," and then he tried to set up.

"Lay still, Larkin," I said.

He was so damn weak, and I could tell by how easy-like he swallowed that his throat must be hurting something bad. I put a cold wet cloth on his forehead and he peeped at me through slitted eyes. "Who's that?" he said, and I was surprised at how hoarse he was.

"It's Arty," I said, "and you've been sick as I've ever seen anybody that didn't die. And you still might, so lay still."

"How'd I get here?" he croaked. "God, my throat hurts."

"When it started to snow, Mary sent Hack Jr. to get Zeke. And it's a good thing she did, or you'd be dead, boyo." I leaned over him with the cold rag again. "They's a foot or more on the ground and it's still coming down."

I could see him trying to study about that, but he could not keep his mind on it. I watched him struggle with it, then he dosed back off and for the first time since they'd brought him in, he slept a good sleep.

I was still setting there when he woke up the next time. "Arty?"

"Right here, honey." I pushed the hair back from his forehead and let my hand stay for a bit. "Good. The fever's broke."

"I'm starved to death," he said.

I had to laugh at that. "No, honey. You *cheated* death as sure as the world. I'll get you some broth."

He was so hungry that I had to fuss at him a little. "Not so fast, Larkin. Take it slow."

When I'd spooned the last drop into his mouth I waved a hand in front of my nose. "I'll get some water and we'll clean you up a bit. You've smelled like yesterday's minners for days now."

He turned his head and looked at me. "Days?"

"You've been sick for almost two weeks, Larkin. And you're weak as cat pee."

He stared off up at the top of the cabin while I was heating up some water. When I commenced to washing him, his face got red as a beet. "I hate you're having to do this, Amma."

I grinned at him and just kept on washing. "That's the first time you've called me that in a long time, honey. And don't you be bashful. This ain't the first time I've scrubbed you down, and I ain't gonna see a thing I ain't seen a hundred times before."

He was quiet after that and let me wash him and was back asleep before I got halfway across the room with the dirty water.

It took two more weeks before he could get out of bed and put on his clothes, and they just hung on him.

I couldn't help but laugh. "Why, we'll use you in the garden come spring. You can scare the crows away."

Those clear dark eyes looked at me and finally, finally I could see a little sparkle. "You remember how Granny would sew that thread through each kernel of corn before she planted them?"

Now that really got me tickled. "Lord yes, and them crows would kick their own heads off trying to get it out."

Now you have no knowledge of how good that felt to set there and laugh with him.

He set down on the bench I'd pulled over next to the fire, and I set down next to him. We watched the fire for a while and the quiet between us was a good one.

He cleared his throat. "Thank you, Arty."

"You don't need to even say that, honey." I patted his bony knee. "My memory is long, and I ain't forgot for a minute how many times you've helped me."

So much flew between me and him as we set there.

"I was a mess, weren't I?" he said.

"You was." I gathered up his hand but kept my eyes on the fire. "Are you better?"

He knew just what I meant. "I believe."

"Then you need to think about going home, honey. They need you." And then I looked at him. "But only if you're better."

He sighed. "I know it. I'll go in a few days."

"Go only if you can, honey. You was born right here in this room and they was times when I thought you was going to die here. I swear I could feel Granny right here with us. At the first I thought she'd come for you, come to get you, and I kept telling her she could not have you yet. But one night I woke up from a sound sleep and just knowed in my heart that she was here to help me. And then I knew you wouldn't die."

"I hope part of me did die, Amma."

I looked at him, studied his face, and what I saw there made me smile. "They's something cleansing about a good sick, Larkin. Just don't do it again anytime soon."

I squeezed his hand and we set that-a-way, just holding hands, for a long time.

Three days later, Larkin went home.

CHRISTMAS FELL ON SUNDAY that year and they was a big preaching at the church. The young'uns always got up and said some little play parts and such, and some one of us would get up and read from St. Luke about the holy birth. That year of all things they asked me to read it and I spent the better part of two weeks studying on it so I would not get up and make a fool out of myself. I figured I would be nervous as a sore-tailed cat in a room full of rocking chairs. And I was, until I read the first verse, and the beauty of that sweet story seeped right into my bones and I was just fine. *And there were in the same country shepherds abiding in the field keeping watch over their flock by night. And lo the angel of the Lord came upon them and the glory of the Lord shone round about them and they were sore afraid.*

There was a big hush when I finished reading and then there was a little commotion at the back of the church, and you could have knocked me over with a feather when I saw Larkin step out into the aisle and head toward the front of the church. I thought he was coming to say something to me, but he did not even look at me. He went right past me and hit his knees right there in front of the altar. It was when Mary began to shout that I understood what was happening.

I HAVE NEVER SEEN anybody commence to loving up on salvation the way Larkin did.

Larkin took to reading the Bible that very night and he sort of whispered the words to himself. *"In the beginning God created the heaven and the earth."*

It was hard reading sometimes, and there were things he didn't understand. Preacher Daniel had told him to read all of Genesis, and through the cold winter days he would come by the house and me or Zeke one would try to help him. Carolina was a good hand at reading, too, and many was the night the two of them would set and read by the firelight. Now, let me say that they was a time or two when I was tempted to quarrel at him for not being at home, but he seemed so much better that it was almost like he'd been charmed, and I did not want to be the one to break whatever spell he was under.

There were times when he got plumb aggravated with it. *Now these are the generations of the sons of Noah, Shem, Ham, and Japheth and unto them were sons born after the flood.* I agreed with him there. I mean, who was all them folks anyway, and why did they have to list every name plumb back to the beginning of time?

There were times when he pondered the words and even I was plumb struck with some of the tales. *And Abraham stretched forth his hand, and took the knife to slay his son. And the angel of the Lord called unto him out of heaven, and said, Abraham, Abraham: and he said, Here am I.*

By spring, he'd finished Genesis. By summer he'd finished Exodus and Preacher Daniel advised him to skip to Psalms and Proverbs. He even carried his Bible into the field with him, and I saw him many a time propped up on his plow right in the middle of a row with it out reading. Why, sometimes he'd set into crying and I could not help myself, I'd cry too. *Why standest thou afar off, O Lord? Why hidest thou thyself in times of trouble?* We both set there bawling like two calves in a hailstorm for a good thirty minutes when he found the words Granny had told us all those years ago when her own Pappy refused to stop singing the old love songs. *Make a joyful noise unto God, all ye lands: . . . All the earth shall worship thee, and shall sing unto thee; they shall sing to thy name.*

In church he took to singing solo, songs he chose from the old singing books. The one he held most dear was the one called "French Broad."

> High o'er the hills the mountains rise, their summits tow'r toward the skies,
> But far above them I must dwell, or sink beneath the flames of hell.
>
> Oh, God! Forbid that I should fall and lose my everlasting all;
> But may I rise on wings of love, and soar to the blest world above.
>
> Although I walk the mountains high, ere long my body low must lie,
> And in some lonesome place must rot, and by the living be forgot.

I allowed as how as long as me and him lived, Granny would not be forgotten. And he wondered how many would remember as soon as me and him went to the grave, and it hit me that he was right. That is not hard to figure if you think about it the least little bit. Recall that he had no memory of his very own mommie and daddy. I reckon that was what he meant when he said that time, "Why, Amma, once we die we might as well have been dead a million years."

But there for a while he seemed to move away from his thoughts of death and dying and put his mind on the living. He spent hours and hours with them two boys, and it was not long before you saw them out working together and hunting all through the cove and yes, you could hear them singing, too. He was finally starting to get back to himself, even if I thought he was leaning a little heavy on the church-going.

Mary had laughed to me and said, "Do you know what that Larkin said to me yesterday?"

And I was so glad to hear her laughing again and putting on weight that I felt like my face was going to split wide open, I was grinning so hard. "What did he say, honey?"

She looked at me and her cheeks was flushed with high color and her eyes was just shining. "He called me a virtuous woman whose price was far above rubies."

Yes sir, it sounded like our Larkin was back, and that he'd come a long way in figuring out how to deal with Mary just fine.

HE HAD STEPPED OUT of doors there at the house one cold winter's day right after he'd started in on the New Testament. I just happened by the table where he had his Bible out and I saw it was open to Philippians. I saw where he'd maked a passage and leaned down to read it: . . . *Work out your own salvation with fear and trembling.*

Now, that's the part of this church business that I do not like. They talk about God as a stern and vengeful one that will break a switch and just go to wearing you out at the least little thing. And it appears to me that all these people what gets a good dose of the religion gets awful high and mighty and commences to thinking that somehow they is only one way of doing things and that would be their way. They always allow that God has showed them or told them this, that, or the other. I am not too keen on this, as God has never told me nor showed me nothing.

It looked to me like Larkin Stanton was not being talked to much by God, neither, but from the looks of how his Bible was marked up, he was hunting for something awfully hard.

## 18

I HAVE HEARD FOLKS say that the biggest calm comes right before a storm. As I look back down through all these years that have made up my long life, I will have to say that this is the way it is sometimes. We'll be going right along and have no notion that things are fixing to change for us and then we'll get blindsided, and our life will just go hind end over apple cart. They was no warning a'tall that spring and summer. And I will even go so far as to say they was indeed a time of calm right before Preacher Daniel set things in motion that would change all the rest of our days.

Zeke and Larkin had gone off that spring and fetched back some tobacco seeds and we had all throwed in to grow it together. See, they was the promise of real money in 'baccer, and Lord knows we had need of that. My boys and Luke and Hack Jr. would hit them fields and work like dogs without Zeke or Larkin either one having to stay after them. And Larkin seemed more like himself than he had since he'd come from the war.

I reckon that's why it was so hard on us when it all come to pass.

ROXYANN WAS A BIG girl that summer and I remember she tended to all the young'uns while the rest of us was in the field. In that way she reminded me of myself. Seems like she was born with her hip stuck out to set a young'un on and she was always tending to and nussing young'uns. That was the first summer I really noticed what a fine voice she had. I was coming from the 'baccer field all sticky and hot and heard her singing to one of the young'uns and it was some of the best singing I'd heard in a long time. I made a note in my mind to learn her some of the old love songs and put Carolina on her as well.

See, that is what I mean about it being a peaceful time, which is not to say I don't go to singing when times is tough. Hell, sometimes that's all a body can do is sing, but it is better when the times is good.

Well, that summer went streaking by and they is several things that makes it stand out for me. I was forty years old and in June I found myself breeding again. This would be Arty's last lap-budding, and he come a big old pretty boy that would be the joy of my old age. We named him Joe Larkin. The "Larkin" ought to warn you that I was in a big way of missing my biggest boy. So here is the story of what and all happened that summer right before Larkin was set to have his thirty-second birthday.

MARY HAD ALREADY TOLD me that he was not sleeping and that he had took to wandering around and about the place in the dark. Now I knowed that meant he was fighting with something that he did not want to share with nobody, but I am sorry to have to say here that the didoes he'd cut back before he got so sick had made me not want to trust him much. I was watching him awful close. He started to fall off and his clothes got too big for him. Zeke allowed as how they was not standing around up in them fields, they was all working real hard with that 'baccer, and that this might be a good time for me to just mind my own business. That flew all over me as how I always prided myself on staying out of other people's business. I told him that sometimes I thought men was blind as bats and it was an amazement to me how they managed to find their own hind ends. So after he looked at me and shook his head and went off mumbling down into the front of his shirt, that is the last he mentioned it. I guess he knowed I was not feeling too good, and that he'd had a big part in why that was so. He pretty much left me alone over that summer. And it is probably just as well that he did.

It was not even daylight when Roxyann come running into the yard that Sunday morning. She said her mommie had sent her to fetch me. Rosalie was sick and her daddy was not home. I went with a heavy heart, scared sick thinking that awful squatting thing had somehow found its way back down the path to my biggest boy.

Mary met me at the door and her face was all pinched up. I went off the end of the porch meaning to find Larkin Stanton if I had to hunt all blessed day. That was not to be the case. I found him right off, as he had gone no further than the spring.

I didn't see him at first as the pearly light of that summer dawn had not found its way in under them big trees that stuck out over the water. I had turned to leave when he called out to me. "Amma?"

"Lord have mercy, you done about scared me to death."

"I didn't mean to scare you. You've got that chin stuck out and I know better than to mess with you now." He squatted beside me and smiled.

I looked at the sheen of dew on his clothes and his hair was wet with it. "What are you doing?"

"Just been out here woolgathering." He scooped a handful of water and wet his face. His eyes was red and he looked so tired.

"How long you been out here?"

His mouth give a little quirk. "Awhile."

I looked at him a long time without saying nothing.

Of a sudden he give me a big grin. "You aiming to paint a picture of me?"

Though he was trying awfully hard to be sweet, I did not even try to take the sharp edges off my voice. I was not going to put up with the foolishness I'd let roll over my head before. "Mary sent Roxyann for me before daylight. Rosalie is sick, Larkin, and you'd laid out all night." I know my chin was way out and I let her stay there.

His face got all worried and on the inside I give a big sigh of relief. Maybe me and God did not have so big a fight on our hands as I'd been getting my pigs set for. We headed back toward the house and he never said a word. And I never neither. I left him going in the house and I went on home. This was a preaching Sunday and I had my own herd to get ready.

PREACHER DANIEL WAS ALREADY in the chair behind the altar by the time we got there. All that running about before daylight had caused me to run late, and my bunch was as grumpy and sulled up as a bunch of possums. Hack Jr. and Luke was setting at the back when we went in, but Larkin and Roxyann was up next to the front and had saved us a seat. I asked Roxy where her mommie was and she whispered she'd stayed at home with Rosalee. I hushed then because the preacher stood up and smoothed back his thinning hair and walked to the altar. He laid his worn Bible gently on the stand, and looked out at us and everybody seemed to set up a little straighter and leaned toward him. He managed to keep my mind from wandering, which in my estimation made him a very fine preacher.

"Welcome, brothers and sisters!" His big strong voice boomed out into the room, and he motioned his hand toward the open windows. "It is a glorious day God has provided us with to come together to worship in his holy name. Amen?"

A bunch of people hollered "amen" back at him.

"Then I say let's raise our voices up to Him in song. Just like David told us to do. Let's sing 'Ninety-fifth.'" He held his Bible up and raised it above his head. He laughed delightedly. "And like the song says, 'When I can read my title clear to mansions in the skies, I bid farewell to every fear, and wipe my weeping eyes!'"

The congregation broke into full-voiced singing of the old hymn.

When I can read my title clear to mansions in the skies
I bid farewell to ev'ry fear and wipe my weeping eyes.

Would earth against my soul engage, and fiery darts be hurl'd,
Then I can smile at Satan's rage and face a frowning world.

Let cares like a wild deluge come, let storms of sorrow fall,
So I but safely reach my home, my God, my heav'n, my all.

There I shall bathe my weary soul in seas of heav'nly rest,
And not a wave of trouble roll across my peaceful breast.

Preacher Daniel had a look of pure-D rapture on his face and he rared back and hollered, "So I but safely reach my home, my God, my heaven, my all! Hallaleuer! Glory be to His blessed, blessed name! Amen! And amen!" He took out his handkerchief and wiped his brow and then his mouth. "As I was riding here yesterday I was a worried man. I usually am led by strong conviction. I *know* what I'll be preaching on before I ever get on that old horse tied out yonder!

The Lord puts them thoughts in my heart and the words come pouring out like He wants 'em to."

Preacher Daniel looked down at us and his face wore a wreath of sorrow. "But not a word come into my heart yesterday, ner last night, ner even this morning as I was coming here. But when I heard that song, that old wonderful song, I knowed what God wanted me to talk about here today. Listen to hit again: 'So I but safely reach my home . . .' No sweeter thought, brothers and sisters, than to know I'm going home one of these days. I'm going home!" He quit talking and looked back and forth at us all. "Do you know whether you're going home one of these glorious days? Can ye say, in the darkest part of the night, to yeself, 'Yessir! One of these days me and old Preacher Dan'l will stroll arm in arm over heaven together'?"

Throughout the room several folks closed their eyes and started rocking back and forth, and a few of them went to shouting.

"Some of ye can say, 'Yes, Preacher! I *will* see ye up yonder!'" He pointed his finger toward the ceiling, then set in to pointing at different people in the crowd. "Sister Ethel! I know, praise the Lord, that me and you will celebrate one of these days around the throne! And you, Brother Carl!" The preacher began to laugh. "Ever single time that door back yonder opens, Brother Carl is pawing the ground to git in. And them little babies, if they went right now, in the blink of an eye, why they'd be rocking in the arms of angels!" He wiped his face and opened his Bible up. "Some of ye knows what hit takes to git into heaven, praise God. You've lived it! Amen! But there's them amongst you that ain't guaranteed your place in Glory. Hit's them that God wants me to talk to today." He lowered his eyes and began to read, "Luke, chapter fifteen, verse seven. 'I say unto you that likewise joy shall be in heaven over one sinner that repenteth more than over ninety-nine just persons, which need no repentance.'" He looked at us and his countenance was sad. "Them's Jesus' words folks. More joy over one sinner that seeks redemption than ninety-nine folks that needs none."

"Bless him, Lord!" screamed out Ethel from right behind me. I swear that scared me so much that my hind end come plumb off that bench.

"That's a big old word, ain't it? Redemption. But that's what hit's all about, friends. Redemption. What did the prodigal son receive from his daddy? Even after he'd took his daddy's gold and squandered it? Even after he'd broke his old daddy's heart? When he come back dragging his tail end behind him, what did his father do? He forgive him. Took him in his old arms and loved him. He give him redemption. And that's what God does fer us. When we beg, and I mean *beg*." He pointed his finger at Carl. "Ain't that right, Brother Carl?"

"That's right, Preacher." Carl answered.

"Amen! And amen!" the preacher shouted. "And when we beg long enough and hard enough, long enough to where"—he laughed and patted his knees—"till they's scabs and calluses on these old kneecaps, then we receive redemption. And we're forgived of all the sins, all the pain of this old life is lifted off us, and we are pure again. Pure as any of these little babes laying in their mommies' arms. All them black spots that sin marks our souls with are gone!"

He smiled. "The Lord's moving in this little church today!" He gazed out at the congregation and paused. "I feel it so strong I want to sing about it. Let's all sing the old song 'Redemption.'"

Come all ye young people of ev'ry relation, come listen a while
    and to you I will tell

How I was first called to seek for salvation, redemption in Jesus,
who saved me from hell.

I was not yet sixteen when Jesus first call'd me, to think of my
soul and the state I was in;
I saw myself standing a distance from Jesus, between me and him
was a mountain of sin.

The devil perceived that I was convinced, he strove to persuade
me that I was too young,
That I would get weary before my ascension, and wish that I had
not so early begun.

Sometimes he'd persuade me that Jesus was partial, when he was
setting poor sinners free
That I was forsaken and quite reprobated, and there was no
mercy at all for poor me.

The preacher looked out at us and waved his Bible. "It's all right
here. The word and the way. You'll find everything you need right
here." He tapped the cover with a gentle hand. "There is mercy and
salvation for us all. All we need do is confess our sins, beg forgiveness.
And then we have it. It's ours." He smiled. "Redemption."

## 19

IT IS FUNNY HOW words can be treated different by folks. I felt it was a pretty decent service and I told the preacher as much as I was leaving that day. And it's funny as I have often said what we recall from days when our life takes a turn from the way it seemed destined to go. I mean, for all the world I thought we was all in good shape— me, Zeke, Mary, Larkin, and all our young'uns. We was doing good with the 'baccer, and money would soon be rolling in. We stood out in front of the church house that day and talked with Larkin about what and all needed doing in the next few days. He never so much as let on that something had settled down right next to his very soul and was taking great big bites out of it. And I am sorry to say that I did not catch it, though I stood right up in his face yapping away about 'baccer and the topping of it. The last I seed of him was his big broad back going off down the road with his young'uns.

It would be almost two years before I'd see him again.

I HONESTLY DON'T KNOW what I'd have done if it had not been for Zeke, God bless him. I was big as a cow with Joe Larkin that fall and though I was not sick one bit in the body, my heart was absolutely broke. Every time Aunt Susan come by the house on her mule carrying the mail I would go rushing out to ask, "Is they anything a'tall for me?" and she would look at me with a world of sadness and say "No, honey, they ain't a thing." You will just have to imagine how it was for me because they is no words to tell you of how I suffered.

When Larkin went walking off with his young'uns that day he'd got about halfway home and then had told Roxy to tell Mary he had to do something and would be on in a bit. Then it was like he'd fell off the face of the earth. All the next day they hunted for him and come up with nothing, and they kept on hunting for a solid week. As you might figure, Mary was perfectly wild. When Zeke made the call to stop looking, she was fit to be tied and I was too. I went up to the cave and they was no sign of him. I stood there in it and looked around at what was there and felt all done in. They was still some of Hackley's things and I don't know, it just made me feel so lonesome and hurt. Zeke finally said, "Arty, you're going to have to let this go." And though I knowed he was speaking the truth, it was hard for me to do. That was one of the few times in my life that all I could do was pray. But as with lots of them times, I did not know if God had Arty on the top of his list and sometimes I felt I might as well be praying to the wind for all the good it done.

I knowed when Mary got a letter from Larkin because Aunt Susan told it to me. I went straight as a shot to Mary and stood around for the better part of a whole day waiting for her to offer to let me read it, but she did not. I went home and cried for an hour to Zeke. Carolina finally said, "Mommie, it is between them." And Zeke said, "Leave your mommie alone, missy." I tried and tried to do that, but finally I had to ask Mary if she could just tell me that he was all right and she looked up at me and I ain't never seen such a look on nobody's face as the one she offered me. "He is in Charleston and is well, Arty." I did not dare ask anything else. At least I knowed he had not gone off somewheres and lost his mind. I done the best I could to comfort myself with just the knowing of that.

JOE LARKIN WAS BORN in March and I knowed in my heart somehow that he would be my last. There is something in a woman that goes to mourning when she births for the last time, and so it was with me. But you know it seemed like I was in a constant state of mourning that next little bit. Mommie died in May and Daddy fell dead at the milk gap that summer. That was an awful time for me as it seemed like everybody I loved was leaving me. They is something that happens to us when our mommie and daddy dies. It is like we have to step up into their shoes and they is no bigger footprints in this world. I grieved and grieved and then grieved some more. And I was watching Mary grieve, too, and she was not like me in that she had no grave to go to and mourn over. A grave does serve some purpose, you know.

LARKIN HAD BEEN GONE over a year when I was out hunting the cows and come up on Mary there on the ridge between the Shop Holler and the Munsen Cove. She was just standing there all wrapped up in Larkin's big blue coat, and I felt sorry for her when I looked in her face. I said howdy to her in my softest voice, and she looked at me with eyes as old as time itself and I was struck with how she looked to have aged ten years in the last two. I asked her what she was doing out. She sort of smiled and said, "Probably for the same reason as you." And we stood for a while looking off back into Tennessee where you could see the snow coming in. And then in a voice as flat as a flitter, she said these words to me that I have never forgot.

"I am so very tired, Arty. I woke up this morning and thought I heard somebody screaming, but it were just the wind hitting the side of the house. I laid there a long time trying to draw comfort from the sounds of my young'uns sleeping, but it did not work its charm on me like it usually does. I find no comfort nowhere."

I went to stand next to her and took her cold little hand in mine. It was like ice and I chapped it between mine till she finally pulled it back. Oh, how I wanted to ask her if she'd heard from him, but I held my tongue. To tell you the truth, I don't think I wanted to hear what she might have to say.

Then it started to snow. "We ought to get in out of the weather," I said.

"They is nowhere I can go that it is not cold, Arty," she said.

That hurt me as bad as anything I'd ever heard, and I'm ashamed to say that I wanted away from her and her cold little hands and her sad little face and her heart that was so badly broke. I went off and left her standing there by herself.

My heart was not just broke, it was shattered, and I could not stand no more.

LATE THAT SPRING MAGGIE come by the house. She was a sight to see and was all decked out in a fine dress and soft leather shoes and had that big mane of glossy hair done up in coils on top of her head. She looked a vision and I told her so. Her and Silas was up there seeing about her house and she asked about Larkin and Mary. Her eyes got bigger and bigger when I told her what had happened. They stayed on for supper and it was a good visit. She wrote to me when she got back home and said they'd gone by Mary's on the way out the next day, and peace had been made between her and Mary. Time does have a way of fixing things up. Though you might not believe that, I will tell you that it does. What she said in her letter is this: "Me and you and Mary has many things between us, Arty, the least of which is your brother and Larkin. We are all women what has eaten us a big mess of life and I suspect they is more of it on our plates to eat before we leave this world. We need to try to help each other as we go along."

And Maggie was exactly right. The three of us went right on eating for a long, long time.

LATE THAT SUMMER AUNT Susan hollered me from the house and she had a grin on her face as big as a mile. There was the letter that had been two years in the coming, but for all that time it were but a short thing.

Dearest Amma,
I am coming home.
Larkin

And it was like a dam busted inside of me and I cried and cried and cried.

I did not feel honor-bound to tell Mary as she had not done so with me. And it were a good thing, as the days passed and he did not come. My heart would set up a great racing with each sound from the road, but each time they would pass me by. By the end of August it was like the letter had never come at all.

Do not get it wrong here. I harbored no hard feelings toward Mary. I loved her better than my own sister. It is just that when you mixed her sad in with mine, it was a heavier load than I could tote. But I did feel bound to help her in any way I could, and when she sent Luke to get me to help her put up her corn, I went with nary a word.

That day was hot as Satan's housecat and we'd been out in the field most of the day and had left the boys to keep pulling corn. Me and Mary was out behind the house shucking as hard as we could and I could hear Roxy out in front singing where we'd put her to silking and washing it. I even recall that she was singing "Little Margaret." And then right in the middle she just quit. Now, my head come up right off, because we generally do not stop in the middle of a song, and my ears was straining for the next words. Mary was, too, and so it was that both of us was listening hard and had no trouble hearing her give a little scream. Quick as lightning me and her was up running for the house. Mary went in low through the back door and I knowed she was going for the shotgun that was always loaded and setting in the corner. I went around the house at a run and did not even stop to think of myself. My heart leapt into my throat when I come out into the clearing and saw Roxy sort of grappling around with a big man with shoulder-length black hair and I thought to myself, *Lord have mercy, what is a Indian doing here?* That is exactly what it looked like. Out of the corner of my eye I saw Mary come out on the porch and bring the gun up to her shoulder. I thought for all the world that she was going to shoot them both, so I hollered, "No, no, Mary, you'll hit her too." And when he heard my voice the big man turned Roxy loose and I saw his face.

Oh, but it was Larkin standing there.

Then a voice called from inside the cabin. "Mommie, Luke is at his back with the rifle and I'm coming out onto the porch." Hack Jr. come out then and stood beside his mommie. From where I was, I could see that he knowed Larkin but his eyes stayed as cold as ice.

It seemed like we was all froze in time. All except for my eyes and it seemed like they was everywhere at once. It seemed like I could see everything that was happening in a glance, and I thought that at any minute Mary would lay down the gun and everything would be as it should. But that did not happen for too long, and then I knowed something was bad wrong.

"Come over here, Roxy," Mary said, and my heart literally quit beating.

"Mommie, it's Daddy. Can't you see that?"

"I see him. You come on over here anyways."

Roxy looked at me. "Aunt Arty?" she said, and then she took a step away from her daddy and I heard the hammers on that shotgun being pulled back and it sounded loud as hell in that little clearing. I did not even think about it.

I just stepped out into that hot sun and put myself in between Mary and Larkin.

"Luke, you get on up here," I said, and I waited until he was standing there with his daddy.

When he saw his boy Larkin said, "Ah, Luke," and reached and gathered him up close to him. I could see Luke's face over Larkin's shoulder, and his eyes held no welcome for his daddy.

"Get on in the house with all of you young'uns," I said. My voice was rough as a cob and I meant for it to be that way.

"Do not interfere with this, Arty," Mary said to me. I felt my chin come out like a rock cliff.

"You make them young'uns go in that house, Mary, and I mean it. They are innocent lambs in this and should not have to bear it."

This give her pause just as I'd hoped it would, and while she was arguing with them I planted myself closer to Larkin. I never took my eyes off Mary and did not even have time to so much as speak to him before the door shut on them young'uns.

"Get out of my way, Arty."

I felt my guts go to water, but I did not move. "No, I will not."

We all stood there and I could feel the sweat break loose and go to running down between my shoulder blades. I could not stand it no more, and I turned my back on her and faced my biggest boy.

His black eyes was watching me like a hawk and his hair was wet with sweat. His shirt looked wet enough to where I could've wrung the water from it with my hands. "Oh, Larkin," I said right low to him, "what is this about?"

From behind me Mary said, "Tell her, Larkin, as I have not."

He flinched at her words. Finally he said to her, though he was looking me eyeball to eyeball, "You should have told her as I asked you to."

Mary give a big sigh and I heard the shotgun thump down on the porch. When I looked back at her, she was setting on the top step with the gun beside her. "What, Larkin? What should she have told me?"

And Mary laughed, but it was not a happy laugh. "Tell her, Larkin."

Larkin reached out a hand to me but let it drop back to his side before I had time to do anything. "Oh, God. Where will I start?"

"At the beginning, Larkin," Mary said and her voice seemed to echo around in my head.

Of a sudden I couldn't stand there in that sun another minute, and I said, "We're coming to set on the porch, Mary. I feel like I'm going to fall up."

Larkin grabbed hold of my arm and I went and set down beside Mary. He moved a little away from us but kept to the shade of the porch. And then he started to talk.

He said he'd been west to Missouri, south to Florida, and north to Boston since he'd been gone. He'd seen some pretty places and kept company with some pretty rough characters and allowed as that was all right since he was every bit as rough. He had even joined up with a minstrel show and had done a fair bit of singing from the stage. But he said he knowed now that every single step he'd made away from home that he was just making his way back.

I peeped at Mary and she was just staring out toward the barn. I couldn't help it when I said, "I know this is bad, Mary, but surely not bad enough to kill him for. I mean I'd feel the same way I reckon if it was Zeke, but I don't know that I'd take a shotgun after him." I have to tell you here that when I set down, I put my hind end right square on that gun and nothing short of Gabriel blowing his horn could have got me off of it. And maybe not even that.

She give me a look. "Quit wallering the truth around, Larkin," she said. "Tell her like you told it to me in your letter. Or I will one."

We set there and all was quiet. Then he give a great sigh and all the hair stood up on my arms, and I almost capped my hand over his mouth to keep him from saying what he aimed to say.

"Amma," he breathed and then he told me.

"It seems I have carried this thing for all my life, but it has only been with me since the day before I brought Hackley home throwed over that mule. Me and him had a big fuss the night before the Battle of Winding Stairs. It seems like that's all we done there at the last was fuss and fight with each other. I did love him." Mary made a little sound on that and he glanced quick at her, but then his eyes come right back to where they'd been holding mine. "You will probably hate me all the more for the saying of that one thing, Amma. But I did love him.

"I didn't hardly sleep a wink the night before the fight. To tell you the truth, I just sort of dozed around dreaming all manner of foolish things. I was up long before we was called to form up. Right at daylight I went to find Hackley and try to put things right between us. But when I found him he was sound asleep and I did not wake him.

"We formed up in a double V on either side of the road as it topped the mountain. Kirk put the tallest of us in the back and the shortest out in front and us sharpshooters was right in the middle. I could see Hackley right down in front of me. Then the Rebels come around the curve below us and all hell broke loose. It didn't take us long to turn them back and of a sudden a big wind come blowing down the hill and took the smoke off with it, and I saw Hackley getting up. He come up on his knees and sort of turned toward me. He was looking me right in the eyes and he knowed it before he hit the ground. I had shot him and he was dead and gone by the time I got to him."

And there it was. Now you might wonder how I felt hearing him relate the death of my brother to me like that, and I will have to say that I am still in amazement to this day. They was a brief little flare of pain way down in my heart and I immediately thought how this would hurt Mommie and Daddy and then I recalled that they was beyond this. So I let that go. Then I thought on their young'uns and I knowed right off that they had all knowed it for a long time and that's why they had acted the way they had a while ago. The only one that would not forgive him was maybe Hack Jr. and I couldn't swear to that. I searched my own heart again and for just a minute Hackley's face danced in the air right in front of me. But he'd been gone for so very long and though I was sorry, they was no way to change it. We have to go on and life is for the living.

I LOOKED OVER AT Mary and she was staring at Larkin. "What is it?" she said, and then she laughed. "Oh, I know what it is. You're thinking Roxyann looks more like me than I do myself."

I saw on his face that she'd caught him fair and square, but, bless his heart, he tried to deny it. "No, no," he said. "You look just like you always did."

And I thought to myself, *You still can't lie worth a damn.* Then I realized that was what hurt me more than anything else about all this mess. He had not come to *me* with it.

Then Mary said in a real soft voice. "Well, did you find your redemption, Larkin Stanton?"

"Leave him be, Mary," I said and my voice sounded old as Methuselah.

"Oh, I aim to leave him be, Arty. I just want to know since he wrote me so many letters about how he was searching for redemption."

Larkin stepped toward her but I held up my hand at him. "No. You leave her be, too," and I meant that as much as I'd ever meant anything in my life.

"Your forgiveness is all that matters to me, Mary."

She laughed out loud. "I think not, Larkin. The only thing that has mattered to you for a long time is yourself."

I could tell that her laughing had hurt him as bad as her words.

"That's not true, Mary. I've always done for everybody else. Amma, you, and, yes, even Hackley. He always had everything, the best of everything. He always got everything he wanted. Even you. He was not a good man, Mary, and he didn't deserve you."

Mary stared at him. "What are you talking about? His women, his not wanting to fight in the war, what?"

"Well, all of that."

She nodded. "Let's talk about that word redemption some more, Larkin." She leaned toward him. "What do you think would've happened if Hackley had lived?"

"Why, I don't know, nobody knows." He was flustered and I could tell this was not something he wanted to talk about, but I was curious and I wanted to hear what she had to say.

"You know what I think? I think he would've probably got shot by some woman's husband or bigged some young gal and left me for her." She pushed the hair back from her face. "I've not aged well."

What he did then reminded me of Carolina when she was in a big playacting fit and was going about the house all draped in one of my quilts and talking foolishness. I couldn't even feel sorry for him, though I did almost laugh. "You are the darling of my life. Will you say you've forgiven me, honey?"

She waved a tired hand at him. "Oh, get up, Larkin. Go on. Leave."

He got up and his face was red as fire. She looked at his big self there in the yard, sweaty and dusty, and she give him the gentlest of smiles.

That sliced him plumb to the bone.

"You wanted a big show of some kind, didn't you?" she asked him. "Me crying, the young'uns wailing and carrying on, you orating, vowing to love me forever and all. Larkin, you have worn me out. Go on and leave. I'm not taking you back."

My head was going back and forth between them so fast that I was making myself drunk, and I swear they were acting like I was not even setting there.

"But you've got to," he sputtered.

"No, I don't. I went from Daddy's daughter to Hackley's wife to your wife and I'll not have it again where a man can boss me and tell me what to do."

And I could not help it, I thought, *Go it, Mary.*

"But, Mary, I can't live without you. You're my redemption."

This time her laughter carried a measure of sadness with it. "No, honey, I ain't your redemption now no more than I was before. I'm just a real tired woman."

"Hackley would've wanted me to look after you. He told me that before he went off to the war."

"I know, I know. Poor little Mary, she needs tending to, looking after. Well, not no more she don't." She stood up. "It's sort of funny, Larkin. How you provided for me and Hackley."

He looked at her. "Lord have mercy, Mary, I ruined everybody's life."

"No, Larkin, you didn't. You give me the chance to be something I always wanted to be. Strong and able to do things for myself, depending on nobody but me."

He gave a bitter laugh. "Well, so I helped you by going off and making you be strong. I didn't help Hackley, though. I just murdered him."

I could hold my tongue no longer. "Oh, Larkin, didn't you hear what she said awhile ago? About what might've happened to Hackley if he'd lived? Don't you see, honey? He died with dignity, not caught in the bed with some man's wife. You give him a noble death in the war. In a way you give Hackley a good, decent way out."

The smile that lit Mary's face offered us the girl she once was. "Now you all go on while I go in and try to make sense of this for the young'uns." A frown puckered her brow. "I can't promise you'uns nothing where they're concerned. Roxy has always been her daddy's girl, Rosalie will go with her sister. Luke I don't know about; he's awfully close to Hack Jr." The frown deepened. "Hack Jr. is not a good age for this. He's all full of piss and vinegar. Larkin, I don't want you to even try to talk to him right now. He's a lot like his daddy was. Arty, maybe you can try a bit later." Her eyes met mine and held.

I give her a little smile and said "Time will take care of it. Just like it takes care of everything else," I said.

Her eyes went to Larkin when he said, "Can I come to see you?"

"I don't think so," she said. "I don't think I want you to."

"But I love you," he said and the truth of it was in his eyes.

"Time will take care of that, too. You go on now, Larkin."

"The young'uns?"

"Roxy will find you, don't worry." I come up off the porch and offered her the gun. Her hand was on the latch when she turned. "You're not a bad man, Larkin. You really ain't."

And she closed the door softly behind her.

## 20

I HAVE LAID THE picture out one more time and have run my hands over it. I do not need to see it to know what it looks like. I wish you could see it. Larkin and Hackley are all dressed up in their uniform suits. They was both such handsome men that you can see why they each got a little piece of Mary's heart. Larkin is setting in the chair and Hackley is standing beside him. I reckon the picture-taking man set them up that way because Larkin was so much higher than my brother. I recall his face looks solemn as a judge and his eyes and hair is black as a crow's wing. Hackley's eyes looks almost white, and it is left for my old blind eyes to remember the color of them, which was like the blue-eyed grass. He is standing with his pistol out and his elbow is resting on Larkin's shoulder. His hat is cocked over to the side of his head and his face is just full of devilment. Hackley's got his fiddle in his other hand. I'm glad in a way that I can no longer see it, as it used to hurt me so. See, the picture was took right before they left for Morganton and Winding Stairs. One month later and the deed was done forever.

I think Larkin did find his redemption. Him and Carolina come by here awhile ago and she fixed supper for me. They sung a few songs while they was in the kitchen and it done my heart good. Oh, I did not tell you that he married Carolina, did I? Well, he did, and though I fought it and threatened all manner of hellfire and brimstone would be throwed at their heads, it has worked out in the end.

Just like everything else. Time has took care of it.

If I live a few more hours it will be 1920. If I live three more months eighty-four years will have rolled over my head. I have hoed a long row. It ain't always been easy, but Lord it has been worth it. I have raised eight young'uns counting Larkin. And never, no, not for a minute, have I forgot the two I buried. My rough old hands was the very ones that eased most of my own grandbabies into this world. I have laughed more than most folks and I have cried just as much. I have lived hard at times, not so hard at others, and even let some days plumb get away from me. But who has not done the same? I have give and I have took. I have had a good run.

The smell of lilacs, cold spring water in my mouth on a hot summer day, the colors of fall, the sound of falling snow.

And what of the greatest of all? What of love? Oh, I have knowed love. Love was blue eyes that growed darker when he looked at me.

My hands move over the wooden bowl of a soup ladle with a broken handle and a verse from an old love song goes through my head.

> So fare you well, my old true love,
> So fare you well for a while.
> If I go I'll come again,
> If I go ten thousand miles.

Some things is just too rich for words.

# Acknowledgments

THIS STORY IS BASED on family history. Hackley Norton was my grandfather's uncle and he did die in the Battle of Winding Stairs in June 1864. Larkin Stanton did survive the war. His grave stone is located at Walnut, North Carolina. Arty was indeed Hackley's sister and she is buried on a hilltop in Sodom. The other names, characters, and events exist only in my very active imagination or, if real, are used fictitiously and are not in any way intended to represent specific persons.

There are so many people to thank for their great insight, inspiration, and support: First and most important—Jim Taylor, my husband, traveling buddy, and Muse—*there hath been no greater love*—and I could not have written this book without his ear and support. My beloved children, Melanie Rice, Hart Barnhill, and Andrew Barnhill. Lee Smith, my friend and favorite writer, for her unflagging support and encouragement. My agent, Stella Connell, who believed in me enough to take a chance. My editor, Kathy Pories, for her genius, her amazing insight and sensitivity, and for helping me to turn Arty loose to tell this tale. Aidan Quinn for listening and then convincing me I needed to write this story. Renni Browne for her editing suggestions in the early stages of writing this book. The ballad singers of Sodom—Dellie Chandler Norton, Berzillia Wallin, Cas and Vergie Wallin, Evelyn Ramsey, Inez Chandler, and Doug Wallin—they were the keepers of the old songs and their voices are heard throughout this book. My sister, June Gahagan, for reading the book in its infancy and for being the calm at the center of what can sometimes be life's raging storm. My much loved and appreciated aunt Robenia and uncle Wayne Adams for being two of my most valuable resource people. My cousin Jerry Adams for jogging my memory and for supplying me with so much important information. My other cousins, Sharon Ray, Janet Adams Crowe, Sue Vilcinskas, and Keith Ray for listening, encouraging, and just setting on the porch with me while I rambled on and on. My uncle Ward and aunt Almarie Adams. Joe Penland, Bobby McMillon, and Marilyn McMinn McCredie for their lifelong friendship, music, old sayings, sharp wits, and unfailing ability to keep me grounded and laughing. Josh Goforth for his keen ear and musical genius. Laura Boosinger for the years of friendship and help with the selections and singings of the shape-note hymns. Wayne Martin and George Holt for over thirty years of priceless advice and sharing of frailties. David Perry and Linda Hobson for their much valued input. Lydia Hamessley, Sandy Ballard, William Jolliff, Bill and Fritzi Wisdom, Mimi Wright, Susan Graham, and literally countless other friends and fans that have helped me in so many different ways. Sonia Wallace, Vicki Skemp, James Leva, Amy Rabb, Susan Smith, Robbie Gualding, and Carol Elizabeth Jones for their encouraging words at the very beginning. Martha Fowler for handing me the little "gem" I used in the book. Randall Garrison, who showed Jim and me where the battle of Winding Stairs took place. Taylor Barnhill and Dave McGrew for sharing their knowledge of what this part of the world would have looked like in the 1800s. The Mountain Retreat and Learning Centers for providing the most beautiful place in the world where I wrote most of this book.

The following books and writers provided me with invaluable information on the political climate during this period in western North Carolina's history: *The Heart of Confederate Appalachia: Western North Carolina in the Civil War* by John C. Inscoe and Gordon B. McKinney; *Bushwhackers: The Civil War in North Carolina: The Mountains* by William R. Trotter; *Kirk's Raiders: A Notorious Band of Scoundrels and Thieves* by Matthew Bumgarner; *The Papers of Zebulon Baird Vance* edited by Frontis W. Johnston; *Mason Jars in the Flood and Other Stories* by Gary Carden.

I so wish these people were still here to read the book since it was from their recollections that I got the bones on which I hung the meat: Ervin and Neple Adams, Wayne Adams, Myrtle Ray, Fannie Leake, Jean Adams Sizemore, Bob and Emily Norton, Andrew and Mirlie Adams, and Father Andrew Graves. As Mama and Daddy so often said, "Family really is the most important thing in this world . . ."

For all those I have not mentioned I can only say this—you are of my heart, my family, my culture, and I love you—thank you for allowing me to be a part of your lives. And I have to give special thanks and a world of respect to all my Elderhostelers for their great wisdom and humor, and for teaching me the valuable lesson that no matter where we come from, we are all family in our hearts.

*My Old True Love*

SHEILA KAY ADAMS

*A Reader's Guide*

# A Conversation with Sheila Kay Adams

*Sheila Kay Adams talks with her youngest son,
Andrew Barnhill, about the writing of* My Old True Love,
*their ancestors, and the traditions they both love.
Andrew is also a writer, musician, and singer of the old
songs. He lives in Mars Hill, North Carolina.*

**Andrew Barnhill:** What inspired you to write a novel like *My Old True Love*?

**Sheila Kay Adams:** The inspiration for the novel came from a story Daddy told me. It was the first Saturday in June and we'd spent it cleaning off graves, since Sunday was our family's Decoration Day. We were resting on the porch drinking water from quart jars.

"WE MUST'VE CLEANED off every grave in Sodom, Daddy."
Daddy laughed. "Lord no, honey. They's old graveyards all over the place. We couldn't get to all of them if we worked a solid week." He pointed off across the valley. "There's one up yonder on the spine of the Pilot. See them pine trees?"
"Who's buried up there?"
"I believe that's where they buried your great-uncle, Hackley Norton, after the battle of Winding Stairs during the Civil War. They said Larkin Stanton brought him all the way from Rip-Shin throwed across the back of a mule."

"Who was Larkin Stanton?"

Daddy got this look on his face that let me know a good story was fixing to be told.

"Well, Larkin Stanton was born an orphan . . ."

IT WAS DARK when he finished the story. Of course Daddy had to take me up there later in the summer to see the graves of Hackley and Mary. And one Saturday on the way home from Marshall, we went by the cemetery at Walnut where Larkin Stanton was buried. Seeing their graves made such an impression on me. Over the years I guess Daddy retold that story a dozen times.

I actually wrote it first as a short story and it was in with a bunch of stories Lee Smith convinced me to send to the University of North Carolina Press. There were so many Civil War stories in the submitted manuscript that my editor culled them and said I ought to keep them for another book. Boy, am I ever glad that happened! Otherwise the story would've been published in *Come Go Home with Me* in 1995.

After Daddy's death in 1998, I felt I needed to do something with all the great stories he'd told me through the years.

In 1999, I was hired as singing coach for the movie *Songcatcher,* and over that summer I got to know the actor Aidan Quinn. We swapped a lot of stories back and forth, but it was the one about Hackley and Larkin that caught his ear. He was convinced it would make a great movie and encouraged me to write a screenplay. We worked together on it over that winter, but my heart kept telling me it should be a novel.

My heart won out.

**AB:** As children you entertained us with stories from your childhood. While reading the book, I must admit I saw parts and pieces of those same stories, and some of the personalities seemed awfully familiar. How does your flair for storytelling influence your writing?

**SKA:** As you well know, we don't have normal conversations in our family. I think you were the one who came up with "story-speak" to describe how we communicate. And in every story there are these great turns of phrase, speech peppered with fine old sayings, long uninterrupted pauses. Listening to Daddy and his brothers talk in "story-speak" was where I developed my ear for catching and being able to tell a good tale.

The only problem with this (if it is a problem) is that all the voices telling stories in my head speak with a mountain accent. So I have a tendency to write with an accent as well. I had to tone it down quite a bit for the book. I had a great editor, Kathy Pories, who worked really hard helping me keep the flavor and flow without making it such a huge distraction for the reader.

Many people who've read the book have also seen me perform from the stage. They all say my voice was right there in their heads the whole time they were reading.

So after having said all that, I guess I would have to say my writing is really just storytelling from the page.

**AB:** Your depictions of southern Appalachia are, at times, both chillingly desperate and vividly beautiful. Describe how such an extreme variety of climates made a difference in the lives of your characters and your ancestors.

**SKA:** I have traveled all over and still feel like I live in one of the most beautiful places in the world. But it can also be awfully harsh. One hard winter in the mountains usually sends folks who aren't accustomed to it scurrying for better climes. And if we think it's challenging now, think what it must've been like when our people started showing up back in the mid-1700s.

I don't think it's really possible for any of us today to imagine what it must've been like for those first settlers. It would've been the harshest sort of existence that would've called for a lot of determination. Mama said they were borderland Scots who moved to Northern Ireland during the reign of James I and from there they came here. They were called Scotch-Irish and they came for land, and they meant to have them some too. Daddy described them as clannish, hard-living, quick-to-anger people who would fight you just as soon as look at you. You know, I reckon they could have left, gone somewhere easier. But they stayed, generation after generation, and figured out not only how to survive, but developed a love of place that is pretty remarkable. And most of the folks I knew had this remarkably dry, sophisticated sense of humor. They were and still are some of finest people in the world.

Arty, the narrator of *My Old True Love,* exhibits a certain resiliency that I saw in a lot of my kinfolk over in Sodom. She has that deep love of and connectedness to place and family. She also has a keen understanding of what she needs to do to survive. There was a sort of gentle hardness about her that I saw in the women and heard stories about while I was growing up over home.

The beauty of the place and the harsh reality of it would've shaped a special kind of people: accepting but very determined, independent of spirit but also with a certain sense of community. That's what I tried to get across in the novel.

**AB:** Edgar Allan Poe, among many others, once wrote of wild races of uncouth men living in the southern Appalachian Mountains. How would you address this stereotype, and how is it different from the culture you developed in you novel?

**SKA:** I remember watching *The Beverly Hillbillies* and *Hee Haw* and howling right along with the canned laughter. I had no idea they were making fun of us. I grew up in such a loving, close-knit community that I didn't realize these stereotypes even existed until I got into college. I was introduced to that business when a girl from Myrtle Beach asked me if we really married our first cousins. I still chuckle at my totally innocent answer.

"Lord, no," I said. "You have to get down to second or third cousins before you can marry."

Back during World War II, Mama and Daddy went down to Mobile, Alabama, to work in the shipyards. Mama said they made such fun of her accent that she practiced in front of a mirror trying to lose it. She thought it was pretty funny that she worked so hard to lose the very thing I get paid to do.

I guess I can understand how folks from outside the area might have seen my ancestors as somewhat lacking in social graces. I mean, let's be honest—they would've been pretty rough characters.

But where outsiders were way off the mark was in assuming these Appalachian people were lacking in culture. They were well blessed with that.

The culture in the book was the one I grew up in, and I wanted to provide an insider's perception for readers to dispel, with any luck, some of the old stereotypes. You know, I'm often puzzled how folks from outside the area still feel comfortable making fun of us. Honestly, I wish I had a nickel for every time a person comes up to me after a performance to share some completely unacceptable joke about mountain people. With a straight face they will say things about us that they would *never* say about any other ethnic group. I think that's pretty sad.

**AB:** At the end of one of her novels, Alice Walker describes herself as an author and a medium. Did you have any similar experiences while writing *My Old True Love*?

**SKA:** That's really interesting, because there were times when I felt like I was channeling Arty, that she was talking through me. I would wake up during the night with her voice talking so loud in my head that I would have to get up and write what she was saying. Sometimes she talked faster than I could write. My husband, Jim Taylor, went over to Knoxville to do some research on George Washington Kirk and found enlistment papers for Hackley and Larkin that had their physical descriptions written on them. Can you believe that descriptions I'd written a couple of months before were right on the money? When Zeke left for the war I swear I felt depressed for days, and I cried the whole time I was writing the chapter when Sylvaney and Ingabo died.

There were days when I would get impatient and try to bull my way through without her and what I wrote during those times was somehow lacking. It just didn't ring true, so I'd have to go back and say, "All right, Arty, let's get to it."

When I wrote the last sentence in *My Old True Love*, she was gone. I went through a period of really missing her, mourning the loss of her, I guess.

When I started working on this new book, which is set later in the nineteenth century, I was worried that the main character would sound like Arty, but that hasn't been the case. Arty is not telling this story. A time or two, I've tried to call her back, but she's really gone. I haven't heard her voice at all.

**AB:** *My Old True Love* was originally written in third person. How did Arty's voice emerge, and in what way did this change to first person affect the overall delivery of the story?

**SKA:** Arty showed up on the first page of the first draft, and I battled with her through several revisions. To be honest, I've never really cared for books written in first person, so I was pretty resistant to the idea. It was actually my editor at Algonquin, Kathy Pories, who convinced me that it needed to be Arty's story. I figured it would take me months to change it from third person, but once I turned Arty loose, it went amazingly fast. I started the first week in August and wrote the last sentence the end of October. I really can't imagine it being told any other way now. Arty's delivery gave it intensity, a richness that didn't exist in any of the other versions.

**AB:** Were you aware when you first began writing this novel that the ballad singing tradition would be as vital to the characters as it eventually became?

**SKA:** Not really. I'm not all that surprised, though. Aunt Arty was a great singer, Hackley really was a child prodigy on the fiddle, and Larkin supposedly had one of the best singing voices in that part of the world. And ballad singing would certainly have been a part of their lives, since the songs were passed down to me. When I was writing the book, I would be going right along and all of a sudden the characters in the book would start to sing. It seemed the most natural thing in the world to write down the song. It was a surprise how the tradition seemed to be such an important part in their everyday lives and how it fostered such an intimate connection between them.

**AB:** As a seventh-generation ballad singer, what do these ballads mean for you, your family, and the culture that keeps them?

**SKA:** For me, singing the ballads provides an almost mystical, unbroken connection to the past that I don't think I could experience any other way. There's this feeling of continuance that truly gladdens my heart. There really is something uplifting about singing a song I know someone in my family sang two hundred years ago.

Sadly, the culture that nurtured the living, breathing tradition of singing the old songs is dead. When the outside world came for us with better roads, radio, telephones, and television, it was just a matter of time. My parent's generation, in their mad dash to escape the crushing poverty of their childhoods, threw away their culture with both hands, the good along with the bad. So, now we have this tradition that's not really a part of anything; it just sort of hangs out there, and we struggle to figure out what to do with it. I guess you could say it's an anomaly.

I don't think the tradition is in danger of dying out anytime soon. There's been a resurgence of interest in the old songs because of the movies *O Brother Where Art Thou?* and *Songcatcher*. The younger generation is starting to turn back to their musical heritage. I find that hopeful. I'm still keeping my fingers crossed that one, or all three, of my children will take it up.

**AB:** The largest source of external conflict in *My Old True Love* is the Civil War. How did the Civil War affect your region of the Appalachians, and what was the general response of your ancestors to the conflict?

**SKA:** Mama said the Civil War provided the opportunity, there around home, to settle old grievances, and there was certainly a lot of that. Brother fought against brother, families broke up, and communities split right down the middle. And they had to deal with roving bands of deserters who spent the war hiding out in the mountains. My family found themselves smack in the middle of the Union Army over in Tennessee and the Confederates down in Asheville and Marshall. From all I've read and the stories I grew up hearing, it was a terrifying time in the region's history.

What I tried to do in the book was keep the focus on those that were left behind using the Civil War as a sort of backdrop. I've always been fascinated with how people survive while the social structure is literally coming apart all around them.

The majority of my family were pro-Union. Based on what all I heard growing up, they pretty much just wanted to be left alone, and given the choice they would've stayed out of the whole affair. My great-great grandfather—William Norton in the novel—really did say he thought it was a rich man's war that would work its way around to being a poor man's fight.

**AB:** How did their Scotch-Irish past influence their views on the major issues of the Civil War?

**SKA:** They had such a mistrust of the government, any government. This would've definitely been a carryover from their dealings with the British. I wouldn't be a bit surprised if they hadn't felt some sort of visceral aversion to owning slaves given their relationship with the English. But in any event they were too poor to own slaves. Recall that Arty says there were no slaves in Sodom except them what were white and female. They were all fiercely independent and just wanted to farm their land and take care of their own. But the war came to them, and when they had to fight, they fought hard. I do know most of the men tried to stay close home to do their fighting. I doubt that they had much interest in states' rights either. As a matter of fact, they tried to secede in the 1780s to form the State of Franklin because they believed they had so little in common with the rest of the state. I always figured it was a good thing they were so isolated here in the mountains for so long, since it was so obvious they couldn't get along with anyone.

**AB:** *My Old True Love* is populated with a great many strong female characters. Was this typical of southern Appalachian culture?

**SKA:** Oh yes. The women were always in charge. The men just didn't know it. They still are, and they still don't.

**AB:** Would you consider yourself a feminist, in the modern sense of the word?

**SKA:** If being a feminist means I think women should have the same political, economical, and social rights as men, then I'm definitely a feminist.

**AB:** You released an album showcasing the ballads and traditional music seen in *My Old True Love*. What motivated you to do so, and what surprises did it hold for you as both performer and producer?

**SKA:** Actually the only choice I made concerning the recording was the title, *All the Other Fine Things*. My husband, Jim, was the driving force behind the album. He produced it, chose the songs, arranged the fiddle tunes, and got some of the best singing out of me that I've ever done. He was my muse during the writing of the book and spent many an evening sitting on the floor of my office listening as I read what I'd written that day. His idea for a CD as a companion for the book happened pretty early on. He felt it would really add something, give more texture for the reader to be able to hear the songs they were reading about. The surprise is how well the CD has done. People say it's like having a sound track for the book. I think this is exactly what Jim had in mind.

**AB:** Traditional Scotch-Irish ballads have been preserved in the southern Appalachian Mountains, truer to the original songs than exist today in England. Will these ballads live on, and what must be done to preserve them?

**SKA:** Well, the ballads have survived into the twenty-first century and all we need to do to preserve them is exactly what Granny told me years ago: Keep singing them and passing them along.

**AB:** What would you like for readers to remember most about *My Old True Love*?

**SKA:** That human frailty is a condition of the heart that only love can cure.

## Reading Group Questions and Topics for Discussion

1. In *My Old True Love*, Sheila Kay Adams uses the dialect of her Appalachian home. Did Arty's dialect and informal way of speaking pull you into the story immediately or did you find it distracting? How would the telling of this story been different if Arty's speech had been more conventional?

2. What does the first paragraph tell you about the narrator? What does it reveal about Arty's personality?

3. How did Arty know her aunt had died? Did you find the exchange between Arty and the midwife believable? What symbolic meaning does swapping the buckets have?

4. The oral tradition of ballad singing is an important and integral part of *My Old True Love*. It makes an early appearance during the deathbed scene when Arty says, "Crazy-like, the words to an old love song run through my head." Over twenty-five songs were written in part or in entirety throughout the book. Did the songs seem a natural occurrence and appropriately placed? How do they provide insight into Arty's culture? How did this tradition influence Hackley and Larkin's relationship?

5. Why do you think Granny allowed Arty to take over Larkin's care? What did Arty mean when she said, "From the day he was

born, my arms had carried him, but that very day was when my heart claimed him for my own"?

6. Did you find the custom of "hanging" someone with a name odd? What customs do you practice in your own family that outsiders might think odd?

7. Why do you think so many of the important scenes in *My Old True Love* take place on the porch? What are some examples?

8. Arty relates many fond memories of childhood. When do you think Arty realizes she has moved beyond these carefree days? Do you think she wishes she had chosen a different path than that of wife and mother? Explain.

9. Why did Larkin live with Zeke and Arty only for a short time? What happened between Larkin and Hackley when Larkin moved back in with Granny? Do you think this would've happened if Larkin had continued to live with Arty? How would this have changed the story?

10. What does Arty do that reveals her superstitious nature? Where else in the book is this revealed? Do you think Arty may be clairvoyant and have what mountain people refer to as "second sight"? Explain.

11. Did the bawdy humor of the women surprise you? The story is peopled with flawed but strong women. Did you most identify with one particular woman? If you could choose to be like one of the women, which would you choose? Why?

12. When Arty says Hackley might have been little but had that way of moving that women just loved, what kind of picture does that

statement paint of him in your mind? Do her expressions and sayings help you visualize other characters in the story? Give some examples.

13. What does Granny mean when she tells Larkin, "You got nothing to lay forever out next to, nothing to measure it against"? Death has always been an accepted part of life in the Appalachian culture and is an important aspect of the book. How does this compare with our attitudes today? What are Arty's religious beliefs, and how do they differ from her mother and those of Granny?

14. How does Arty describe Mary, and when does she realize the extent of Larkin's feelings for her? Is there any indication that Mary is encouraging Larkin? Explain.

15. There are so many complex relationships in the book that resolve in one way or another. Do you think there was a relationship between Larkin and Julie and how (or was it) ever resolved?

16. There are so many opportunities for Arty to tell Mary about Hackley's womanizing. Why do you think she chooses not to tell and advises Larkin to do the same? How might the story have been different if Arty had told Mary about Hackley and Maggie at the political gathering on Shelton Laurel? What would've changed had Larkin told her?

17. A large part of the population in western North Carolina was pro-Union during the Civil War. Often it was truly brother against brother. What were Arty's feelings about the war? Was she ever in support of either side? Explain.

18. When Zeke leaves for the war, Arty is expecting her seventh child. Why do you think she struggled to hide how she really felt from Zeke? What does this say about Arty? How do the war years change Arty?

19. Arty often says there are situations in our lives that change us forever. In your opinion, what single event in the story brings about a profound change in Arty? Explain your choice.

20. How does Arty cope with the deepening relationship between Larkin and Mary? What decision does she finally make? How does this affect the outcome of the story?

21. Arty has such conflicted feelings for her brother, Hackley. She obviously loves him but strongly disapproves of his behavior. Give some examples of this. How does she react to his death?

22. Why do you think Larkin avoids Arty when he returns from the war? When he tells her he's no longer a boy, she responds with, "Don't wind up being a stupid man." Why does she say this? What happens after their conversation?

23. After Mary and Larkin marry, Mary tells Arty that she feels that she has somehow betrayed Hackley. Arty replies, "Life is not for the dead and gone. It is just for the living." After the birth of Roxyann, Arty is troubled by Larkin's behavior at the spring. How are the two connected? Explain.

24. How does Arty try to intervene as Larkin changes? What does she mean when she says that Larkin's sickness was "the greater sick of his soul?" What happens that seems to cure this? What was Larkin searching for?

25. How did Mary change when Larkin left? Why wouldn't she share Larkin's letters with Arty? How does Arty's final letter from Larkin set the scene for Larkin's homecoming?

26. Were you surprised by Larkin's story about Hackley's death, or did you suspect it all along? Did you believe Larkin when he said he loved Hackley? What were Arty's feelings?

27. Did your opinion of Mary change in the last few pages of the book? Explain.

28. Arty's growth and development were irrevocably connected to nature and the land. How does the summing up of her life support this? Do you think the last sentence is an appropriate ending for the book?

SHEILA KAY ADAMS is an acclaimed performer of Appalachian ballads passed down for seven generations through her own ancestors. She has been a featured performer in several documentary films, served as technical director for the film *Songcatcher,* contributed to *The Last of the Mohicans,* and was cohost and coproducer of Public Radio's *Over Home.* She performs year-round at major festivals throughout the United States, as well as in the United Kingdom. She has three children and lives with her husband, Jim Taylor, in Madison County, North Carolina, where she was born.